NUBARA

By

Alex H. Singh

This is a work of fiction. Names, characters, places, and incidents either are a product of the author's imagination or are used fictitiously. Any resemblance to actual persons, living or dead, events, or locales, is entirely coincidental.

Copyright ©2015 by Alex H. Singh

Cover Designer: Jennifer Munswami
Formatting: Book Bangs

All rights reserved. This book contains material protected under International and Federal Copyright Laws and Treaties. Any unauthorized reprint or use of this material is prohibited. No part of this book may be reproduced or transmitted in any form or by any means, electronic or mechanical, including photocopying, recording, or by any information storage and retrieval system without express written permission from the author / publisher.

Printed in the United States of America

First Printing, 2015

Dedication Tree

The dedication of this book is split many ways.

To Oupary, Isabel, Katie, Richard, Daniela, Liam, Ashley, John, Michelle, Paul, Jeff & Laceigh.

And to all that have stuck it out with "My Creative Thoughts" from start to the finish.

Thank you For Believing in Me & Above All Thanks for Believing In Nubara.

Table of Contents

Prologue	vii
Chapter 1	1
Chapter 2	15
Chapter 3	33
Chapter 4	49
Chapter 5	61
Chapter 6	75
Chapter 7	87
Chapter 8	101
Chapter 9	117
Chapter 10	129
Chapter 11	143
Chapter 12	153
Chapter 13	171
Chapter 14	189
Chapter 15	201
Chapter 16	219
Epilogue	235

Prologue

Hatred builds up to the point where you can't feel anymore. That feeling lingers causing you to get stronger and enable you to tackle hardships to come. I've reached that boiling point, where nothing matters and nothing is ever the same again. Here I find myself standing on the far side of the world. Maybe it's all the sparkling ice; white and hard as bone. Within moments, my head starts to feel heavy and after some difficulty shifting my thick red scarf, I gaze down at my silhouette, and wipe the ice crystals from the corners of my nose. The spread of endless white overwhelms me, and I'm overcome by the whirling ache of vertigo. Voices foreign to all but me echo in the great depths of my mind along with the images of my short life that dwell and stir.

Here in the middle of this cold, flat, dark and dense wasteland, I picture my life with angst and fury.

There's a deep hole in me from which nothing escapes. How could I ever know who I truly am? It seems that whenever I meet anyone for the first time, they see my glossy black hair, tan skin and their first reaction is to shut me out. Their mouths twist slightly as they try to put a finger on what they think I am. I'm half Thai, of course. Sure people say I'm far from dull, but that's just how I was born, not how I feel. The truth is, I'm not like everyone else.

My name's Soliel Oupary—a typical clueless twenty-something grad student. Today was a cold one, a frosty chill constantly blew my hair on to my face stinging my eyes and as I pushed the strands away, I spotted my classmates trembling in a colorless huddle like a flock of gray geese. The cold doesn't affect me since I feel nothing, the hate has left me cold and numb already. For me, hate and cold are my closed companions. Therefore, I feel nothing.

Why are we all shivering in zero degree weather in the middle of the arctic you may ask?

An age old mystery. A preposterous myth about an ancient civilization and the annihilation of all human life. Or, maybe it's nothing but a harmless waste of time...

To summarize it up, we're here to see if the legend of 'Nubara' is true. It was a place - an island - that once stood proudly on top of the waters of the Atlantic Ocean. Rumor has it that the descendants of Atlantis once lived with the beings from Planet X - a.k.a Nibiris.

We've all heard different renditions of the story that Earth will one day be impacted by a wayward star or asteroid and it will cause great damage and destroy all of us by reversing life.

Scientists believe that an asteroid is speculated to wipe us out of existence. I guess you could say the universe likes to course correct from time to time. Yet my heart tells me there's something in all this doom and gloom that we're not seeing; something special. Undoubtedly, the universe is immense enough to have people out there who, like us, wonder about the point of it all and are just as curious to know that they're not alone.

Everyone around was zipped up to their eyeballs and almost swaddled themselves in their fleece blankets. Another gust of wind ruffled the puff ball on my red beanie. I sure as hell was in no mood to stand shoulder to shoulder with some of my more obnoxious self-involved classmates. We were specially selected to go on this little expedition, since we were the brightest of the Myth and Reality 101 class. Not that I was feeling special right now, since I'd spent the last few evenings with these blue-blooded dullards.

"Where can I get a coat like that?"

Again, I was lost in my own thoughts. I do speak. I promise. I like to observe and think far more than socialize. I speak when I have to. I hope that doesn't make me aloof?

I heard a voice from behind as I was adjusting a pair of warm gloves on my hands. A half-smile stretched across my cheeks as Shoba Ali elbowed me in my side.

"Come on; don't hold out on me, Oupary! I'm not exactly pleased to be standing out here freezing my knickers off..." she pouted. Shoba had faint lines that traced around her eyes as she chuckled and shuddered. Despite being a few years older, she still possessed virtually flawless bronze skin that most East Indians are known for. Shoba didn't rattle easily, and I secretly admired her free-spirited disposition.

"What are the chances we'll actually find anything way out here?" I asked.

She arched her eyebrow at me. "Find what, exactly? You don't still believe in those fairy tales about the mystical alien kingdoms of Nibris, do you?"

"The signals we've been triangulating, they're too strong to be written off as coincidence." Shoba and I met eyes. "I'm sure of it."

"You're obsessed by it," she replied.

After a moment of thinking about it, I spoke up. "I'm not the one who left London, remember?"

Shoba abandoned her life in "Albion" to attend the highly prestigious Rolling Hills University. Even she would admit that it wasn't the University itself, but specifically our Dr Dr. Michaels. No matter what the full scholarship offers from Oxbridge, she knew the thrilling research in astronomy & myth, especially Nubara, would change a world where things rarely changed. In fact, she enrolled on a razor's edge. Apparently, the class had been already filled, but rumors swirled that the brilliant Dr had a sore spot for the "South Asian mystique." Shamelessly, Shoba used it to her advantage. Regardless of being a genius; men will be men, it ever fails.

Within seconds, the sunlight faded from the sky. Orange hues are stripped into shadows of violet and black. Then a terrible thought flushed over me.

Surely, what we find here won't have negative unexpected consequences, right?

And with that came another thought.

If something does go wrong, could we fix it?

"Oupary, are you okay?" asked Shoba as she rubbed her hands together.

Shoba elbowed me in the side, harder this time. My mouth was half-parted and my mind was in deep thought. I must've zoned out in my troubles again. I've spent long stretches of time in silence. Even though I have a handful of friends, I much preferred my own company over that of others. I lowered my eyes and stared down quietly at my feet. Dr. Michaels wordlessly waved his arms to hush us up and cleared his throat.

"We've established two voluntary divisions before we trekked up here. The first division is back at the Rolling Hills studying the seismic tremors occurring with much greater frequency in the heart of the Foxe

Basin. The second division which are all of you fine people, are spending the night here to observe activity we find in this cave."

"He's just so cheeky I want to yank him by that scruffy fox-fur lining," Shoba whispered in my ear.

I felt a small knot in my throat at the very thought of it. Oupary & the opposite sex? Never. Instead of thinking about boys, I worry over dissertations. Instead of primping for awkward first dates, I spend my "wild" and "crazy" nights perfecting my abstract. I don't have time for cuddling or fun. Not if I want that coveted research scientist position at the Natural History Museum. If I lose focus, it means losing out on my dreams. Nevertheless, men don't look twice at me. Unless by some deranged neurosis, gleaming green eyes and stringy hair are all the rage these days. If my class mates weren't swooning over Dr. Michaels, they were hyperventilating over his brother who I'm told, was a dashing man who loved Asian girls. *Lucky for me, I guess. I'm of Asian descent. Apparently, we Thai women are supposed to be sensual and spicy. Sadly, I'm more of the geeky and intellectual type. I'm definitely not spicy. As for sensual? I'd have no clue where to begin unless it came with an instruction manual.* Like I said to myself before, I just don't have time for that sort of distraction.

A smile stretched across my face as I remembered Shoba's words.

"—oh boy," I coughed. "You're awful."

We all stood back as flames burst up as Dr. Michaels lit a small pyre.

For whatever reason, I felt sick and was desperate to get some sleep. The emotional rage that consumed me from the get go was starting to wear me down.

"Everybody pack in. By the time this burns out tomorrow morning, we will be heading further into the cave. Make sure to keep emergency water and rations—just in case. The last thing we need is another delay. Okay? Good. Shoba Ali your partners with Soleil Oupary, You two are going to decipher any texts or murals you see, understand?"

I gazed at Dr. Michaels, scowling now. No matter how many times I've reminded him not to, he always insisted on calling me by my first name. The reasons why I preferred my last are indescribably personal. Certainly, it's none of his business. Still, I nodded, forcing a smile.

Our Dr looked at us both with probing stares.

"Can't you see it? This is our moment."

Shoba was good at finding out dates, but not so much as to origins of the writings or images. Hence why we were paired I guess, we did make a good team.

The Dr finished rattling off names and assigning teams. John was paired with Terrence for brute force and heavy lifting. Sexist? Then again, who wants to move ice boulders around? *Not I.* They slapped each other a shivery high five. They looked like two little boys who discovered a toy at the end of the Cracker Jack box.

Many of us bundled by the fire and unfurled our sleeping bags. Seconds later, my eyes fluttered. I felt drained and strung out, as if my body was losing control...

My feet were covered in scabs. A trail of blood leaked on the muddy ground. I couldn't see myself but I knew that I was running from something or someone. The air smelled so crisp and felt so misty until suddenly blood spurted out my mouth. There wasn't a single crystal of ice. I could only feel wet earth squish between my scarred toes. My cheeks blushed from the warmth of a bright sun. A muffled hoof beat trampled over bramble and fallen limbs from trees. *It's coming for you, Oupary.*

A sturdy beast charged out of a thicket, half-horse and half-human. A swift kick smashed into my stomach, and I lost the ability to breathe. I collapsed—slamming my back first—in a disorienting haze. I could only make out small things like wild flaming hair and black beady eyes. A strange symbol, an Emblem, was etched in the center of his chest. A grin stretched broadly across his face as he reared on his stiff hind legs. It spoke from its throat.

"I will stop the rot from spreading. Lunati must die!" At once, something felt hot in my hands. *A Crossbow? An arrow?*

Sweat dripped and burned my eyes. I've never used a crossbow in my life, but somehow I felt calm. The arrow glowed white hot in between my slender fingers. I aimed straight for his bulging neck. He doubled back, kicked dirt in my bloodshot eyes and escaped underneath the shadows of the trees.

"Soleil? Hey!"

I immediately bolted upright and gasped for air. Shoba loomed over me holding a lantern and before I could explain what I saw, Shoba patted my shoulder. I knew she would be awake as she hardly slept herself. Insomniacs rarely do.

"Look...listen carefully, it was a bad dream. Nothing more. Nothing less."

I sat up now, removed my hair from my hat, letting it flow freely. I noticed my face was damp - *all that sweat from one dream. Always the same one, but this time was slightly different. I saw something - something familiar yet not.* I got up out of my sleeping bag and decided to sit in front of the cave entrance so I could have a breather.

Shoba smiled to herself as she looked down into her lap. I could tell she had a question on her mind. I was waiting for her to say something, but she didn't. I knew what she wanted to know. "If you are wondering why I don't go by Soleil, I can tell you if you're curious..."

Shoba nodded her head. It was a topic she knew that I tended to shy away from. Not because I am shy, but because the pain is still fresh in my heart and showers my soul

"Tell me the reason, the truth that no one else knows," she said softly.

"My life changed when I was thirteen," I began still in shock. "Who I am now wasn't anything like who I was then. I remember how warm it was, how everyone laughed and danced. I swayed to the music, the hem of my sundress swirled above my knees. My parents hadn't arrived to pick me up from the birthday party. I can't even remember whose birthday it was anymore. Abruptly, the earth shook and rocked underneath my feet. I hid underneath a table and comforted a screaming boy by holding his hand. Another little girl stared at me in this certain kind of way. She wasn't frightened and didn't flinch at the chaos unfolding around us. When the tremors stopped at last, everyone's parents showed up, but I still waited. Hours later, my brother Rex pulled up, his eyes were red and his face was soaking wet. He didn't say a word, he just pulled me close. Too close. I could hear his beating heart. That same young girl gazed into my eyes from outside Rex's car. I knew, from that day forward, I would never see my parents again. That's probably why I feel the way that I do. There's lots of anguish of being left alone in this world."

"What about your brother?' Shoba asked.

"He's never been the same. Our lives were ripped apart."

Shoba sniffled, fighting back the glistening in her eyes.

"Do you two still keep in touch?"

"Not as much as we should, but that frightened boy left me a letter a few days after."

> Dear Soleil,
> Know that losing someone doesn't mean they are lost. Without you, I never would have found my way. I hope your heart heals itself like the cut on my shoulder.
> —Cal

Shoba clung to me, and I didn't realize it until I felt her embrace exactly how much I needed a hug. The quivers still trembled through our bodies as warmth started to spread. Shoba lifted her eyes and saw a golden glow rise near the pyre as it died down into smoldering embers.

I glanced back into the unexplored depths of the cave. Shoba never let go of my hand as the rest of the crew groggily rose from a deep slumber. Shoba pointed towards the sky.

"See, there's your sign that things will get better." I looked up to see the sun rising. *The darkness was always only temporary - you just have to wait for the light to rise.*

Chapter 1

Soliel Oupary

I walked forward, gazing at the shadows cast by the dripping icicles. Although, I had slept for nearly eight hours, I didn't feel rested. Restless is a more apt description, my intense anticipation brewed for what we might find down here in the frozen depths. Just as Shoba promised, she stuck by my side. You could tell she was much less interested in the expedition, and "discoveries of a lifetime," and more interested in keeping a wandering eye on our Dr.

Echoes from the other students ricocheted off of the surrounding icy walls, weakening as the distance grew between us. My thick rubber boots scuffed along—making each step more exhausting than the last—but keeping me from slipping and fumbling. Pinching cold nipped at the exposed slivers of skin on my neck. I felt Shoba trembling so violently, she wouldn't dare let me go.

"Oupary, *slooowww dooownn*," Dr. Michaels called with his hands cupping both sides of his mouth. "You know what they say about people who always need to be first..."

I cocked my head clueless. *That they get all the spoils? That they're not interested in wasting any more time lollygagging and running the risk of getting frostbite on their asses?* I pondered. He flashed me a look.

"Well, they say people who are always rushing to be first, always find love last. There's more to life than the admiration of your colleagues."

I forced a smile. "Hardy-har-har."

We've already established that love and I are at impossible odds. No need to play a broken record twice. Terrence Polo, another one of my classmates, whipped out his camera and took pictures of the inside of the cave. It hardly looked any different from most caves I'd seen. Although, to be honest, I hadn't seen very many. While the others tried to catch up, John McBeatty seemed to be concentrating on the search much harder than I. Even amongst all the lively commotion, I caught him deliberately pressing his head against the wall.

"McBeatty... always was the mad one," Shoba muttered, her teeth chattering.

"Sorry to tell you Shoba, but some of us actually came here to find out if the legend is true. "

Shoba quickly sucked in her teeth and waved her hands in my face.

"Please, it's possible to be smart and have a life, okay Oupary?"

I relaxed my arm and withdrew from my best friend's side. Shoba slowed her pace, confused. I couldn't even look her in the eyes. I'm sick of everyone telling me, in one way or another, that I'm a boring and a joyless future cat-lady; it is really grinding my last nerve.

Shoba wrinkled her nose.

"Was it something I said?" Shoba asked rigidly holding out her arms.

I spun around and paced backwards.

"Hah!" I laughed. "No, tell me more about how boring and loveless I am since it seems to be your favorite subject...seems to be everybody's favorite subject these days..."

I noticed a fearful look in Shoba's eyes. "I wouldn't do that if I were you." It was hard to hear her, it sounded as if she was far from me but I thought she was just whispering so I responded in my normal voice.

"What speak my mind? Stand up for myself?"

"No, no, no—that!" Shoba yelled out.

Darkness surrounded me as I stumbled into the shadows, it would seem that I tripped into an alcove and that's when I realized my folly, I had walked a bit too far away from Shoba. In a quick motion, I grabbed my flashlight and slammed my palm on the back end; it swung it in all directions.

What have you gotten yourself into this time? I asked myself. The circle of soft light waved across the smooth gleaming walls of ice. Whispers filled the air and swirled all around me.

"Just another dead end..." I mumbled. I spun, illuminating the small chamber and quietly cursing myself for getting in this predicament. My eyes squinted at something glittering from within the cold walls. It had a scratched golden surface with an opal-colored gem in its center. The shadow-shaded jewel had an imposing smooth gloss. It felt almost as if I was staring directly into an eye. The logical part of me was screaming for me to turn and run.

Yet, the scientist in me wanted to examine it and hold it in my hand. I traced my fingers along the Emblem searching for something, cracks, an inscription or even something altogether unexpected. Then as I squinted for something I finally saw what looked like an image on the inside of the Emblem.

All of a sudden, I felt a heat warming the back of my neck. A growl. No, a snarl, vibrated into my ears. *Just move very slowly.* I told myself. With carefully timed movements, I rooted around in my backpack. *That's it! The flare!* A pair of unholy eyes glistened before me. There was no telling if the creature hunting me down was either a man or a beast. My finger twitched over the trigger of the plastic neon orange gun. I aimed it dead center, right at the lurking savage.

The creature thrust out of the pit of darkness. My heart-thumped heavily in my chest as it knocked me over and wrestled me on my back. Terrified, I scrambled up, trying to feel my way out.

I had one shot, and I took it.

BOOM!

A stream of crackling embers and white billowing smoke hurtled towards the ceiling. The flare exploded like stardust, crashing right above me and filling the cave with a glowing red light.

Less than a second later, the beast turned, threw me down and flung me against the icy wall. My back pressed right on top of the mysterious Emblem. Tremors shook the cave and rattled all around. My stared frantically down the cracks forming in zig zag pattern under my footsteps as chunks of ice crashed in all directions. Then ground gave way, and I flailed my arms desperate to grab hold but failing to do so. I could hear myself grasping for air and trying to scream but managing nothing more than a thin whimper as I was swallowed up by total darkness.

When I tried to move, a piercing pain stabbed through my entire right side, it felt as though my rib cage had been chopped in half; it hurt to move at all. My eyes widened after slapping my hand over my mouth to stifle a shriek. I was sure I wasn't alone. Tears watered in my eyes as I clutched something fragile and glossy in both hands. *The Emblem?* So, I just held it, rocking in the dark and praying that someone would find me.

Somewhere far away from the Arctic was a young woman who was being quizzed by her peers to test her genius skills…
"Hydrogen."
"1766."
"Krypton."
"1898. You're going to need to try harder than this, David,"

Ashley Boylan

I SMILED NEVER HAVING LIFTED my pen from my paper. It had been raining all day, and for whatever reason I was transfixed by the streaks of raindrops left on the window pane. David sat with his mouth agape, shocked at how easily I retained it all.
"Alright, how about this one? What year was Schrödinger born?"
"1887."
David gasped slapping his left hand on the table.
"How does she friggin' do it? I can't remember what I ate for breakfast let alone know the exact date of Schrodinger's birthday. Just admit it, you're secretly a cyborg."
"Am not," I said punching him softly in the shoulder, "I just kinda don't forget those type of things. Dates intrigue me."
I bit down on my pencil and pulled free a hair band and then tried to comb my frizz back. The keyword is try as a few blonde wavy locks escaped and fluttered into my face. I smoothed it in one swift motion and my shining blonde hair drifted down into my eyes. It was times like this, those long hours we spent in the lab that I wished I was curled up somewhere no one could find me, instead of reading about planetary myths, I could get lost in the pages of my history's reference books: St. Aquinas, Tesla and Einstein. That's the only time I have ever felt at home, all the other times, I felt like an impostor. I can't shake the feeling of being unwelcome in my very own body.
Still, it's best not to get hung up on the little things, after all we're only human and it's natural to feel out of place.
"Got anything new to report?" I asked our leader Christopher Palace Michaels.
"We're getting pretty close to a breakthrough," he told me.
"That's what you said a month ago," I replied slapping him on the back. Palace turned to me, and I looked in his bright blue eyes. He

had that kind of tan like he was always coming back from a long vacation from some faraway paradise. He and his brother were nothing alike. Palace always seemed to have a more level-head about most things.

"Hold it right there, this is different."

Palace gestured me over.

"Come look, these waves are decreasing in elasticity."

"You mean they're compressing?" I asked.

He nodded. "Something is forcing higher velocities in these waves."

"Check out these arrival times."

I pointed."The waves are so close. It's like they're stacked on top of one another."

David, Curtis and the others on the team came around to sneak a look.

Curtis Anderson was almost too stunned to answer.

"Oh, come on," he said. "You can't tell me this is normal?"

You only see these sorts of numbers as a pre-cursor to quakes of a 9.0 magnitude," I replied.

"Hang on a second, when was the last year the earth's surface had this much activity?" Palace asked me.

"Judging by the data, we haven't had anything like this since 1960."

"Woah, this is just getting freaky," George said with extremely terrified eyes.

There was no denying that the waves were dangerously choppy. Uneven waves translated to trouble. I quickly lifted the transparent read out from the table and made a fast path to the map on the wall. Wasn't sure where yet, but I had a hunch. I smoothed the seismic read out against a street map of downtown New York City.

Paula Legest spoke up, she always took pleasure in trying to best me every chance she got, "Judging by the alignment of the waves, it's most definitely central to the Upper East Side metro area."

The expression on Palace's face began to change.

"These readings should pinpoint the locus, but all we can tell is that it's coming from within city limits."

I chuckled. "Yeah, it should, but when was the last time any of the print outs were a hundred percent accurate?"

I stared at all my colleagues in the lab that all had worried looks on their faces. Clearly, whether these readings would actually occur in the heart of downtown or not; made everyone a little touchy. I rested my arm on Palace's shoulder. Now, as far as I knew, nothing had happened yet, and the situation was still under our control. He was the first to speak.

"Solving this one could be a long shot."

"Maybe." I shrugged. "Maybe not."

Of course, Paula had to share; she couldn't stand being ignored, and had to add her own two cents.

"Yeah, nice try Ashley, but I don't think you completely understand the gravity of the issue here," she said dryly.

Paula stood no chance going toe-to-toe with me.

"Let's say that these readings are right, and the tremors that have been affecting Rolling Hills University are as apocalyptic as they appear," she began to explain.

I shrugged. "...go on."

"I'm just saying that an earthquake, even a hypothetical one, on a 9.2 magnitude would destroy not just destroy Manhattan or the Upper East Side, it would level the entire city!"

I simply gazed at Paula with a blank stare. Paula darted her eyes around the room looking for some sort of affirmation.

"We're talking about a body count like you've only heard of in Richard Matheson books. We can't just go on a hunch that things will just fix themselves," she finished.

David, Curtis and George looked at me.

"It's like I said, we have lots of evidence but no clear answers. So, let's tone down the hysteria and avoid jumping to conclusions, okay? We still haven't heard from the research team out in the Foxe Basin. They said that phone over there would ring if anything happened. "

Hot fires of frustration burned in Paula's eyes as she took a seat in her chair.

Brrriinnnngggg!

All six of us turned and faced the single phone. Palace, no doubt saw me shifting nervously in my seat. The phone kept ringing off of the hook, and none of us were prepared to hear who was on the other line.

"Somebody pick it up for heaven sakes!" Paula shrieked at the top of her lungs.

No one moved. Finally, David muttered something to Betty, but I was way too distracted to concentrate on what he was saying.

"Well, what are you waiting for?" I asked everyone in the room attempting to sound calm. Palace scratched his chin and let the phone ring a few moments more.

"Well?" Paula pushed waiting for somebody anybody to step forward.

"Let's just get it over with…" I said marching toward the phone. I felt someone tug at my shoulder, it was Palace, he tried to hold me back, to no avail, so he stood to one side realizing that, once he picked up, nothing would be the same. On the last ring, he answered it.

"Christopher P. Michaels, how may I help you?"

Soliel Oupary

BACK IN THE ARCTIC…in the darkness…

There was a constant ringing in my ears and everything was blurry, I can't remember clearly how I ended up alone in the dark. The back of my hand was sodden with blood. Nervously, I turned around and stroked through my ripped jacket and soothed my aching right side. My body felt sluggish as I scrambled to press my back against the wall. There was no telling if I could get up without searing pain ripping through the inside of my body.

I had a few moments to regain my bearings. I inhaled a deep breath, ignoring the swelling where I cracked my ribs. I stuck out my hand and felt around for my flashlight. Something must have knocked it loose, because the light flickered on an off. Adrenaline throbbed through my chest from barely surviving the fall. *Would anyone find me? Will I be left here to die all alone?* After wiping the cold sweat from my forehead, I maneuvered my gloved hand around frozen hunks of ice.

Something scratched the inside of my elbow, and I couldn't figure where it was coming from. All I knew at this point was that I needed to get out of this cave and fast. I tilted back my head and shone the fading light onto the cave wall. The icy ceiling twinkled eerily, and I wondered if everyone else had made it out alive.

What shocked me, when I tossed the light to my other hand, was the streaks of dried blood drying into the creases of my skin. I hadn't realized how severe it was until I stared hard at the glistening deep scarlet wound. It stained not just on my hands but pooled all around my body. I panicked and patted my body down with feverish speed, desperate to know where the blood came from.

Stop it, Oupary. I told myself coming down from a fear induced high. I nodded, calmly and noticed the blood wasn't even my own. It seemed more likely, that something had fallen and died somewhere nearby. I swung the flashlight slowly, inching along the panorama of the collapsed cave. I bolted back and dropped my light on the ground. It rolled on towards the rocky terrain and stopped. A radiant glow reflected on a hulking furry beast. A stiff body, sharp claws and slobbering jowls lay still on a jagged slab of ice.

Its once menacing eyes were made less intense by a thin layer of frost. I could only stare into them briefly, afraid that somehow, it would jolt back to life and tear me limb from limb. There was something familiar underneath its dense shag of fur. I pushed myself up from the wall and on to my tender feet as I kept my hand clamped on my side. I waved my light further down the polar bear's lifeless body and saw where some of his fur was stripped clean from his skin. My eyes fixed on the sticky clumps of red fur. Three deep gashes carved up the animal's throat. All of this trauma between me and the bear begged a single question.

What did this?

These scars were shaped exactly like my own. Its ripped throat exposed the tendons and bones jutting out of his neck. I tried not to think about what I just saw. When I turned my attention to the hard frozen wall, I noticed a sliver of light poked through. I grabbed my sides to keep the heat from escaping from my body. Maybe this was it for me. Maybe this was really how I was supposed to die. I thought of Shoba and wished I could see her again, just one last time.

O...upary!

A muffled cry broke through the thick ice.

O...upary!

I heard it faintly again. Almost certainly, if I stayed trapped down here for any longer, I'd start to hallucinate and have no hope of ever getting out. I ignored the stinging aches, and pressed my ear near the ice.

"It's Betty. Betty Tavish. We're going to get you outta there, stay strong!" she shouted.

"I'm in here!" I screamed back, in near tears, hoping to the heavens and the universe that someone could hear my raspy voice. No matter how tightly I wrapped my arms around my sides, it still felt like my blood was quite literally freezing in my veins.

"Stay back, we're coming in!"

I rushed back, hearing the sounds of impacting metal crash through the fortress of ice. A giant metal pick axe erupted through the ice. Betty Tavish took a vaulting step in, and my eyes darted right to her. Shortly after, she embraced me and inspected me more closely.

"If I hug you any harder, I'm afraid you'll break," she joked.

I tried to work up a smile.

"Everyone's going to be so relieved to know you're alive."

Alive. Those words were like music to my frostbitten ears.

A crew of EMT carefully picked me up and gently placed me on a red stretcher. When they carried me out in slow and steady stride, the harsh sunlight felt like a thousand needles in my eyes.

"We're flying you out tonight and you'll arrive in New York early tomorrow morning," An EMT said. My ears were still ringing, and I was forced to read his lips. The whole research team stood by frightened with their hands cupped over their mouths. Shoba pushed Betty aside.

"I'm right here, Oupary. Just as I promised. I will never leave your side."

The terror I now felt started to subside after hearing my best friend's soothing voice. My eye lids weighed a ton, and I could hardly keep them open.

"That's right, just close your eyes and get some rest. Soon it will all be over," Shoba told me while stroking my matted hair.

I had a hard time staying awake until finally sleep overtook me.

Callum Morrissey

AN EMERGENCY HELICOPTER SOARED above the skyline on a humid misty morning in the heart of New York City. Horns, police sirens and the extraordinary dissonance of swarms of stop-and-go traffic played out in its own urban rhythm. Every morning bike riders, tourist and anybody in between felt the rush of charging through the throngs of people. When wandering through the soiled streets, no matter how many people pass by, you still feel incredibly alone. It's a wonder how anyone in this faceless crowd struck up a friendly conversation or got to know deeply the lives of the harried and overworked pedestrians around them.

Callum knew this better than anyone else. He was new to New York, a fish out of water. While gliding through the hordes of strangers, he felt utterly invisible. Hardly the life he had imagined for himself at his age. All he desired was to move out of the small town life and pursue his dreams of living in the big city. Callum took a step back allowing the traffic to clear the lane, than pushed up the glasses sliding down the bridge of his nose, pulled his weathered army green jacket in close and sprinted across to the other side. His pale complexion matched well with the atmosphere of the city, at least. Often, he felt it intimidating to even look into the eyes of strangers. Callum swallowed hard as he inhaled a short breath and leaned against a corner.

A car alarm went off nearby and pierced his ears; startling him. Near paralyzed, he forced his nerves to calm down and then ran his fingers through his hair. He often would people watch and wonder what their lives were like. Callum wondered if the strangers embraced it more than he did. Unexpectedly, a glimmer of something broke through the crowd. A woman surged toward him and passed so close that a brisk chill ruffled his hair.

She stepped on the tip of his left loafer. The young woman was neither moving too slowly or in a hurry among her hectic surroundings, she moved entirely at her own pace. Tendrils of her flame-colored hair swooped over half of her face. Esabelle never felt more at home. She wasn't the slightest bit skittish having lived all of her life in the city. She had a single rule; live by your own rules. Esabelle had always been a very clever girl, unafraid of the challenges of being one of millions in a place like Manhattan.

Totally unexpectedly, both Esabelle and Callum rushed down a flight of stairs side by side. The pair of complete strangers were headed for the subway at Grand Central Station. A second later they both idled on the platform listening to the voice on the intercom rattle off the arrival times. If she happened to be late to where she was headed, Esabelle wouldn't worry. Callum, on the other hand, concentrated on the ticking clock scheduling down to the very last second. He hated to be late and above all else, he had to be on time.

The train screeched into the station and they both shoved through the morning rush of people and got on board. They grabbed on to a silver pole in the middle of the train, missing each other by mere inches. Callum grabbed the pole near the top and Esabelle took hold near the bottom. Silently, they stood there. Just riding. Just two people going about their daily lives oblivious to each others' presence.

Esabelle glanced over at the flickering light at the front of the train. Strong turbulence shook the car on its rails and quickly lurched the subway car violently forward, forcing the riders to cling on to whatever they could reach. A blaze of electric sparks fired against the glass windows as the car collided into a concrete wall. The passengers' screams were muffled under the sound of crumpling metal and screeching brakes. Esabelle swung madly on the pole and Callum grabbed her hand. She felt relieved and begged him not to let go. The glass windows shattered, ripping riders out of their seats. Others lost hold and flew out of the windows, catapulting them onto the deadly electrified tracks.

Callum held her tighter, finding a courage he didn't know he had. They gazed at one another for a long time and finally, Esabelle got her resolve and pulled herself closer to the steel pole. Neither of them would have fathomed that their everyday routine; waking up and heading off onto the subway could spell the end of their lives. The train rocked from side to side and then a fire exploded up ahead in the tunnel. Concrete blocks tumbled down at harrowing speed as the tremors of rumbling concrete muted out the surrounding sounds in the car. Callum shouted something, but Esabelle could not hear. They just held on, kept their eyes open and waited for an end.

Hours Earlier...

No one in the room breathed as Palace hung up the phone. Emotions were running high and the last thing we needed was for this team to unravel any faster.

"It's the expedition," he started to speak in a shaky tone. "One of the students was caught in a cave collapse."

"Who? Who was trapped?" I asked.

But Palace lingered in silence, leaving us to the worst of our imaginations. *Could it have been Shoba, Terrence or Betty? Or, God even Soleil?* I thought running through all the names in my head as he rested his hands on his desk, clenching his jaw.

"Soleil Oupary couldn't escape in time."

I've had enough. I didn't even care if it was true. It's not my nature to brood too long on misfortune. Palace looked at us all with sorrowful blue eyes.

"We've still got a job to do here, guys. As long as the mystery about the tremors remains, we haven't accomplished a damn thing yet!" I said trying to push the focus back on the task at hand.

"I mean it's not like the reason for the tremors is simply going to fall in our—"

The beeping on the seismometer screamed a shrill high-pitched noise. Paula immediately covered her ears.

"Make it stop!" she screamed.

The ground underneath us shook and rattled. I grabbed for anything I could to stabilize myself as instruments flew everywhere and beakers shattered on the floor. Our research rolled half-way across the room; here we thought we had it all figured out. *No way* would tremors happen here? *Yeah, right*. David looked up terrified that the rickety old building would collapse on us all.

I squinted in pain, biting my tongue and that bitter iron taste flooded my mouth. In a last ditch effort, I ran for the window and little by little things started to settle. Until finally, everything stopped. We all glanced at each other in various compromising positions.

"Is it over?" I asked.

Palace loosened his grip from his desk and looked us over.

"You guys alright?"

"I've been better."

Everyone else in the room moved from the walls and back towards the center.

Beep. Bip. Beep. We were all on edge when the seismometer wailed again.

"Don't be alarmed, that's not a warning for imminent danger. It's processing data from that tremor. The sound of the scratching of the needle against the transparent paper was like nails on a chalkboard and when it finished, Palace ripped the results from the print tray.

"Well?" Paula asked. "What does it say?"

I couldn't wait for Palace to answer. I peeked over his shoulder to see the readout myself. A breath tickled in the back of my throat, and my eyes were so wide I thought they would fall right out on the floor.

"It's the source," Palace said exhaling a staggered breath.

"It leads us right to the nexus of where the quakes originated…"

Paula, David, George and I grabbed the read out. We looked at it together and placed it over a map of Manhattan.

I spoke first.

"Grand Central Station. Right in the heart of Manhattan."

"Are you sure?" George asked.

Palace shrugged. "There's only one way to find out."

Chapter 2

Soliel Oupary

When I opened my eyes, and finally came to, everyone stood around my hospital bed. Shoba, my Dr and my research colleagues idled next to each other; shoulder to shoulder. Their probing eyes made me feel more than a little uncomfortable, but at last I was home.

"Please stand back and give her adequate breathing room. Now let's have a look at you," the physician, Dr. Colfax said as she flashed a light in my eyes and mouth.

"She's a little banged up, but she'll recover just fine. By the way, you have another guest who wants to see you."

"Don't scare me like that again, kay?" Shoba insisted poking me in my shoulder.

"*Ow!*" I cried.

Everyone except Dr. Michaels walked out of the door, but one person walked in. Dr Michaels introduced him to me.

"Soliel, this is Dr. Claus Schuster the Department Director of Interplanetary Studies and the leading researcher on some of the most elusive mysteries surrounding our universe.

"Feel free to say something at any moment," Claus told me with a smile.

Honestly, I thought all of this attention was too much. Of course everyone meant well, but I'd had my fill of it quite frankly.

"It's weird. I'm back but I don't feel back, y'know what I mean?"

"All I know is that we have a lot to thank you for," Claus replied. He sat in a chair against the wall.

"What do you mean?"

"When you were out cold we found something on you..."

It didn't realize what Claus was talking about, until I reached in my pocket and nothing was there.

"No," I said breathless.

"Yes, the Novae Emblem. It was the missing piece. The piece that completes the puzzle. Astrophysics is going to evolve way beyond anything we've ever imagined all because of you."

My throat was too raw to scream in a fit of joy. I lowered my head back realizing this moment is what I'd been working for pretty much all of my life.

"You'd need to know we found something else."

"What else?" I asked.

The last thing I wanted to hear was any dire news. I groped my hands along the bed rails, bracing myself for whatever he was going to say next.

"For the longest time, there was a myth," Claus began. "A myth that said that the destruction of time, and all we know, will happen because of the trajectory of an asteroid. This asteroid will travel so fast towards our surface that we will have absolutely no way of stopping it. This means we have absolutely no way of keeping it from wiping out all of humanity."

"I don't understand," I replied I was still confused. I didn't truly understand how the prophecy of Nubara connected with the Emblem I found in the cave.

He pointed to the obsidian-colored stone in the middle of the Novae Emblem.

"It's a sort of spectro-stone. You see these indentations? These deep grooves? They're what are called spectral lines. Think of them as fingerprints, better yet, as unique identifying markers for different multi-verses."

"Wait, that black rock is a key to other time lines in the universe?" I asked.

"It is part of a key. We're still not sure exactly how it works, but hell, this is the closest we've come to time travel in centuries. Are you getting the picture now?" he asked.

Just before I could consider this discovery further, the half-digested food churned in the pit of my stomach. A gurgle lurched in my gut and I felt flush. Bending over, I crammed my pillow over my mouth to avoid spewing. Dr Michaels knelt at my side. He tilted my head, holding a glass of water to my lips.

"Sip," he urged.

I swallowed light sips of water, letting it moisten my tongue just so. Then the sensations finally subsided.

"These convulsions are only getting worse and worse," I muttered under my breath.

"Wait." Claus narrowed his eyes. "You mean to say you've had this problem before."

No one's ever asked me that question, but come to think of it, I never considered it a problem before. Throughout my life, I'd suffered from these spells; bouts of pain for no reason. Once I resettled back in the bed, I no longer felt like my stomach was tangled in a Gordian knot.

Dr. Claus leaned back.

"Tell me Soliel, have you had any hallucinations lately?" he asked.

I faced him with my lip pursed, utterly confused, then I remembered the creature attacking me as I forged through the wilderness with scars on my feet. How could anyone know about that? I thought. Memories of an electric blue arrow, charged with powerful static energy, flooded right back. With the two of them looking at me the way they did, the last thing I needed was to seem like I'd bumped my head a little too hard. Even if I hadn't kept these visions to myself, how could it help me? How could telling the truth help anyone?

Claus stared me down with inquisitive eyes.

"What does any of this have to do with me?" I asked.

Claus stood up. "The Novae Emblem is said to cause seizures when someone has been exposed to it directly. That is why it's kept in this case. However, if one comes in contact with it, they may see their lives in an alternate time line."

I was shivering now, hoping I hadn't accidentally exposed myself to something that would change my life forever.

Esabelle Matthews

A FEW WEEKS LATER, Esabelle was sitting in her chair and entertaining her class of toddlers.

"Colin that's *stellar*!"

I thought I'd sounded sincere enough. Then I forced a smile, clapping softly while four year old Colin trotted back to his desk. Daisy hopped up next with a macaroni "masterpiece" grasped in her tiny hands. Show and tell again. I walked over to the desk and took a seat.

"Go on, Daisy, tell us about what you're holding?"

Daisy squeaked at the top of her lungs, but something else caught my attention. At that particular moment, my cell vibrated inside my purse. It was a text message alert and it read:

> Need my stuff. Meet u later—T.R.

After stifling the urge to roll my eyes, I returned my attention back to my class. For all the glory of my new position, I still only substituted a few weeks out of the month. Even though the charter school left narrow room to deviate from the curriculum, the actual lessons plans, thankfully, were all mine.

What could Tyson possibly want anyway? I thought after four years worth of missed dates, forgotten birthdays and complete lack of intimacy that I'd learn to leave well enough alone. Worst of all, meeting up with Tyson also meant being late to the hospital. Chelsea Huang, my friend who works red-eye shifts at Holyoke Medical, had been dying to get back in touch. She just survived a divorce from hell. At this time, what she needs most is a friend not a flake. Daisy finished her presentation and lifted her art work high. It was hideous, but naturally, I grinned and nodded. Not all toddlers can be a prodigy. Finally, the bell to signify the class was over rang and at once the whole group of children began clearing the room, scurrying madly towards the classroom door, and I quietly follow after.

There he stood, hanging around my door and as I made eye contact, I stumbled on a frayed corner of my welcome mat. We haven't seen each other in several weeks, but Tyson Roberts had a fondness for simply "dropping by."

"You have your own key. What did you text me for?"

Tyson couldn't help but have a somewhat delighted look on his face.

"You need to hear something."

I raised a brow. "Oh do I?"

"What was it about us?"

After dealing with squealing five year olds all day, there was no way I was ready to endure this conversation. "I swear to God. Why are we always having this conversation?"

Tyson straightened up from his crouching position next to my door.

"You know why. I'm smart. Courteous. I've never hurt you. Essie, I'm—I'm a neurosurgeon for Palacet sakes! I want to know precisely why we broke up."

I chuckled handing Tyson my second pair of keys.

"Because you're dry." He pulled back furrowing his brow.

"Dry?"

"Yes, like stale toast. Imagine dating someone who doesn't feel passionate about anything? Really? Ask yourself that. You're boring, Tyson. You spend your life learning. I spend my life living."

We paused, and an awkward silence ensued. His face contorted with confusion, he couldn't utter a word. So, I simply kissed poor Tyson on his cheek, said my goodbyes and slipped down the stairs.

Without a moment's hesitation, I ducked past the hospital reception and headed straight for Chelsea Huang's office. The stark white corridors felt suffocating. No doubt Chelsea hated the idea of coming back to work so soon. After casually tossing my jacket onto the back of a nearby chair, I made myself known.

"Wow! You look awful," I announced.

"That's a funny way of saying 'Hi'," she replied glancing up weakly. Chelsea had puffy rings circling her eyes. When I looked further down, faint tear stains dotted her scrubs. If Chelsea sneezed, I feared she might collapse. I leaned over her desk.

"Well, you know I've never been the type to sugar coat the truth."

She sniffled. "Bastard! Should have known it wouldn't last. We've been together for seven years. I thought that it meant we would stay together forever."

I softly poked her in her shoulder.

"That's your problem right there. Look, nothing lasts forever. Hey, maybe you should think about getting a dog? I've thought about it. Course, my place isn't exactly huge..."

Chelsea didn't say much more, and I thought it my might be good to keep letting her spill out all those pent up feelings. In fact, I knew she'd be blubbering about that bastard for as long as it took.

"Oh, I'll just give you a minute..." I said feeling a tad uncomfortable. I'd feel a bit mean pushing the subject of moving on already too much longer, instead I took a few steps back.

Oomph!

Then in the next second something or someone charged at my back. As if out of the blue, a woman with dark thick hair—almost violet underneath the harsh light—slammed into me and damn near knocking my purse to the floor. To be honest, she looked a god-awful mess, like perhaps she'd been standing there waiting for someone all day. Her eyes possessed an icy gray intensity, daring me to challenge her or put her in her place.

I just stared at her as she walked away. Underneath her shirt, I could make an outline of something but I quickly shift my whole body around when the strange woman suddenly turns and glowers and at me with her intense eyes. A thought instantly infiltrates my head - "who is this woman?" - as she storms out into the sunshine.

Soleil Oupary

BEFORE THIS MOMENT, I'd spent the last thirty days in the ICU. My head still hurts, my body still aches all over and my hope in those I love is diminished. I'm not sure what came over me, but I collided into a woman—a stranger, nearly trampled all over her. Okay, granted... There's a part of me that's upset. No visits? No calls? No one comes to pick me up when I finally reawaken? After having spent weeks lying in bed, all I wanted was a way out. I didn't even know my sides could hurt so much. My hand brushes over the tight gauzy wrapping with careful tenderness.

Somehow, I know that no one is coming for me, *alone as usual Soleil*. Given all that's happened, maybe it's for the best and seeing as I almost met my doom, it was a good idea to move forward rather than dwell on the past. So I decided to dawn my first name and leave my last name as it was. I snaked my hands across my collarbone...

Oh, God! It's missing! Where's the Emblem?

Robert Michaels

MY FRUSTRATION LEVEL was rising to a new peak…

"Will anyone tell me what the hell is going on?"

The murmurs in my cell phone don't even answer my question. Holyoke Hospital has had me on hold for hours, and rage boils deep inside my bones. One answer. I only need one.

"Where is Soliel Oupary?" Why can't these people give me a simple answer?

I'm close, and I count the cars ahead one by one. I feel numb with anger, praying she won't hate me for running late all this time.

A voice cuts in again, after I'd been placed on hold.

"Ms. Soliel is gone; she left our care hours ago."

My mouth parts, the words on the other line warble into a sort of white noise. It's as if all time and space has been interrupted. I find myself—spinning, ragged and breathless—waiting in the infinite stop-and-go traffic. I can tell too much time has passed, and no matter what, I'm too late. Soliel is a smart girl I am sure she will find us, better to go back as there's a reunion to attend to.

Concerned gazes sweep across the floor of the room.

"No doubt, you've heard of the news," Palace said.

The students from the expeditions and the students at the Rolling Hills University lab finally together again. I look over to my brother Robert while holding the list of registered students in my hand; I mentally take a head count and then inhale a shallow breath of air.

"That's odd," I said keeping my eyes on the registry.

"What's odd?" Ashley Boylan asked.

"Shoba Ala, where is she?"

Robert distracts me, softly resting his hand on my shoulder.

"It would be better if we addressed it in private, brother."

By the sounds of it, something pretty grim took place. The last thing we needed right now is anymore bad news. I nod at the students.

"Give us a minute."

We relocated to my office. Robert closed his eyes for a moment. I almost didn't know what to say.

"Shoba's had to take a leave of absence."

I leaned in. "Is she—"

Robert dispelled my worries.

"Yes, she's fine," he assures me. "It's her mother." Before I can continue, I ask my brother a simple question. "Given everything that's happened, Are you okay?"

He just looks at me while taking inventory of the books on my shelves.

"Let me put it this way, I hope I never relive anything similar again."

That was on par with my own feelings. Whatever our differences, my brother and I always put our students first.

The both of us rose out of our seats; we hear a knock at the door. Betty Tavish swung open the door and stood still in the doorway; her chest was heaving heavily and she had a shocked look on her face.

"It's her! She's back!" she whispered.

The two of us walked side by side out of the office. I can't help but stare at her—Soliel. I don't know how much time has passed or how much will change after, but I'm thankful for now. This moment. I'm thankful that's she's alright. Soliel regards me with a quick glance as the class storms around her. She smiles, but not fully. The other students, glad to see her smother her for a few minutes and finally step back and give her some air. Then she finally makes her way towards my brother and I.

"Well, well, speak of the dead..." I said with a wolfish smile.

Soliel flashed a lopsided grin.

"Not yet. Not dead yet."

Robert comes around, as if he just realized something.

"We got an extra room. I mean, if you're not just ready to go back home."

There's a definite look of surprise in her eyes.

"Are you sure?" She asked with uncertainty in her voice.

"—just know the option is there," I replied.

At this, Soliel nods and shrugs.

"Maybe it's not such a weird idea. Can't say I'm looking forward to getting back to my crummy apartment..."

"Then, that settles it."

Everyone in the room shifted to get a look at me. Have you ever felt that? Felt weird or odd to all those around you, except not to yourself?

"Soliel? What's wrong?" Robert asked

I could already see I've made them uncomfortable. Feeling like a victim—a charity case—is the last thing I wanted. *I guess I wasn't dreaming when I left the hospital after all.*

My voice cracked. "It's missing. The Emblem."

When I caught my breath, an epiphany came to me. That moment in the hospital. *That woman...*

The chills I felt were that of those waking from an awful dream. We hit each other so fast that the impact could have knocked the Emblem free. In my head, I replay the scene over again and again. That weird gaze she gave, as she shuffled her purse on her shoulder. That's it! My steps quicken and I go to grab my coat.

"Are you going to tell us where you're headed," Robert asked.

"Where ever she's headed. She's not going alone," Palace replied.

Then an intense air filled the room. Palace gathered his things too. Not long after; everyone else in the room followed. Absurdly, my colleagues were all getting whatever they had and then were right behind me.

"She mentioned the subway," I told them.

At this point, I knew they didn't have a clue about whom I was speaking of, but they trusted me. They trusted my word and once my colleagues gathered their things, we left to go find the woman.

Callum Morrissey

"BY ORDER OF THE COURT, this case is dismissed..."

Callum cut the judge off. "What?"

"Do I need to repeat the order for you, Mr. Morrissey?"

These swift motions were all too familiar for me. I rubbed my hands together, until they got hot. In cases like these, the criminal defense attorney only contented themselves with manipulative legal loop holes. I sighed and shook my head.

"Your Honor, there are no grounds to move for a dismissal. Picture this. A full grown-man stands on the same route a twelve year old boy walks every day. Every day that man has a choice. He can watch that child walk home or he can take that child home with him—"

Judge Mathias straightened herself up and sat listening for a few moments in silence.

"—how is it that when the victim walked that same street, on his way home from school, all witnesses remember him passing by except at the corner exactly where the defendant stood?" I asked.

"Correlation does not equal causation, Mr. Morrissey," the judge pointed out glancing over the frames of her glasses.

I approached the bench uncertainly; needing her to hear me out. Hoping, somehow, I could convince her not to let this criminal go. The mere sight of me—standing so close—wrinkled her brow in the most undesirable way.

"Frankly, we can't afford to dismiss this case. That's not what this city wants," I pleaded damn near almost on my knees. "It's the city I fight for!"

Her nature still cold, the judged lifted the wooden gavel, saying nothing else. The sound of its flat hammering echoed through the courtroom. Then she found her voice. I centered my attention on her eyes.

"Case dismissed!"

I just stood in uneasy quiet while the entire courtroom shuffled out of the doors.

Another case lost. Another criminal on the street. I've long since gotten past drowning my inadequacy in a bottle.

Actually, between all the young professionals heading out to dimly lit bars and those of us just calling it a night, there really didn't leave much for those who wanted a little something in the middle. People like me. People who have gotten too old to crawl to a pub, yet still wanted a relatively quiet evening out—it hardly seemed fair.

Maybe I should just leave early. Go home. There are a hundred paged briefs calling my name tomorrow morning. As I tried to forge a path through the endless city traffic, a car rushed past me, inches from striking me down dead in the street. Midtown. The city was packed full of hordes of strangers all trying to head in one direction or the other. New York maybe dirty, but it oozes character. The rich mixture of culture and colorful backgrounds are what makes this urban mecca better than any place else. Through the scattering crowd, the steps for the subway caught my eye.

I resumed ahead quiet and introspective, sticking my hands deep down into my pockets. A clamor of muffled footsteps rush down alongside me as trash, pages of a tabloid with Hollywood's latest gossip strewn all about my path.

"Oomph!" I cried out. A woman thumped into me at the speed of a wrecking ball. We watched each other clumsily swerve around. Not once did we exchange a single word. She and I both slowed, gazing into one another's eyes—without being too obvious. A surge of recognition fired inside me. *Do I know this woman?* I wondered. This sense of déjà vu, something close but also far fascinated me. She wobbled on her feet. I grabbed her hands to help break her fall.

"Gotta be sure to keep your eyes up," I told her.

She gave me a slow suspicious nod. "Falling down is my badge of honor, I'm afraid."

"Where are you headed?"

"Rolling Hills."

"That's not too far from me."

She resisted some more. "Look, I'm fine. Really."

"I'm Callum."

"Soliel."

All of a sudden, the intercom announces the oncoming arrival of the connecting train. She relaxed a bit, and I released her hand. We stand next to each other for minute. The train comes to a screeching halt. A green light dings. Throngs of densely packed people erupt from its hissing automatic doors.

I waved my hand. "You first."

"HEY! Hey—get a clue!"

A woman, with long scarlet hair, shrieked at the top of her lungs before the doors closed behind us. We both drifted towards the left side of the car, watching the entire odd spectacle.

A man stood close—too close—to her back. We heard a scuffle and two voices shouting at one another.

"Oh, Come on; just admit it sweetheart, you liked it."

"Yeah, suurree.! After working eight hours with screaming kids, the first thing I'm absolutely dyyyingg for is for some jackass to grope me on the K-train!"

The dark haired woman nudged me in the shoulder."Should we say something?"

"It looks like she has it handled." I shrugged.

Needless to say, I only wanted to stay out of it. The woman was wearing a sea foam colored dress and had a bullish attitude, she was pivoting fast, teetering left and right at the mercy of the turbulent train. She was seething, trying to hold on to both the metal pole and her composure. Startled, she squinted at us both. Then she acknowledges us with a wagging finger and shot an intense look at Soliel.

"Wait. Wait. Wait." she insisted, the hem of her dress swinging.

"You look like you've seen a ghost," Soliel said.

"—you...I *know* you."

Soliel's eyes darted left and right.

"How so?"

"Holyoke Hospital."

For whatever apparent reason, I must have been invisible. The crazed woman barely uttered two words to me, but no one else on the train appeared to be bothered. Typical New Yorkers.

Soliel, was suddenly breathless; she recognized her too. She felt weak and grabbed hold of the dingy metal pole to support herself.

"Do you have it?" she asked with wide eyes.

The fiery-haired woman nods, digging through heaps of junk in the purse tucked under her arm. At this point, I'm still bewildered on what's going on.

"Found it!"

The loud woman reaches out her arm with some sort of, what looks like a stone, in her hand.

I gazed over at Soliel with a curious interest.

A jerk shakes our train car. People slightly spill out of their seats. The hothead holding the stone falters but catches her balance.

"Esabelle."

She shakes Soliel's hand. I stopped myself from stumbling onto the disgusting subway floor but still not taking my eyes of the exchange between the two girls. Esabelle turned her hand over and Soliel gave up her palm. The small jewel plopped in the middle of her hand and she clutched onto it. She was instantly calmer now than the when I first met her, no longer the frantic woman rocketing down the subway steps.

"Do you guys want to meet up? Some other time, I mean?" Esabelle looked around. "Not like this on the train, but someplace we could sit down and talk?"

Honestly, I didn't do small talk. I barely could stand being in a crowd of people. Soliel didn't wait for my reply.

"It's the least I can do. There's a place right next to the entrance of the station a coffee place, I think. Why don't we all meet there?"

My nerves twisted a bit at the thought of having an articulate conversation with two, by any measure, attractive women.

"What say you—" Esabelle prodded hoping I'd finish her sentence.

"Callum. My name's Callum Morrissey."

Esabelle swayed slightly trying to figure if she's met me someplace before.

"...Callum Morrissey...Callum Morrissey..."

Something must have sparked in her brain because her face flushed once she looked me in the eyes. She had that same blinding rage from earlier when dealing with the subway perv.

"Oh, so it's you!"

"Me?"

"You're the damn fool that knocked your beer all over my dress!"

The twitches of electricity in my head pulled it all together.

"Ohhhh, that."

Esabelle pushed me with a single shove of her hand. Seething in rage, she clenched her eyes shut. Before, Esabelle's tirade boiled over, I caught a glimpse of Soliel texting on her phone.

Soliel Oupary

> I'm here. At the stop.
> —P.M.

I SWALLOWED HARD, and my mouth felt dry. Palace waited for me somewhere near the side of the platform. The whole of the subway lobby was filled with people I didn't know. Honestly, I knew zilch about where I was heading. A man in a cotton lavender colored button down stood with his back facing me. I couldn't tell for sure, but I thought I'd give it a shot anyway.

"Palace?"

A man turned, broad-chested with a charming grin on his face. I looked at him with relief and disbelief.

"So, we meet again?" he said his voice thick and sultry.

I stiffen at the sight of him unable to speak.

"That was just a joke. Y'know like ha...ha..." I half-smiled hoping I wouldn't get too dizzy.

"Oh, sure. I guessed half as much." Seemed like nothing would dig me out of the deep hole I'm in now. He stuck out his elbow.

"If you'd like you can hold on, and I'll walk you to the car."

At my age, I should be able to put one foot in front of the other. I thought. I hooked my hand through his and we walked lockstep beside each other. Palace's presence alone made me feel like somehow he could keep me safe. I felt as though, we had this strong connection. Maybe he knew it too. Maybe he didn't, but there's definitely something high voltage between us. At the street crossing just before his apartment, Palace let me know that Ashley was already there. I'm sure this whole thing started with her. My instinct tells me that those inscriptions might have finally been cracked.

"Hhhhheeeyyy!"

A springy figure answers Palace's door. Ashley is all smiles, and her wired energy is infectious. Palace leaned back on the kitchen island. I slunk on his couch. So excited, the poor girl could hardly get out a word.

"It's cracked!"

Palace began to think before he asked his question. He simply collected his thoughts, scratching his chin. "Good news or bad news?"

"Not sure," Ashley replied. "The translated words aren't sentences or phrases, really. You guys, they're something entirely different."

"Like..." I said trying to help Ashley articulate her ideas.

"Beasts."

He cocked his head to the right, confused.

"Beasts?"

"Yes, the inscription is the word Gar'Neim in ancient text's concerning the history of Nubara, the Gar'Neim, or Centaurs, are an intricate part of protecting their most precious jewels. When, I looked down on my neck and examined the small gap where the missing stone was—something else she said came to mind.

"You said beasts. Do you think there's more than one?" I asked.

"I know there is," she insisted. She held the stone under the projection microscope. "There are at least three different Centaurs being described here. I figure they must be some sort of mythical guardians...what they were guarding—I don't know."

I folded my arms picking at the loose tethers of memories floating around in my brain. The inference from the message on the jewel could only be that that creature I saw in my dreams, visions or whatever. The point is, it did in fact exist. I strode to the other side of the room realizing that, at least for me, the fabric of reality completely changed. The arctic, it turns out, hid more secrets than we may have known. Those beasts wanted desperately to protect something, otherwise, why would they try to kill me? I jumped when Palace walked behind me and squeezed my shoulder.

"No worries, you'll be alright," he reassured me.

But will I? Given that angry supernatural beasts dating back thousands of years had it out for me, I'm not sure I'll ever be safe again.

Chapter 3

Ashley Boylan

Stepping before the subway entrance, Ashley was trying to think how she felt about investigating the tunnels alone with Curtis. According to the most recent data read out, the tremors all lead here. I unfurled a subway map with intricate details of all the interconnected rail networks underneath the city.

"Where are the shock waves originating from?" David asked me.

"Couldn't tell you," I replied. "Wish I did, then we would have a much better idea than ever about the general area of where the seismic activity is coming from."

David rolled his eyes.

"General idea? Good one, Palace. That's *really* helpful..."

I flashed him a scathing look.

"Then tell me, David. Where's your plan? I don't ever remember you suggesting one, *hmm*?"

We both squabbled on like this for a couple more minutes until I noticed a woman crouched near the steps. She gave me a fearful look then dodged out of view. While finding the tunnels was priority number one, we needed to take some drastic measures. There are people who live along the dark tunnels. People who would know more about the more off-beat corridors rarely traversed by the likes of the 9 to 5 train riders.

"Hold on," I told him. David quieted, watching me quickly make my way down the steps and approach the woman where she squatted. The woman's intense piercing green eyes peered at me through a sea of red that was normally white. The skin around her eyes was puffy and dry as if she had just woken up, but most likely she'd been awake for hours. Her clothes were tattered and stained, and seemed to hardly keep her warm. She muttered as I approached her.

"It's...It's alright. I'm not here to hurt you." I said.

She pulled away as her eyes widened, there was no doubt, and she had been abused before by people passing through. Police harassed her for loitering and passengers harassed her because of the smell so to them and her state of utter poverty; she no longer deserved to be treated like a human. She glanced at me obviously pondering my intentions.

"Please. I sincerely mean you no harm. I have a question which I think you may know the answer to."

She panicked breathing fast and scuttling further away with her back against the wall. Despite my best efforts, she didn't trust me, which meant we needed another plan. When I began to walk away, I heard a squeak of a voice.

"You a cop?" she mumbled through cracked lips.

I turned around and saw her huddling.

"Me? No. Not all. Just a scientist, I'm afraid."

Although I couldn't see it, I was sure David had no idea what I was doing. I moved closer.

"I'm looking for something, but I need help from someone who knows how to find it."

The pale faced woman wheezed and hacked a nasty cough, she was obviously dealing with some sort of long-suffering illness. *Poor thing.* I thought

"What you looking for down here?"

"We're trying to pinpoint where these shocks are coming from down here in the subway?"

She peered carefully over her holey sleeve.

"Yes!" she exclaimed. "Oooh, those shocks. They keep all of us MOLES ducking for cover."

She paused balled her hand over mouth and coughed.

"Spare a cigarette?"

"I—I—don't smoke."

Quickly, she shuffled back against the wall. I felt I'd lost more ground than I gained. David rushed to my side, rooting around deep in his blazer breast pocket. He plucked out a single cigarette along with a cheap plastic lighter. The homeless woman snatched it fast out of his fingers, propping it between her lips. There was a slight pause as David lit the end. We let the woman take a puff before continuing.

"So, tell us about the...MOLE people," I said.

"There no different from you two, just they make their lives in the caves. In the caves, we can be who we are without being gawked at by the whole world. Usually, it's safe. No one bothers us. But—"

David and I stared at her, waiting impatiently for her to finish. David urged her on. "But? But what?"

"The ground started to crumble underneath us, chunks of concrete rained down from above. Charlie's leg got crushed during the first couple of nights it happened."

"Could you lead us down there? Down to where the quake happened?"

She shook her head at me.

"I ain't going back down there. Why risk my life again? Only a crazy person would go into the depths of the tunnels."

Just like that, we were back to square one, needing answers and having no earthly clue how to find them. David got up from his knees and dug into his pockets and pulled something out. He stretched a hundred dollars in between his hand, tugging it tauntingly at its corners.

"Could you lead us there for say...one Benjamin Franklin?"

The woman grinned, "Now, you're talking!"

I glanced over at David finding his "solution" more than a little crass—but it worked.

The woman pushed herself up from the wall.

"Call me Molly. Follow me."

Soliel Oupary

I POPPED MY HEAD out of the window as we idled in the mid-afternoon traffic. Pedestrians shouted at taxis cutting through the crosswalk. My nerve returned much stronger now, things have gotten emphatically much better. Palace and Robert have been nothing but gracious. Now, I'm off to catch up with Esabelle and Callum—the two strangers I met off chance on the subway. It felt nice to be doing what normal people did again. We were meeting up to just sit and have a chat. Then something flickered in me, this twinge of panic. *What would I say about myself, really?* I thought. I never found it easy to yammer on about all things Soliel. A part of me felt more at home sitting quietly in a cafe corner than being in center of a crowd. A muffled murmuring went off in my pocket, making a whirring noise as it vibrated against the driver side door.

I felt my phone vibrate so I pulled over and checked my phone. It had a text and it read......

> Can't make it. Gotta work late. Sry—Callum.

Callum wouldn't be there. Understandable, this sort of worked out, in a sense. Now, Esabelle and I could have a chat alone. She had this presence about her, something I can't quite describe, but it lingers on the tip of my tongue. This energy between us seemed almost kismet. First things first, I had errands of my own to run. Shoba was still in England and left in such a manic rush, I never did have a proper chance to say goodbye. I pulled a letter tucked in my jacket pocket and headed straight for the blue drop off box nearby. Her mother had come down with a serious case of bone cancer and could hardly walk without suffering great pain. How anyone can muster to find hope amongst all that tragedy—I don't know. The letter tumbled into the dark depths of the post box. I just needed to help in some small part. I needed my best friend to stay strong.

After parked the car, I coursed up a narrow flight of stairs. On the next landing was the entrance to the subway, and the cafe wasn't too far ahead. Esabelle sat right next to the window. Once again, that now familiar pounding intensity started to throb through my body. Esabelle drew me to her somehow. Immediately, I shuffled inside and greeted her.

"Hope I didn't keep you waiting too long," I said smiling.

Esabelle looked up from her coffee, almost as if I'd caught her by surprise.

"Nooo, not at all. Just been sitting here daydreaming."

She placed her coffee back on the plate.

"Where's our boy, Callum?"

"Won't make it. He said he had last minute work."

Esabelle craned her neck up slowly. "Ah, I see. Also, please don't take this the wrong way or anything..."

The warning piqued my interest. Usually such warnings were a precursor to something bordering on offensive.

"You just seem so guarded," Esabelle said.

I shrugged. "People say I'm hard to get to know..."

"Why is that?"

No one's ever asked me that before. It's like she had this deep connection with me even though we just literally met.

"Yeah, I'm just so much in my head. Guess that's why I ended up being an anthropologist."

I meant that to be a joke, but Esabelle didn't laugh. She simply eyed me up and down as if she thought I should have said something more.

"I can hear it in your voice, there's sadness there," Esabelle replied.

I gave a half-hearted shrug. "Everyone's got a sob story. I'm no different."

Esabelle forced a grin. I'm sure she detected the tension brewing.

"So, when you gonna tell me about that necklace?"

She looked at me as I stroked the pendant she returned with my thumb. She reached out her hand. "Do you mind?" She wanted to touch it. I didn't mind so much as I wanted to be careful not to lose it. Once I nodded, she caressed the opal gem and the previously missing piece.

"Aagh!" Esabelle jumped.

"What happened?"

"I don't know."

By the time her arm settled back on the side of her table, I could tell something was different. She gazed longingly at her fingertips. Her eyes turned electric blue for a few short seconds.

"Do you feel that?" she asked.

Certain I didn't feel a thing I asked her, "Feel what?"

"The energy..." she replied.

"It's about time for me to take a hike," she said.

Feeling terrible for running late, I gently clutched her arm. She merely pulled up her purse from slipping down her shoulder.

"I got to go, but I'll call you sometime."

I looked away, deflated. "Okay. Bye."

She skipped out of the doors running towards the subway exit. I watched her until she vanished in a crowd of people.

"Well, that was abrupt." I wondered why Esabelle was so awkward, maybe it was just me, maybe this is how New Yorkers are in general. Not sure. Strange girl. But I still think she is interesting to say so the least.

Callum Morrissey

I SLIPPED MY CELL back into my pocket. Soliel should have gotten my text by now. I could hear the other attorneys bickering over insubstantial minutia. Here I am. Stuck. I'd much rather be relaxing for two hours engaged in conversation with strangers. I pulled my jacket over from the back of my chair and folded it on the desk. Believe me, today I could have used the escape. I replayed meeting Esabelle on the train again in my head. My heart slowed slightly at the thought of her flowing red tendrils of hair blowing freely in the wind. I wish she could see how I saw her.

Esabelle had something more than beauty she had heart—fearlessness. All the things I lack. I let my eyes close and pictured her as if she stood right next to me. Even the thought felt a little scary, but I imagined her standing there anyway. If only she could see the other side of me, the side of me that's a capable prosecutor...most of the time. Maybe then I might have a chance. Anyways, that's enough fantasizing for now.

The door of my office swung open, and a man I knew from an old case entered. He'd been mistakenly accused of committing a robbery. He had olive-toned skin, wore a fitted jacket and smiled big from ear to ear.

"Pablo Martinez, it's been sometime. To what do I owe the pleasure?" I asked.

About three years ago, Pablo's ex-girlfriend, Tamara Ortiz, robbed the Lucky Nine's convenience store on Broadway. There were two cameras on opposite ends of the convenience store. One camera clearly shows Pablo sitting in the car driving away from the scene. From the looks of the initial evidence, it would seem like an open and shut case.

Yet the other camera, thought to have been busted, recorded Tamara bolting out of the store with plastic bags of stolen money gripped in her hands. The second footage surfaced only after I'd spoken with the store clerk. He spoke Armenian and, of course, the cops didn't take the extra time to understand what he was trying to say.

I had the bright idea of hiring a translator to tag along and give me a detailed account of what the clerk saw on the day of the events.

"Mr. Morrissey, sir. Thank you, thank you so much. I'm a free man because of you and your incredible work." Pablo said as he eagerly shook my hand. I smiled. "We're not out of the woods yet. The jury still has to deliberate over the evidence when we present it in court."

Pablo stepped back, nodding. "Yes. Yes. I understand. My ex put me in some serious trouble. If the jury convicted me, they could put me away for nine years." He finally stopped furiously shaking my hand. "Not as long as I'm representing you and not as long as we have the second video tape. Are you busy? C'mon let's go for a drink. Just one." Unable to hold back the smile, he dove right in and hugged me. I gulped gingerly patting Pablo's right shoulder. "There. There." Once he pulled away, Martinez gave me one last grateful look. "I'll see you tonight, Mr. Morrissey," he said and left my office.

I hid the two digital copies of the footage on my thumb drive. The rain outside poured against my window, without an umbrella I'd get soaked. The best thing I could do right now without calling our overworked security guard is fish through the items in the "Lost and Found" in our office. Before I left, I stowed away the thumb drive in my desk for safe keeping. When I turned the corner, the Lost and Found was directly ahead. Just as I figured, a couple of forgotten umbrellas, and a stash of other knick knacks that had no chance of being reclaimed, were ready for the picking. I greeted passing colleagues on the way out to meet up with Pablo. God knows I needed a stiff drink.

The clock inside steadily ticked as I sat in my seat. A brief had been left on my desk, but I didn't have a pen to sign it. As I rummaged through my drawers, I felt a jolt of unease. My hands scraped the bottom of the drawers, and even though I knew I put my thumb drive inside... I felt nothing. It was empty.

Where could it have gone? I wondered, feeling my temperature rising. Then my body flinched as a surge of adrenaline shot through my arms. When you get a feeling this bad, you can't just ignore it. I rifled through each drawer. I dug through my boxes of case notes. After that, I dropped fast onto the floor and crept around examining its cracks on my knees.

Where could it have gone!? Then it hit me. Martinez will go to jail without the introduction of that tape into evidence. The smell of bourbon on my breath had my head spinning. A man's life and freedom literally slipped from my grasp. The chances of him getting off now plummeted exponentially. Now, as it stood, it was the claims of one man against twelve, and the odds were not in his favor.

THIS TIME I WAITED.

It wasn't long until Esabelle arrived. These meet-ups at the cafe happened with surprising regularity. Esabelle immediately came to suspect we had more in common than what meets the eye. She shuffled into the booth and plopped her purse beside her.

"How's your coffee?" she asked.

"Lukewarm," I replied.

"That's why I always wait until they make a new pot. I like my coffee boiling."

I stifled a chuckle before taking another bitter sip.

"Let me ask you." Esabelle looked directly at me. "We've been hanging out for the past few weeks. Why haven't you spilled the beans about why you stayed in the hospital?"

After spending weeks drained and broken, I didn't really want to face it anymore. Languishing for weeks on end with broken bones needed to be a far off memory, but I knew I'd never develop a friendship if I kept bottling everything in. So here it goes.

"As you know I'm a grad student studying to be an Anthropologist," I began. "A few weeks ago, a select few of us from my class, Myth and Reality 101, took an expedition to Foxe Basin in the Arctic..."

Esabelle just sat there quietly listening. There was something about the way her red hair glowed in the warm sun. She just allowed me to talk freely, without making me dread if I've talked way too much.

"So, we get in the cave, and being the super klutz that I am, I trip backwards and fall. Before anyone can help me out the whole thing collapses and I'm buried under the ice for several long lonely hours."

She looked at me through a furrowed brow.

"Am I boring you?" I asked.

"No, it's not that. It's just that your injuries don't entirely to match the story, is all."

Bewildered, I reply, "Gee, thanks."

"No, it's not like that. The type of break that cracked your ribs, that sounds very deliberate."

Telling her the whole truth would only make me sound crazy. So, I avoided it like the plague.

Esabelle leaned over the table clinking her mug against its plate as the waitress came and refilled our coffee to the top.

"What were you all doing out there in the frozen arctic anyways?"

"We were in search of something; we wanted to prove if there was any validity to the legend of Nubara."

Esabelle, impressed, pointed her finger.

"Ohhhh, I think I've heard of that. My memory is a little rusty, but isn't there some theory that an asteroid or more than one at some point will be going to impact Earth making it go BOOM

"Yeah, something like that," I replied. "We wanted to see if there was any truth to it."

Of course, I skipped the whole thing about having visions. Visions of creatures chasing after me in a mythical forest, verging on delirium. Esabelle leaned in closer completely entranced.

"Is there?"

"We're still not sure. Our only hope is a small rock with an inscription written in a language that no one has spoken for thousands of centuries."

I looked down at the locket around my neck and twiddled it in my fingers.

"Esabelle."

"Mmhmm."

"Would you mind taking the locket?"

"You sort of just met me," she said a little taken aback.

"—But I feel like I've known you forever. I just think it will be safer with you."

Esabelle glanced at the locket I dropped in her hand. No doubt, it was a little forced. No matter how crazy it seemed, I knew I made the right choice.

Ashley Boylan

PALACE & DAVID STILL haven't caught up yet. And to my side there was Curtis helping me investigate the point from which all the tremors emerged. The dust in the air was so thick you could choke on it. The colossal spaced had long since been abandoned. Pieces of thick suspension cable and unsalvageable rusted tracks twisted in all directions. Curtis glanced at his watch.

"Where are those two?" asked Curtis as he watched Ashley's curls roll into her eyes. "I dunno," I whispered, hushing Curtis to keep his voice down.

My shoes were soaking wet from sloshing around in the pools of lubricant and rain water that collected on the ground. If I had to vote for the worst place in New York—and possibly Earth- this place would be it. Everything felt damp, but the air had a stale moldy odor.

"How exactly will we know if we found the nexus, the spot where all this stuff began?"

"Weak traces of radiation should set off the scanner." I said lifting the heavy metal device.

Curtis muttered something, foul I'm sure, tired of searching blind on this wild goose chase.

Thud.

"Did you hear that?" Curtis asked as I simply carried on walking.

Thud. Thud.

"There it is again!"

This time I heard it too. I held my gaze firmly, peering out into the sullen dark. The air around us grew thick and thicker until either of us could hardly breathe. Although, I could not see it, someone was following us using the shadows of as cover. I'm not sure what scared me the most, the fact that we were being watched or the fact that I didn't know why.

Callum Morrissey

I SLIPPED AWAY OUT of my office, knowing Pablo waited just outside. He took a reeking drag from a cigarette. The looming stream of smoke filled the air. In a half-hearted gesture of solidarity, I inched up to his side.

"Can I get a hit?"

Pablo passed over the cigarette, and I inhaled deep leaning against the wall.

"You're not going to like what I'm going to say next?" I warned him. His eyes glared at me in the worst way.

"What do you mean?" he asked.

I didn't even want to talk about it but the god damn thief gave me no choice.

"The security tape."

"So, what about it?"

Before I say anything more there's a silhouette of three figures running through the back of my office and out into the street.

Pablo plucked the cigarette from his lips. "Is that? Is that Tamara?"

Tamara Ortiz charged through the afternoon rush of people. Each step she took only looked more pitiful in her stiletto high heels.

Pablo chucked his cigarette and stormed after her. I helplessly followed.

Soliel Oupary

PEOPLE BRUSHED PAST me while I stood in front of the entrance. I scanned the whole parking lot, searching for Esabelle. Then she walked up with her hair tied in a bun, ready to go.

"Don't worry, I know shopping isn't really your thing, but I promise when we get there you're going to have fun.

I just agreed trying to let me talk myself out of it. I wasn't old but I didn't think I was young anymore to hang out around the "food court." Esabelle steadily gathered her train fair in her hands. We stepped forward and headed down deep into the train station. The swarming crowds of people triggered nausea in me; I tried to ignore it. We didn't reach the platform yet and Esabelle hadn't paid for her transfer card.

Esabelle tapped me on the shoulder. "We'll get the next one, kay?"

I nodded.

A rush of people entered the subway car. Another train screeched, roaring into the station. When we gazed through the windows, we saw practically no one stood inside.

"C'mon, let's get a seat before it gets full."

As we approached the turn style, a woman gut checked us with her elbow, almost shoving us to the ground. Beads of sweat dripped down her face and in her hand, she clutched a thumb drive of some sort. She breathed so hard you could hear the wheezing deep in her chest. Where ever her destination, she was in hurry to get there. Hyperventilating, she sprang through the air like a javelin then hit the ground running and didn't even pay.

Esabelle snorted. "And people wonder why everyone thinks New Yorkers are jerks..."

Esabelle held her ticket out in her hand, but two men startled her.

"Callum!" I exclaimed shocked.

She too couldn't believe her eyes. Callum and some man who smelled like nicotine barged right through us.

Ashley & Curtis

"GOD," CURTIS RAISED his voice. "Where is it already?"

Ashley too—on so many levels—couldn't remember the last time she ever had this much trouble. After clattering over the crumble of cement, Ashley came damn near ready to just give up. By the time Curtis caught up to her side, that bizarre noise started up again.

Thud.

THUD.

Curtis and I ran, we didn't know where, but we couldn't stop. Nothing but a flat swift clamor hurried after us. The spotlight from my flashlight expanded about three sizes as a wall cut us off ahead. This will result in one of two outcomes, either we escape or we die.

Curtis and I lined our backs up against the wall. We paused and waited for our doom.

"Doesn't look like we'll ever find the source of the tremors..."

We stood close, our shoulders touching. I glance over at Curtis and he glanced back at me. We shut our eyes.

Thud.

We gasped.

"You two have no permission to be down here!"

We blinked.

A man wearing a Transit authority security suit stood in front of us with a scowl on his face.

"This area is restricted—off limits. It's not safe down here. Time to leave," he grunted.

"Damn it!" Ashley cursed under her breath, careful the cop wouldn't hear her. She yanked out her phone and sent a text...

> **Caught by cop.**
> **Heading back to HQ.**
> **Don't worry. I'm**
> **tracking all of you—**
> **Ash**

The cop brought us back all the way to ground level back to the sprinting hordes of people. The train still idled near the platform. Curtis and I winced at the incredibly loud noises. The transit officer watched us walk a few feet and finally boarded the train.

Soliel Oupary

AS SOON AS WE COULD gather ourselves on the train, I spotted a familiar face. "Oh, hey!"

Someone called out to me. She didn't say my name, but I recognized her voice.

"Ashley? I thought you were searching for the source of the tremors?" I said

She shrugged her shoulders. "Those plans got canceled, at least for now. Everyone say 'Hi' to Curtis."

Curtis waved. Esabelle and I waved back.

Then it occurred to me I had my own introduction to make. "Guys, this is Esabelle."

When Esabelle smiled, Ashley said nothing for a moment. Like she had a feeling about her too. She saw the jewel Esabelle held in her fist. "You gave her the Emblem?"

By the tone of Ashley's voice I didn't know whether she thought it was a good or bad idea. She then silently understood my decision and in agreement she spoke.

"We just met and I feel like I can trust you." Esabelle softly smiled. "Believe me, I get that a lot."

She turned away from me and Ashley.

I just moved my back and settled in, thankful to have a seat. I still ached a bit, even though I remained in the hospital for a while.

"Something's going on back there," she said, blinking hard.

She stood up, balancing and then peered through the window on the car-connecting doors.

"Wait, what are you doing?"

"Soliel, you need to see this?"

Esabelle stretched out her hand, and I grabbed a hold. After backing out of the way, I had a look for myself.

Two men slammed Callum into the subway window. Callum's hair ruffled over his eyes and he shoved back gritting his teeth. Esabelle, Ashley and Curtis witness the scuffle too and now, she had a manic rage in her eyes. Esabelle pulled the connecting door open with one forceful swing.

"Pablo, grab her!" Callum shouts trying to steal the thumb drive away from Tamara.

Tamara taunts Pablo. "Is this what you want? Wait, till the jury has the evidence hearing tomorrow. You won't have a chance!"

Callum swallowed hard shifting away from Tamara while she squirmed underneath his grasp. Something fast caught his eye, as Tamara's kicked and caught Callum in the gut and he heaves back throwing up his hands with the impact. She bulldozed through the other passengers milling about, heading for the connecting doors. One of her goons did everything to stop Pablo and Callum in their tracks. Esabelle jumped in swinging her arm in the man's massive clenched jaw. With one hit the man doubles back, grabbing his bleeding nose before collapsing on the floor. Callum tried to catch his breath as he looked at her. She looked back, whatever drama they had in the past, they put all behind them. Callum found his balance and started to speak.

"Than—"

A clanging noise pierced everyone's ears. Callum reached for her but the speeding jolt of the train knocked Esabelle straight down. He locked his arms around the first thing he could grab. Not once did Callum take his eyes off her burning red hair. Nor she him. The lights blacked out and sparks flew across the window as we all collided with the concrete tunnel.

Chapter 4

Soliel Oupary

Loud cries echoed through the train so naturally, I poked my head out of a broken window on a hunk of twisted metal. In doing so, a million tiny shards of glass sliced my hand as I tried to sit upright. The woman Callum cornered before the crash, fell out of the train car and hobbled down the tunnel. A massive wall of crumbled concrete cut us off from where we crashed and a lingering gloom of dust and gasoline frightened me deep to my core. I surveyed the scene and spotted Callum hanging from a bent metal pole as a high pitched shrill sounded along with a flashing light lit up the room. It got louder and louder and the light flashed faster and faster.

"Callum!" I shouted, my voice hoarse.

Callum's attention seemed averted, he was having trouble focusing.

"There's somebody out there, Soliel. Can't you hear them?"

He unlocked his arms and tumbled free. We both heard someone calling out from the wreckage. The train itself was crushed and flipped onto its back; the engine was still hot and the heat was distorting the air. Ashley and Esabelle were just getting up after being tossed around like rag dolls on the floor.

"Is everyone okay?" I asked.

I heard my voice echo down the tunnel.

"I've been better," Ashley replied.

Esabelle raises her hand. "I'm alive."

Pablo exploded from beneath a pile of rubble and frantically rubbed his head.

I was relieved and happy that I didn't have to flounder alone in the dark, as each of my colleagues staggered out from the smoke and shadows. Callum led the way in the search for the voice we heard. My lungs felt suffocated by the dust and smoke caused by the crash and as I struggled to breath I noticed Esabelle grab Callum's hand so she wouldn't lose sight of him again; we climbed over the writhing limbs of bodies until we found the mysterious voice.

It was a man, conductor of the train. He got tossed near inches of a crackling electrical wire.

"Can you get me up?" He asked.

A cut on his head bled all over his face. I peered down and grabbed his hand while the rest of the gang helped me haul the injured train operator to his feet.

"What's your name?"

"Henrik."

"Do you know if the radio's working?" Esabelle asked.

"Busted," The conductor said. "I've been calling the head authority since I came to. No response so far."

I fanned my face; the heat literally constricted my throat.

"How about walking? Can we walk our way outta here?" Ashley urged.

"It's possible, but there are so many damn path ways. Without a radio, it could take weeks to find us. Plus, I can't just up and leave all these people; they need me to stay."

"No—," Callum cut the conductor off. "They need you to find help or we all die down here. You're the only one who has some knowledge of the tunnels."

Everyone turned, shocked at how Callum instinctively took control of the scene.

Henrik scratched his chin. "I suppose you're right."

"Well then, lead the way."

Callum waved his hand, gesturing for everyone to squeeze through the broken glass window. I was the first through and as I did so, my shoes kicked crystals of glass when I hurdled myself out. Once we were all safely out of the train, we walked a few yards, then stopped and gawked at the scene we were leaving behind. Since I was at a slower pace than the rest of the gang, I was positioned further back, so I was the first to hear the faint noise that broke the silence. Maybe it was all in my head, but the pitch was so high and so shrill, that someone else had to of heard it? The awful noise sounded like screaming, like people were in pain. Still, I didn't dare stop. I kept going, running to catch up with everyone else.

We had been walking only 30 or 40 minutes but it seemed like, yet no one talked, we just marched one foot in front of the other. There seemed to be no interest in saying a word. I leaned on to Ashley, since I almost having died in that crash, I needed to confide in something I've kept buried, until now. Without Shoba, I no longer had that shoulder to depend on, but I couldn't keep it bottled up anymore. Not with the chance that I may die here and my secret with me. Once I was positioned at Ashley's side, I pinched her arm.

"Pst...pst..."

Ashley eyed me with unease.

"You okay, Soliel," she whispered. "What's going on?"

"It's killing me inside. I can't hold it in anymore..."

"We have to keep up."

"I need to tell you something." I urged.

"Are you hurt?"

"It's something about what happened during the cave at Foxe Basin."

Ashley kept nodding and stopped, but the others continued forward, taking with them the light. Needless to say, I had a few seconds to say what I needed to say, before we were surrounded by darkness......again.

"You know that inscription on the Emblem, the one that talked about the monsters, the Silver Cannabis—the beasts?"

"Yeah," she said.

"That's not some wild ancient fairy tale. I've seen them myself."

Ashley leaned in to get a better look at my eyes, making sure I hadn't gotten totally delirious.

"Centaurs aren't real, Soliel."

"It attacked me. Almost killed me."

"You had a hard fall. It knocked you out and you saw things that weren't there."

"No," I insisted seizing her arm. "It chased after me. It was as real as you and me standing here right now."

Ashley looked back, watching the light from the group fade into the dark.

"We can't stand here much longer. We must keep moving," Ashley said speaking kindly as if trying to calm down a raving lunatic. She took my hand to keep up with the vanishing glow ahead.

At the end of another long tunnel, everything seemed to blend into a muddle of black and gray. One by one, we followed each another in a line grabbing and feeling our away through the endless shadows. The air stung the back of my throat as if a sulfurous acid cloud was lingering in the air. Ashley held my hand tight, and I held on just as tightly with just as much trepidation. We both hadn't said a word to each other since I "came out" with the truth—a truth she couldn't believe even existed. Esabelle and Callum led the way with Henrik right behind them. Esabelle suddenly stopped and Callum just about ran her over, it took him a few seconds to recover and then he turned to looked at her, concerned that she may have slipped or tripped on something in the darkness.

"You okay?" he asked.

Esabelle shrugged and slapped her thighs. "I'm lost—we're lost."

Callum thoughtfully arched his brow, he understood that wandering around down here for hours on end would annoy any rational thinking person. They have been heading this way without any real directions. The abandoned railway tunnels were deserted for a reason; much of what was here was built centuries ago. Common sense didn't sway Esabelle, she crossed her arms and sighed with a grimace on her face. Callum gazed at her while he stood alone on some twisted iron girders, waiting patiently, very patiently, for someone to acknowledge her discontent. He clutched the flashlight in his other hand and spoke.

"No kidding, we've been trying to find our way around for hours...what do you expect? We don't exactly have a map."

She shrugged. "The very least thing I could expect is a plan. I'm thinking if anyone should be leading, it should be someone who is good at finding her way around things. Someone who isn't afraid of taking charge."

"Taking charge?" he asked mockingly while cocking his head slightly to the side.

Callum flashed the light directly in Esabelle's face. She held up her hand to shield her eyes.

"Yeah, that's what I said."

After an odd silence quieted them both, since no one else could be bothered to get involved in their feud. Ashley and I just shook our heads. The wisp of light flickered in and out, causing shadows to dance all around us as if taunting us to come towards it. We were painfully aware that if we lost what little light we had, it would swallow us all whole.

"No, what you're saying is you think I'm just screwing around. Look, I'm just trying the best I can. No one here, except—that guy." Callum pointed to Henrik "—has the slightest clue about this place."

Henrik wasn't exactly sure who should lead. To him, all that mattered is that we stopped standing around. There was no exit going back the way they came.

"Stop being so sensitive for a change. Drop the ego and just let me lead," Esabelle demanded. Callum inhaled deeply, laughing right after. Knowing all this time that's exactly what she wanted.

"Now I see! If you think you can find your way better than I can, so be it. Lead the way."

Callum happily got out of her way. He would let her find out on her own just how difficult it is to lead a bunch of strong-headed people.

Esabelle climbed down the collapsed girders, strolled over to Callum and snatched the flashlight out of his hand. He stepped back, tripping slightly but waited for Esabelle to make her move. Callum gritted his teeth, seething as Esabelle lollopped past him.

We all shifted in place, unsure of what would happen next. Neither of them had the personality for leading, if anything, they argued more than they ever made amends. Soliel didn't think wasting any more time listening to the two of them gripe was in the best interest of anyone. Callum hated people like that, know-it-alls, the kind of people who got bored if they weren't listening to the sound of their own voice.

Esabelle gestured for us to follow.

"What are you waiting for? Follow me."

Callum Morrissey

WHO DOES SHE THINK SHE IS? The woman with the fiery red hair had me scratching my head. Esabelle sped far ahead of the rest of us, splashing in pools of foul smelling sewage toward the deeper end of the tunnels. All the other times when I tried to make any decision, she'd cut-in shaking her head, sighing loud enough that everyone knew how fed up she was. As a lawyer, you see this same type of larger than life personalities pretty much everyday. When I looked behind me, I saw Ashley, Soliel and Henrik climbing over the concrete; being careful not to fall. The gaps between the rails extended several feet down to a heap of mangled metal below. When I returned my attention forward, Esabelle had rested her hand on me, then stuck her fingers in her mouth and whistled at everyone else.

"We've walked a lot. Who's up for a break?"

Everyone nodded or just found a piece of wreckage to sit on.

And annoyingly, she glanced up at me with those deceivingly innocent blue eyes.

"So Cal, what's your story?"

As a man who had just quite literally been humiliated only minutes ago, I wasn't exactly in any mood for chit chat. Esabelle seemed like a walking disaster, the sort of person who cared nothing about the opinions of others. The thing is, she wasn't afraid to let her confidence show.

I tried to look down but discovered that I couldn't avoid her eyes.

"There's no story..."

"*Psh*, everyone's got a story. What type of law do you practice?"

"I'm a public defender."

"Really? You know what... I can see that."

Her frankness had a mild gleeful factor about being impolite; it was the most surprising thing about her. She smiled at me, and to be honest, it made me sweat.

"What about you? Do you have any hobbies? Besides being a pushy know-it-all, I mean..." I asked.

Esabelle snorted and punched me in the arm.

"Kids."

"You have some?"

"I teach them."

"Oh now, the whole 'control' thing makes a helluva lot more sense," I said.

She burst into a fit of giggles and hit me much harder this time. Our eyes met. She inhaled quickly to catch her breath, and I know I felt something at that moment standing beside her. She locked her arm around mine and we continued to walk forward: together. It was surprising how a minute can change things, one minute I couldn't stand the sight of her, the next minute we were laughing and chatting like we're old friends. It's almost like I stumbled into something without even realizing it. She gripped my arm tighter, and my stomach twisted in knots. It's been months now since I've spoken to another woman for more than a few minutes. Most of those minutes are work related. If I say anything more, I'll probably go too far. Esabelle wiped her lip with the back of her hand, holding the flashlight in the other. She probably knew what I was thinking. I've never been too good at wrestling with those vulnerable thoughts. Don't ask me why, I have no problem standing in front of a judge and jury. But when I'm standing anywhere near a woman, my throat tightens, and I break out into cold sweats. When a woman looks at me, they see a scrawny, terrified man too frozen to speak. Esabelle released her tight grip on my arm. *Was it me? Damn, did my eyes linger too long?* I wasn't sure, but she stepped away looking curious. Esabelle stretched out her arm tentatively—squinting as she stepped—and shined the light on a nearby wall.

Ashley, Soliel and Henrik stopped just at my back. The flood of light waved across a tattered and torn map on the wall. There have been many times I've seen a map of the city; this was no ordinary map. It had rail lines I'd never even heard of before. Through the misty darkness, the lines blurred, but before I could take a closer look at it, Ashley shoved me out of the way. She obviously spotted something on the map that she recognized because she yanked the map away and then pulled something out of her back pack. I wasn't exactly sure what it was until I saw her unfurl it in her hands.

"We're getting close."

"Close to the exit?" I asked.

"What? No. Closer to the seismic activity radius."

Ashley kicked through the dirt, holding out the palm of her hand. "Give it to me, I need to see something," she said looking at Esabelle. Then Esabelle waited for some reassurance. I just nodded, trusting that whatever Ashley had in would work.

Ashley watched eagerly as Esabelle dug through her purse. It took her a few moments of rooting in her bag, but she finally fished out a locket. Ashley's body trembled as he inspected the necklace closely in her hand. She turned it back and forth, and then she unexpectedly stopped. Whatever she struggled to find, it didn't appear.

Soliel grabbed her hand as Ashley looked up and scrunched her lips in frustration.

"Are you going to explain what's going on?" Soliel asked.

"I thought it would be here," She huffed ruefully. "It's nowhere to be found in the inscriptions."

Curtis glanced at his watch wondering how long we'd been wandering down here.

"There should be etched engravings pinpointing where the location of the quakes originated from. How could they disappear?"

Curtis and I stepped out into the light to get a good look. I've seen the Novae Emblem up close before. It's true. The engravings were missing. Its matte surface was entirely smooth. Maybe the clues weren't quite as clear as we thought. Ashley fussed with the insistence that eventually, something would show. I gathered around with everyone else. Everything happening tonight is like nothing I've ever experienced before. I whispered in Soliel's ear.

"Do you have the slightest clue what's this all about?"

Soliel stroked her fingers through her hair.

"It's a long story. You wouldn't believe it even if I told you."

"Believe me, I've got nothing but time," I replied.

We trod off together talking as we went.

"There's a legend of an asteroid primed to collide with earth. That locket she's holding is a jewel called the Novae Emblem. I went on an expedition to see if there was any correlating scientific evidence that would prove whether its trajectory with earth was inevitable."

I NODDED TRYING to logically piece everything I had just heard into mentally digestible chunks. I had no idea, when I ran into Soliel and Esabelle on the train that I'd come face to face with the end of all life on the planet. *Can you imagine?* It sounded absolutely insane! I almost didn't even believe her.

I scratched the back of my neck. "You don't need me to tell you how crazy it sounds?"

"As a scientist you often realize...reality is often more frightening than fiction," Soliel replied.

"Is that all?" I asked. "I didn't sign on for this..."

Soliel made eye contact with me. I imagined she had something more sinister to reveal and I had a terrible feeling that whatever she was going to say next wasn't going to make me feel any better.

"Now forget all this science stuff I just told you."

"—Okay," I replied warily.

"There's the legend. The love story of the ages. Stories of ancient queens and kings of the galaxies…"

"Uh-huh."

"The legend has it that a powerful Queen Marietta of Atlantis—from tales of old—fell in love with another species, an alien from Planet X. A planet known as Nibris. The two had a torrid breathless love affair until it was discovered. As punishment for the shame she wrought, she was cast out, banished into the unyielding emptiness of the vast universe. She and her love created Nubara, the earth-destroying asteroid, together."

I heard mumblings from behind us as Soliel was telling the story; it was Esabelle, who flashed a skeptical look.

"You're telling that 'love in space' story again?"

Soliel spun around annoyed. She didn't believe in tragic folktales either, but something was happening to her that she couldn't deny. The burst of intense energy flaring between Esabelle, Ashley and herself was so intense, it almost hurt. I couldn't feel the unexplained power that Soliel did. Yet, there's a connection I detected immediately when I saw all three women standing there. I pulled my coat tighter, my nerves shaken. I wasn't sure what to believe.

"Has anyone heard from Dr. Michaels?" Ashley asked.

Soliel shook her head.

I eased my way further out.

"I find it hard to imagine a woman like you studying far flung planets and ancient legends."

Soliel didn't look me in the eye, her hair shrouding the left side of her face. "I've got my reasons." I was also struck by how defensive she had become all of a sudden. Soliel's eyes gave off a dark glistening shimmer as she glided away like something not of this world. The women caught up again. Curtis and I stood back and watched them work.

Soliel Oupary

ESABELLE EAVESDROPPED IN most of my conversation with Callum. We still didn't know much about each other yet. *Where did the feisty girl with the Venus red hair come from?* Esabelle and I seemed to emerge from two different worlds—neither of which was Earth. I cocked my head slightly as she looked at me, but it didn't seem to deterred her. We locked gazes and stared deeply into each other's eyes. Her skin glinted in the hollow dark and her round focused eyes followed my every move. Esabelle quick-stepped over to me; a smile stretched across her cheeks.

"I couldn't help overhearing," she said.

Her voice vibrated through my entire body. But I could not understand why.

"I don't mean to 'butt in', so to speak...but I overheard something about the legend. The legend of Nubara."

I simply refused to let it slide. "Esabelle, you've been kind to me. But I'd appreciate if you could give me my personal space."

That was the most judicious way I could say it. She didn't even flinch.

"Sorry, I get that a lot." She shrugged. "People do say I'm a bit intense."

No doubt her behavior was bizarre, but if Esabelle was anything else—she was genuine.

"Have you ever had dreams? Dreams so intense you felt overcome with a sudden shock, a faint pressure in your head that never disappears? Do you dream of grotesque monsters? Warriors who attack you in your sleep?"

Everything. Everything she said I had experienced. While everyone else waited for Ashley to decipher the inscriptions, Esabelle and I talked further from the group. My guess is that she wanted to be out of earshot of others. Before now, I'd felt so alone. Not too many other people can say that they've had nightmares like mine; having Centaurs charging after them in a strange land while using weapons made of pure electric energy. Strange visions of people and places I did not recognize. Things up until now, I thought were merely lunatic thoughts in my head.

Callum stood too close. No doubt our conversation stuck out like a sore thumb. He must have heard everything we said and likely didn't understand a single word. He gazed at Esabelle, watching her talk with her hands then stepped in and interrupted our conversation.

"Maybe it's best if we just all take breather, eh?"

"AH!"

We all glanced over at Ashley, waving a satellite phone in her hand as she rushed up towards us and grabbed a hold of me by my shoulder.

"There's signal—see it!" She veered off in the other direction swinging the phone high and low to keep the signal from falling. "It's faint, but it's there."

I only caught a glimpse of the caller ID. Ashley looked nervous about losing a signal. The muffled snowy sound of white noise transmitted through the receiver.

"Who is it?" I asked.

"Dr Michaels...Palace," she replied.

I was relieved but at the same time felt panicked about seeing him again. The Dr made it difficult for me to keep my thoughts in line. No matter, I instinctively knew that having more than professional feelings could destroy things, although, I still allowed my imagination to run wild.

"Is it someone closer to the surface? Can they call for help?" Henrik asked over Ashley's shoulder.

Ashley hit the sides of the phone with the palm of her hand, probably to keep the weak signal from breaking.

"Ash..l..ey..."

A garbled voice escaped from the static.

"Ash..l..ey, Can y..ou hear m...e?"

Ashley yelled into the phone, it was obvious that the phone had merely seconds until it would cut out. The path ahead of us was closed off, so our options dwindled. Something needed to happen and fast.

"Yes!" Ashley coughed inhaling a cloud of soot. "Yes, we're in the tunnels. There's been an accident; a train crashed. We're trying to make our way back to the surface."

We all listened closely as a loud beeping noise sounded in the background. Ashley immediately recognized that sound.

"The seismometer?" she asked under her breath. "Why is it transmitting?"

None of us really knew what was happening. We looked to Ashley, and judging by her expressions, we knew things weren't going too well.

"...Ashley, David's mobile seismometer is getting strong vibrations two miles from where you're currently located. We've been tracking a seismic frequency close enough for you to get to on foot."

Ashley shouted into the phone."What about you where are you?" Ashley asked.

"We got stuck. We never made it past the platform. So, we just headed back to our place to keep an eye on the trackers you installed. We'll send every one down there to find you, whatever you do, DO NOT—"

The signal jumped again, making it difficult to understand.

"Wait. Wait." Ashley shook the phone back and forth. "Can you still hear me?"

She hit the phone again and checked the signal. It appeared the battery was dead since the voices cut out. She didn't seem to want to accept the fact that the signal was lost.

"That's it, Ash. It's over," I said rubbing her back but she walked off; at a loss for words.

Something wasn't quite right about the situation. We all knew that but we didn't know why.

"What's the status?" Esabelle asked.

"There's another quake coming. Our Drs are trying to send the rest of the archaeology team down here to rescue us, but their stuck at the surface with no way in."

I didn't know whether I should feel relieved or terrified that we stood at the epicenter of an oncoming disaster. Ashley finally accepted that her satellite phone wasn't going to work and pocketed it.

Callum scratched his head. "So, what do we do until they get down here?"

Ashley shrugged. "We've got no choice but to wait."

Wait? That's it? Wait for rescue? Wait to die? Esabelle stood next to me, that mysterious energy we felt seemed to jolt right through us. She's got this wild energy that burns through anything and anyone who stood close to her. The screen on Ashley's phone lit up again; it was David again and he had sent a picture of the most recent seismic read out.

"Do you understand what this means?" I asked. Ashley gave us all a serious look.

"It means there's a quake coming that might be worse than the one that flipped our train."

"What are we? Sitting ducks until then?" Esabelle asked.

I exhaled a deep sigh. "Let's hope not."

Chapter 5

A loud dreadful snarl rose up out of the shadows, as creature slithered out from underneath the dark gloom and cut through the soot-filled smog. A paw reached out and climbed down the hulking twisted metal. Drool poured down its gaping maw. *Voices!* It was the sound of fresh meat echoing along the hollowed tunnel's concrete walls. The pack of rabid dog's caught the scent of humans and they set off to find where they're hiding.

"Honestly, I vote we turn around," Henrik said. "I mean we can't keep going forward if we don't know where going forward leads."

Henrik wasn't the only one losing his patience. Ashley had had it up to here with going in circles, following paths that lead to dead ends. Callum didn't say much, but he took a slight satisfaction watching Esabelle's leadership fall apart—especially after she had criticized him. I had avoided the conversation entirely. Instead, I just walked around kicking rocks, thinking about how far Tamara must have gotten. My mind was way beyond impending earthquakes, I was more worried about impending jail time, especially if she got away with the security footage.

Pablo walked away from the group, as everyone else debated on what to do next. How could I have known, my ex-girlfriend, the woman I once thought could be my wife would betray me like she has? I walked a few more paces forward before his foot hit something hard. He stumbled, waving his arms in the air before splashing down in a puddle. A loud rattling clatter echoed right after. We all turned and saw a pipe clanging against the uneven floor. I could hear it rolling down the hall before coming to a complete stop. Drops of sewage water oozed down my shirt and soaked my jeans. I flicked my hands to shake off the foul stinking water.

As I struggled to my feet, I heard a low rumbling noise that originated behind us.

"I thought the trains stopped working here?" Esabelle asked Henrik.

"Umm...That's not a train," he said. "That's something else."

All of us scrambled back when the low rumbling noise approached us. The first thing we saw was sharp glistening teeth as the pack stepped into view. They had cloudy red-rimmed eyes, snarling lips that curled up and revealed their sharp yellow teeth.

"No one make any sudden movements!" Callum shouted. We couldn't imagine all of us fending off the diseased rabble.

"We've got only one chance. We have to separate," Soliel told us. "It's the only way. If we scatter in different directions, they can't attack us in a group."

The last thing I needed was to face off with blood thirsty dogs. The group took a few slow steps back as the dogs closed in. Soliel spoke softly.

"On the count of three!"

"*One...*"

They strode nearer; crushing concrete underneath their claws.

"*Two...*"

Ashley gulped feeling her heart ceaselessly pounding in her chest.

"THREE!"

We took off charging through the wreckage and the ruins as the ravenous dogs snapped at our heels and howled like savages that only can be found in our nightmares. I slipped underneath the downed scaffolding and leaking pipes, limping swiftly and wincing with each step. The further I ran, the less bellowing echoed behind me. *Just keep moving, Pablo. Don't stop. Don't you dare stop.* I told myself as I ran forward gasping for air praying I'd make it out alive.

In the distance, I could hear the dogs shriek. Something must have run them off. Finally, my heart settled down, and I leaned over to catch my breath.

"Are they still there? Can you see them?" Henrik asked. Too afraid to turn around, I didn't dare look back. The way this day was going, I'd be lucky if I survived to the next. We stopped. Sweat dripped down our faces. The barking stopped, as well as the howling. Silence. I had an unsettling feeling that suddenly overwhelmed me. Something was wrong. Henrik hunched over in exhaustion as he struggled to speak. He pointed at me. I looked back confused.

"Do you...do you think everyone else made it out alive Soleil?" he asked.

The question was too big to answer. Hoping everyone made it out okay may just not be realistic. And unlike most anything else I've experienced, this stretched far beyond normal territory and into the twilight zone. I was sick of the smell of raw putrid trash, the choking air and standing hundreds of feet underground. Now we were all separated, god only knows how far apart we were. There's no way to keep track of where we all could have run off. Ashley had the map and the phone. Esabelle had the jewel. And Callum had...*well...* I winced feeling the muscles straining in my legs. I peered out to the pathway behind us hoping everyone was okay.

I've never seen anything like what lied before us. We stood in a silver tunnel that was drastically different from the others. The walls seemed coated with something, some sort of metal. I hung the loop of the satellite phone on my wrist. Without getting to close—or touching it—I inspected the construction of the tunnel walls. Pablo didn't seem to really care what I did. He just felt great relief to still be alive. No longer did the fast pattering of rabid beasts follow from behind us. Ashley scraped muck off of her shoes. Water sluiced out from a pipe, draining through a nearby grate.

"My shoes feel all spongy," I said gazing at my porous leather boots squishing out water with each step I took. Pablo didn't seem to hear me. Or, perhaps just wasn't listening. He stared at the strangely built tunnel.

"What do you think all of this is?"

"I'm the last person to ask for answers."

I leaned forward, slipped off of my shoe and turned it over to pour the excess water out.

"It even smells different in here, not like all the other places."

"...okay" I replied.

"No, really. Take a whiff yourself."

I glared at Pablo not sure if he was joking. Then I closed my eyes and inhaled deeply. Fully expecting to hack at the stench; I didn't. Instead, just as Pablo said, I couldn't smell anything at all.

"This doesn't make any scientific sense..." I told him.

He marched by my side. I craned my head up and examined the ceiling. There's no way of knowing, but this place couldn't have just been discarded by the tunnels. I felt stupid for not having seen it earlier. Good going, Ashley! Over the other side of the tunnel some sort of white light reflected off of the wall. I told everyone in my Myth and Reality 101 course, that no matter how much we won't admit it, there are some things that science has yet to explain. A part of me liked the mystery. That meant I could wake up each morning working to unravel its secrets.

We both stumbled father down the silver plated tunnel not knowing what we would find.

"God, will you please stop pushing me!" Esabelle cried.

Callum pushed her some more."I would, if only you would stop getting into my way,"

Both Callum and I were caught by surprise as we looked back to see if anything was following us. Callum blinked, stroked back his unruly hair and stepped too far back catching his lace in a drain. Fortunately for him, I grabbed his hand just in time and he looked at me embarrassed that he had to take my hand to straighten up back on his feet.

"Might want to think about being a little more careful next time," I said as she poked him in his side. Callum found he couldn't take any more of the small jabs, the backhanded compliments and the nasty rudeness general. It all had gotten on his last nerve.

"Listen, I get it. I'm not the most cool or confident person. Trust me, I get it. But for the next few minutes, do you think you could give the tired jokes a rest?"

I watched Callum slump against the wall retreating from me with a scowl on his face. I've had enough avoiding the obvious. I took a stand and said what was on my mind.

"Do we have a problem here?" I asked.

Callum clutched a part of the wall behind him to steady himself as he took a seat. Callum looked like he said everything he'd already wanted to say, and instead, would simply avoid me.

"C'mon, I thought we already got over this drama already..."

He craned his neck in my direction. "You would think you could catch a hint. I'm *done* talking. No matter what I say, you'll just find some way to humiliate me."

I sloshed my way to him and shoved him in the shoulder.

"OW!"

"Why do you have to be so sensitive about everything anyway? Don't you realize you're much stronger than you look?"

By the look on Callum's face, he'd wait all day before he'd forgive me.

I wanted to clear the air. "Alright, I'm sorry."

It took a momentary second, but he finally looked me in the eyes.

"Yes. You heard me right. I'm sorry."

The way his cheeks relaxed a bit, I knew he was relenting. We wouldn't get out of this if we didn't at least stay on the same page. Even he knew that. I tottered over some trash and slid down beside him.

"So, the question is....what do we do now?"

Tamara Ortiz

A LOW HOWL ECHOED in the depths of the tunnel and instantly I knew it was from what came after me from the shadows. I clutched at the gash oozing blood from my stomach, wetting the gaps between my fingers. I heard a pattering noise echo behind me and as looked over my shoulder, the only thing that came into view was the haunting black cloud of dust that rolled through the silent tunnel. Keep *going, Tamara. Just a little further.* I told myself. Just a few paces more. The creature from hell attacked me. It raked through the flesh of my gut. I could hardly stand but at least I have it now. The footage. Pablo will take the fall instead of me.

Cough.

I didn't want to betray him. But I had no choice. I got caught up in a bad deal, and I needed cash fast. I couldn't reveal the truth to Pablo without confessing to what I'd done. I look down and the palm of my hand was soaked in blood. Droplets trickled down my arm and fell onto the ground below. If the dogs lost me, they'd find me now. The scent of fresh blood was so thick; I could taste it in my mouth. I was clinging desperately onto conscious now. Each minute I forget where I was as stare down the tunnel, unblinking, tired and facing death. Whatever happens to me, I just hope Pablo can understand that I didn't want any trouble.

Cough. Cough.

A light shined, forcing my eyes closed. Have you ever gotten that feeling? The feeling that the worst is over? After walking for hours finally, a light came through. I've reached the end. Soon, I'll be home again. Soon I'll be safe. No more dark caves. No more having to runaway. No more. Each step I got closer to the end, I felt myself trembling as the whole tunnel narrowed around me. Closer. Tighter. I felt a breath constrict in my throat and swallowed it hard. Everything had gotten smaller and smaller all around me. *What's happening? Why can't I breathe?* A panic attack set in, I freaked out in terror induced madness. What if the tunnel won't let me out? What if it won't set me free? Think of what you're saying Tamara. *That's just crazy.* I thought. But the closer I got, the more I'm reminded that I can't stand small places. By the time, I stepped out of the tunnel, I felt as though I had a noose hung around my neck. Maybe this is just me feeling guilty for everything I've done. I can feel my heart slowing; the blood I've lost…it's way too much. When I collapsed on the floor I reached out my hand but no one is there to catch me. The blood flowed over my tongue and only the iron aftertaste remained. My breathing was slowing too and I doubt I can make it any further. So, I stop and kneel. Will anyone help me get out?

Palace Michaels

"EXCUSE ME!"

No one listened. I was breathing fast as I knocked my fist on the window. The woman behind the window turned towards me.

"Can I help you, sir?" she asked. I could hardly hear her voice muffled by the thick plated glass. I dug in my pockets to find my Rolling Hills University ID and pulled it out in one fast move then slapped it against the glass. The woman in the Transit Authority office leaned in close to inspect it.

"Tell me, why a Dr is trying to get in contact with the TA?" she grumbled.

She switched off her radio frequency so she could hear my voice.

"I've got students trapped in the abandoned tunnels beneath the working subway routes." I read her name off of the plastic white name tag pinned to her left shoulder. Delilah.

"Sir, we're already getting teams to access the restricted areas. There's been a train accident, and we're doing everything we can to get the victims out to safety. There's no way to access those tunnels. That area has been closed off for what seems like eons. No one gets in there. No one gets out."

Without a second thought, she turned away from me. Again, I rapped harder against the glass. She spun just as quickly.

"Whoa, Woah, Woah! Step back please!"

Delilah pointed her finger at me. "Keep doing that and you'll break it."

"Listen, in the next thirty minutes there's going to be an earthquake. An earthquake so powerful it could rip this entire station apart. If you ignore us, you're putting everyone's lives in danger. You've got your own crisis you're dealing with I understand. But you'll have a bigger problem on your hands if you don't get us down there. Get the point?"

The woman sat considering it for a minute. My mouth twitched. There was no way to be sure she'd let us through. We were running out of both time and options. The doom and gloom spiel I gave her must have worked, because she immediately turned on her radio and spoke.

"James, do you copy?" she spoke with the radio right at her lips. "Do you copy?"

My brother Robert and the rest of my grad students stood next to me; waiting to hear answers.

David tapped on my shoulder. "How much longer is this going to take Dr. Palace Michaels? We've already wasted too much time."

I hesitated for a moment on what to do next. It seemed like no one had any idea what was going on. Robert held the track monitor in both hands. Surprisingly, it still got a signal. A part of me feels guilty for sending them down in that hellhole in the first place. There was nothing I could want more than to see my students alive again. We had to get down there. We had to reach them.

Delilah grabbed a flashlight from her chair, exiting her booth. She stepped up to us.

"HQ has given us the green light. Keep up with me, I'll take you there."

The damned signal was still too weak. The concrete walls must have been blocking the signal. But a flickering blip blinked on the monitor, giving us hope that my students we're still alive. *What the hell happened here?* I thought. The smoking pile of twisted wreckage shocked us all. *They survived that?* Transit Authority personnel searched through the scraps of metal, searching for any and all survivors.

"How many survivors have you found so far?" I asked watching the TAs walking around with their flood lights.

"Right now, we haven't found any...." Delilah replied.

"It's like you said, there was some kind of tremor. How does that happen in New York City, I dunno. But it shattered the platform which caused the whole thing to collapse in the tunnels."

No survivors? No, that couldn't be right.

Those words replayed over and over in my head. Ashley checked in with me from somewhere so she, at least, had to be alive. My mind reeled at all he nightmarish realities that I could face if none these kids came back alive. David led the way; holding the tracker device signal in his hand. Within seconds, it bleeped out for a strong signal much further beyond where we stood. David took a few steps forward hearing it go faster and faster—then it slowed down.

"What happened?" I called to him. He looked up from his monitor screen. Three hollowed out tunnels stood between him and finding the rest of our crew.

I pocketed my ID. To be sure it could easily be found. "Which one is it?" I asked.

"It wouldn't matter anyway." David shrugged.

"Why's that?"

"Ashley's the only one who's got a tracking bracelet. With everyone else, if they survived, we're flying blind."

Paula came between us. "There's no way we're going in different caves? Getting lost isn't going to save anyone. It's only going to put us in danger."

There's no denying that, Paula had a good point. When Ashley wasn't around, she was always the voice of reason. David, George and I watched her crouch down with a soil testing kit in her hands.

"What are you doing?" George asked with a raised brow.

Paula didn't immediately reply. We waited until she rose to her feet with the testing results in her hands.

"Do you hear that?" David asked.

"Hear what?" George replied.

"Exactly. This far down there should be rats practically running the place."

I didn't even realize it until David had mentioned how odd it was. It was true. These tunnels should be crawling wall-to-wall with rats gnawing and eating their way through the sewage.

"Where could they have escaped to?" Paula asked.

David shook his head. "The scarier question is why?"

There could be no other explanation beyond the earthquake. Tremors, no matter what magnitude, weren't anything new for rats. I looked back to the TA crew, moving lifeless bodies to be accounted for. Soliel was the first person I thought about. She had to be okay. She suffered enough already. It was just her luck to get stuck in a cave again, after having survived already once. From the choices we had left, there didn't seem like there were any good options. Fear is the only thing that could have driven those rats into hiding. Fear of a hungry predator lurking in the dark. There appeared to be a presence down here. A presence that is not natural. As crazy as it sounds, it's the only rational explanation.

Callum Morrissey

A DISTORTED ELECTRONIC noise warbled from somewhere out in the dark.

"Shhh," I waved my hand, stopping Esabelle in her tracks. She heaved back throwing me a sidelong glare. I knew that noise. That scratchy noise. It must have been the satellite phone Ashley lugged along in her backpack. My eyes peered out into the shadows as I carefully stepped over any rusted pipes to be sure I didn't bring any attention our way. We moved fast until the noise got louder and louder. Scratchier and Scratchier. A shadowy figure appeared to float in the dark. Neither Esabelle nor I could make out what it was.

"Wait, it's coming right for us!" Esabelle shouted.

I threw my arm around her, held her close.

"Don't be scared. I think it's someone we know."

Esabelle shoved me, trying to get free. I only gripped her tighter, keeping her still and preventing her from getting too far. The silhouette in the dark strolled further and further into our light. Esabelle dug her nails into my shirt on the verge of a scream. Bouncy blonde locks caught my attention first.

"You alright?" Ashley said, relieved.

"We're not dead..." Esabelle replied.

"Pablo, is he—"

Ashley grabbed Pablo by his arm. He clumsily stepped into place. "He's fine."

All of us stood back together after having gotten lost in the depth of the tunnels. I'm still trying to figure out what was the point of coming down here. The truth was, I thought it was about time to turn back. Earthquake or no earthquake. The group already was torn apart, who knows what could happen or how many more dead ends did we need to walk into before we gave it a rest? The whole thing struck me as silly and naive.

"Once we find Soliel and Henrik, we need to get the *hell* out of here," I said.

"Callum, I realize this is sort of out of your element," Ashley stated slowly nodding her head. "But we came here to solve a mystery. Not turn tail as soon as things get a little hard..."

For whatever reason, Ashley's words cut deeply into me. Is this what I've become—a skittish man-child who runs away when things get too hard? Pablo muttered something.

"There's a weird smell here I can't quite put my finger on it. But God, *it stinks!*"

Baffled, I took in a deep breath, but coughed before I could fill my lungs. Looks passed between all of us. Something foul for sure saturated the air. Ashley eased away looking at the floor. Fresh blood, still warm to the touch, was splattered all over the floor. Ashley dipped her fingers in it then just as quickly pulled them out. She sniffed.

"It's someone's blood," she said a little shocked.

"That can't be right," Esabelle replied.

We all thought the same thing. *Was Soliel okay? Was she still alive?*

"The blood goes all the way down," Ashley said weakly, doing her best not to feel hopeless. That's what we all did. We couldn't imagine if anything had happened to Soliel or Henrik.

"Let's follow it and see where it leads," Pablo suggested. Esabelle led the way, of course and the rest of us followed. The blood was scattered all over as if Soliel had been ripped to shreds. God, I hope I'm wrong.

Solid Oupary

WE FELT DEFEATED. "We are seriously lost..."

I mumbled under my breath. Most my curiosity, about the source of the earthquakes, had faded and Henrik could barely keep himself awake. We just wanted to find our way out, but we had nowhere to go. The dogs had since turned tail and ran, even though we didn't know why they were spooked. To fill the time I asked Henrik a question.

"Why were these rail networks built if nobody uses them?" I asked.

"There not unused. They were overused. These old train rails were used so many centuries ago, before newer better functioning train tracks were constructed on top."

It's just everything down here just seemed so dead. A ghost town of iron and concrete. For how long we've been traveling down here, it almost felt like there was no way out. Like this ghostly train station didn't want us to leave. There's something I find strange about this whole thing, it was almost like it wasn't even of our reality. These caves feel like traveling in a maze. I looked more closely ahead and noticed a split in the path.

"Which way?" Henrik asked.

I'm not sure, I thought.

I'm afraid of taking the wrong path and getting more lost. Or, taking the right path and finding you're the only ones that made it out. Either way, I saw this ending bad.

Henrik grinned. "Wish I had a coin to toss. Would make this choice a *helluva* lot easier."

I didn't want to waste any more time and just pointed behind me. I decided to take neither.

"I'm done wandering, I say just go back."

Henrik agreed. "Going forward hasn't done us much good anyway."

I figured what's the point of getting farther and farther away from where anyone could find us?

We both doubled back down the way we came. Someone would have to find us eventually. Someone would have to get us out. In my head, I pictured someone waiting for me if we did get rescued. I could picture his hair, his sapphire colored eyes....*What are you doing, Soliel? Are you really thinking of your Dr that way?* Part of me found it hard to believe, but deep down I did like boys. Of, course I did, maybe almost dying had me thinking more about my life. Maybe almost dying had me opening my eyes a little wider.

A feral growl broke through the dust haze. I swooped under Henrik's arm, and he didn't dare let me go. I breathed so hard that I'm sure Henrik felt it on his neck. My skin prickled at the thought of being eaten alive. The animals lurched forward. Slow. Menacing. They're drooling lips curled back and we both stared into their raging wild red eyes.

It slipped out of the dark—*faster*—with hasty steps. It craned its head up, looked directly in our eyes, ready to gnaw down to our bones. The fur stood straight up on its shoulders, creeping up ready to strike and rake through our flesh. The feral dog lunged, teeth bared, snapping at our necks. Henrik shoved his way in front of me seconds before the dog gored into his arm.

"HENRIK!" I screamed grabbing at the beasts thick wiry fur. Henrik threw me down to the floor. I slammed in the slurry of sewage and rainwater. It splashed in my face and streaked down my cheeks.

"Get out of here Soliel! Run. Now!"

First I fumbled, and then I ran. I bolted far away from the throaty screams. My stomach heaving, I charged ahead my arms swinging at my sides. *Don't stop, Soliel. Never stop.* My pants are soaking wet. I've got muck and dirt stinging my eyes, and I keep moving—still—as fast as I can. Everything whirled in a blur when I started tumbling face first on the ground. My legs flew up in the air, landing on something soft and warm. Something squirmed underneath my back. For a moment, I shut my eyes afraid to look down.

Then I turned and saw that a woman lay underneath me. As I lifted her up by the shoulders, I recognized her face. She was the same woman on the train. The one Pablo had chased after. I shook her and her eyes fluttered open.

"Tamara," I finally remembered her name. Her body went limp and fell back. Her head flopped over onto her shoulder. She was fading fast, and if I didn't think of something quick—I would lose her. I swung my hand back and slapped her face. Her eyes snapped open and she took a deep wheezing breath. She was hanging on to life by a thread.

Tamara whimpered in my arms. When I first met her, I couldn't' see her as a person. Not after what she did to Pablo. But as he she lay twisted and broken in my arms, she just seemed so harmless. Tamara mouthed something, and I could barely hear the words.

"Thank you," she whispered from her throat.

To be honest, I didn't quite know what to say. I saw her dying and she needed help. It's not that we've become friends all of a sudden. It's just that I simply did what was right. A darker part of me half-considered just leaving her after everything she's done. Instead, I remained calm and stayed focused. I would wait with her here for as long as it took.

"You must hate me," she mumbled.

She said it so startlingly frank. It's almost like she read my mind.

"I don't hate you."

Not entirely. I thought to myself.

"What I did," she paused to take a breath. "It was wrong. I had my reasons, but Pablo trusted me. I ruined that."

Tamara lay there confessing to me as if I were diocese. You could tell by the hoarse crack in her voice, she'd probably been lying here screaming for hours.

"Who did this to you?" I asked.

"I'm not sure. A big thing, it stabbed me in my gut. I found the exit, but I tripped and couldn't move."

A big thing? The list of blood thirsty creatures just didn't seem to have an end. When would we finally escape? When will the insane nightmare stop? Her soft voice spoke up.

"If you see Pablo, tell him for me—"

"Tell him what?"

"Tell him, I'm sorr—"

Something large and bulky emerged from the depths of the shadow and knocked me aside and flung Tamara to the drenched floor. It was a hulking creature, carrying a long dull sword with powerful muscular arms that rippled with power. In a flash of blinding speed in plunged a large sword deep into Tamara's chest. Blood splattered in all directions including on me. I locked up with terror, as I felt Tamara's warm sticky blood splatter all over me. I could taste it fully in my mouth, I was horrified! The stood just a few feet from me and it was a half-man half-beast looking monster. I recognized it right way, it was a Centaur. It reared up on its hind legs and flicked the blood off of his sword. Tamara gurgled her last few gulps of air, until then she breathed no more. That glazed look in her eye would haunt me forever...

"Soliel!" Ashley shouted, seeing me standing there utterly frozen. A bunch more splashing steps drew closer and then a hand gripped my arm and guiding me through the dark. Everyone rushed from the galloping Centaur that was trampling everything in its path.

"Do we even know where were going?" Esabelle panted trying to catch her breath. That's when I realized the second tunnel. The tunnel before Henrik and I tried to go back. After all, what other choices did we have left? Escape in the tunnel, or get hacked to death. We curved around the bend splitting the paths and clung on to each other's hands linking up in a human chain. Let's hope we can make it to the cave.

"I can see it! We all need to get there!" I pointed to it. Everyone headed right for the cave illuminated in their sights. Warm water squished in my shoes, but I didn't stumble or stop; then we saw him. He was charging around all of us. The Centaur was rearing forward and blocking our escape. Flecks of water hit us in the eyes as he slammed his front legs back down.

I stood there with my friends, looking up, my mouth agape. The monster unsheathed his sword and pointed it towards our heads and smiled at us. It was a wicked smile that was stained with blood. The Silver Cannabis laughed and we cowered in his presence. He spoke. "Which one should I rip apart first?" His voice was so deep it vibrated our very core.

His booming voice echoed so loud it could be heard several hundred miles away. We looked, up suddenly aware how close we stood to death. He stomped his feet and is long braided hair swung wildly with each step. We all saw pure evil standing right there in front of us. *What did it want from us? Why was it blocking us?* I tried to reason with it and convince it to let us go.

"Please, we mean you know harm. Please spare our lives." The smell of blood and sewage was fouling up the air. I tried to hold on, hoping I wasn't facing death. For whatever reason, the creature leaned in close to my face, blood dripping from his teeth. He spoke.

"Now, I have you. All of you."

Chapter 6

Soliel Oupary

I felt my whole body shaking uncontrollably and my face glistening with cold sweat as I opened my eyes. The worst seemed to be over. I wish that was true but deep down I knew it wasn't true. My body wouldn't stop shaking in Esabelle's embrace and as I came in and out of consciousness, there was someone I wished very dearly to see again. Shoba.

Being lost down here without her broke me in two. Nothing seemed more important in this moment than telling her how much I missed her. I wished I could say sorry for all the petty fights we had. Esabelle rubbed my arm with her hand. She looked at me as I hunched over with my face buried in my arms. A foul smelling breeze drifted past us. The smells and the moldy water seeped from every crack and crevice. I pressed my hand, wincing as I touched my bruised wound from the fall. It hurt so bad.

Esabelle just loomed close and didn't let go as she held my hand. "Hey Soleil, we lost that thing somehow. We're okay; you're going to be fine."

A creeping delirium swirled in my head, making it impossible to stay focused. It took me longer to open my eyes each time they fluttered shut. My cracked ribs hurt me so much I wanted to cry out in pain. Instead, I swallowed it. My face softened as Esabelle held me close. Held me tight.

"Don't worry, I won't let you go," Esabelle said stroking her finger through my hair. I turned to my other side, shuffled around and pulled my knees into my stomach. Ashley stared down at me with tears streaking down her cheeks.

"We waited too long, we should have gotten here sooner," she said.

It was a nice thing for her to say, but this was nobody's fault. No matter what, I still felt like I was responsible for everyone that died. Ashley still had some enthusiasm in her voice.

"You'll be okay, just stay with us. We will keep you safe."

In this moment, I felt myself becoming lighter than usual. The concerned expressions on my friend's faces vanished from my eyes. Only darkness enfolded me in the deepest corners of my mind. The sensation felt like something crawling out of my head

When I came to, I was surrounded by shadowy silhouettes looking down at me. I stood up and began traveling along an unpleasant road in the depths of the dark forest. *Am I dreaming?* I wondered as I looked out into the grim landscape.

"Aagh!" I muttered under my breath, looking down at the scars on my feet. There were quite of few, twisting and gnarling all the skin between my toes. No! Not this. Anything but this! I knew this dream. I knew this dream because I've dreamed it once before. This is the nightmare where I almost died. The filthy handed Centaurs might come after me again. In a split second, I charged forward knowing that I needed a head start. I knew that in any second, the Centaur could come after me and chase me down. Streaks of my black hair stuck to the sweat glistening on my face as I pressed forward.

The sound of heavy footsteps echoed behind me, and the smell of pond scum filled my lungs. On each side of me, a Centaur with a sharp-edged sword bolted through the trees. The man-beasts raced forward with swords and torches in each of their giant hands. I didn't have much time to think about what to do next. I saw an electric bow lying on the ground. I immediately picked it up as it got closer footsteps behind me drew closer. *Would I at least be able to get the shot this time?* I thought swallowing the lump of fear in my throat.

When I looked up, two hulking Centaurs clicked their hooves on the hardscrabble earth. Their mottled gray skin reflected in the sun. They spotted me, hissing through their bloodstained teeth as blood dribbled down their thin cruel lips. I stood my ground and rose up the blue glowing arrow. I steadied my shaking hands; my forearms ached and my veins were throbbing as I pulled the glowing arrow back. The foul beasts peered down at me with foaming mouths. *Now! Do it now! Soliel! Do it!* The arrow slipped from my hand and whistled through the air at a rapid speed leaving a mesmerizing blue trail as it streaked towards one of the beasts. The creature smirked and swiftly dodged the arrow. When I reached for another arrow, it smiled at me. We watched each other....

Challenged each other...knowing for certain only one of us would die.

Our feet scraped through the dirt. Esabelle moved so fast that she barely landed on her feet. I picked up a broken piece of a cinder block. I knew the only way out would be to face this beast head on. Esabelle grabbed the piece I handed her and raised it high above her head. The Centaur swung its sword over our heads disrupting the air and making a disturbing whooshing sound. I half-turned, not sure what I was doing, and threw the cinder block at its head. The Centaur reeled in pain as the corner of the cinder block crushed his right eye. That was our chance we needed to escape. It was completely blind.

Its tail swung madly, whooshing from side to side. Pablo stepped back with his left foot then his right. He stumbled a few steps more, turning around and running alone down the tunnel.

"I'm leaving. I'm not staying here any longer..." Pablo shouted.

Esabelle and I both watched him escape until he disappeared and vanished from view. *Figures.* We stood awkwardly side by side. Esabelle clutched my arm, and I hunkered down to embrace her. We watched miserably as Soliel lay there unconscious and unable to wake.

"We can't leave," Esabelle sighed looking at Ashley hugging Soliel. "There's no way out."

Who were we fooling? I thought. We had been searching for what seemed like countless hours. No rescue. No nothing. A sudden gasp could be heard, like someone just had their head pulled free from under water. Soliel shuddered. Clearly disoriented, she couldn't recognize us or tell where we were.

"It's okay. Just listen, we're your friends. You're going to be alright."

Hearing Ashley's soothing voice must have been the trigger. The confused look in her eyes subsided and her face relaxed. She clung on to Ashley's flannel shirt, holding on for dear life as tears streamed down her eyes. Ashley drew her in closer, rubbing her hand gently on Soliel's back.

"It's going to be okay," she whispered into Soliel's ear.

George raised his hand right away.

"I see something. The tracker is moving not far from here."

Palace Michaels

MY TEAM AND I MANAGED to ease up from under the Transit Authority's restricted zone. We've been closely following the tracker beacon for hours and George kept the monitor open at all times so we know how far we have to go. We couldn't shake the eerie feeling of an ominous presence all around, a presence I have never felt before. Throughout all the years I've spent traveling to the darkest places on earth and solving unsolvable mysteries, proving impossible theories, nothing could prepare me for what I saw in these tunnels.

The damp and desolate landscape had wreckage and trash strewn all about. I struggled not to gag at the musky odor. It smelled like death circled all around us. *How could they all have survived down here?* I thought. I missed seeing Ashley in the lab calculating insane amounts of data in her head. I missed Soliel for being skeptical—always questioning—but kind hearted.

Without them, nothing would fix the holes their absence left in our team. The misty smog clouded our eyes as we kept to the pathway. Paula stood near George, to get a glimpse of where the tracker was taking us. A ghost-like silhouette faded in and out ahead. George's eyes widened. He darted out in front of us, desperate to find out if Ashley was out there roaming about lost.

"Ashley, we're over here! Over here!" George yelled flailing his arms.

He looked like he'd gone crazy, truly. Especially with the way he ran into the dark carelessly. His yells cut of abruptly. I locked gazes with Paula, we knew something was wrong. George shouts stopped so quick that it seemed as if someone had flicked off his "off" switch. Without thinking, Paula and I ran into the mist to find George. We quickly discovered what had silenced George. The beast's eyes glowed with an unnerving intensity as it focused its gaze seemed to stare right through us. It was a creature you only heard about in the myths I studied. It smelled foul and as it stared at us, we could practically see through its silver tinged translucent skin.

Ashley almost couldn't even get the words out. "Oh God!"

There was George lying in a pool of his own blood. The creature looked like a demon drawn from hell—it had black soulless eyes burning with hate, it silver skinned body was a man's set on the lower body of a horse. It raised its giant hand that was holding a large broad sword, reared up, and charged straight at Paula. She swung her arm up to protect her face as it slashed at her skin like a jackal attacking its prey. Thinking fast, I grabbed my coat and hurled it over at Paula. For whatever reason, it forced the silver skinned monster to jump. It hissed at me for a second then scrambled back into the dark. I slid down and rushed over to Paula and wrapped her arm in my jacket as I looked in her eyes.

"Just breathe. Stay calm," I told her.

If we didn't find the crew soon, there would be no hope for her.

Beep. Beep.

The flickering monitor lay next to George's dead body. I picked it up and gathered Paula in my arms. Once I found my balance, I continued further along in the caves. I felt something rough brush against my back and then it knocked me over. Paula fell from my grasp as the Centaur Silver Cannabis steps out in front of me. When it spoke, it was something indecipherable; I could smell the blood on its breath. I notice the tattoos across his broad chest; they're the same ones Ashley deciphered on the Novae Emblem. In a lightning quick action, its fist swung full force at my head. It connected with me directly in the face, raised its hoof and stomped on my chest. The world went black all around me.

Palace Michaels

"USUALLY, I STAY OUT of these things, but I didn't know why Robert decided to split up."

I haven't found anyone yet who came down here searching for the source of the earthquakes. I've already tried contacting Ashley's satellite phone. My eyes went wide when I saw someone teetering towards me from the edges of the dark. It smiled at me. I stepped back, blinking abruptly, and afraid we'd come face to face. The voices it made sounded confused. It reached out for my hand. I shoved it back. It grabbed for me again. It pushed me aside, and then I yelled its name.

"Curtis!"

He hooked his arm around me. His eyes were wild like he had been wandering down here longer than he intended.

"Palace..." he replied dully.

Before I said anything, I dug through my pack, fished out a bottle of water and handed it over. Curtis snatched it from my hand, unscrewed the cap, and guzzled it like he was a dehydrated man wandering the vast desert.

"You know where everyone else is?"

He wiped his mouth with the back of his hand.

"We split, but I'm not far behind. I'm pretty sure Ashley had gone somewhere down in this tunnel."

Curtis knocked back some more water. When he finished, He gestured for me to follow. I did my best to keep up with his speed. Curtis curved around a bend and saw a flashlight rolling across the ground. A group of people stood in a circle. I waved my light and Curtis stopped running and stooped over, panting at my side.

"Show me your faces!" I yelled.

Slowly each of them turned. I couldn't make out there faces for a brief moment and then after they made eye contact; recognition set in. The only face I didn't know was that of a strange woman with red hair. That didn't matter because the next two faces I saw was who I was hoping to see! Ashley and Soliel ! They rocked together while hugging each other on the floor. I rushed over to them; Soliel refused to lift her face from Ashley's shoulder. I hated seeing her crying. I get it. She didn't want to seem weak. I stepped forward slowly and stroked her cheek. A minute later, Soliel shook her head, and I saw the watery red tinge in her eyes.

"So, many people are dead..." she muttered.

"Have you seen anyone else from the group?" I asked. "Robert, anyone?"

She shook her head again.

Robert hasn't gotten here yet? Something's really wrong.

I heard something running out from the shadows towards us. ARGGHHHHH!

I gently released Soliel as I heard the steps get closer. Everyone turned. Esabelle and Callum ran right for us with—what looked like—rusted pipes.

"Woah, whoa, what are you doing? Trying to ambush us?" I asked. Esabelle and Callum paused silent for a moment. It's like they just became aware of who we were. It's not too crazy. We've been separated for so long, and under the constant threat of beasts who wanted nothing more than to rip us to shreds and feast on our bones for all I knew.

They set there make-shift weapons on the ground. Callum rushed to me and lifted me up in his arms.

"I thought that you were dead, Ash," he said constricting me in a hug. At this point, I totally lost hope on discovering the source of the earthquakes. No matter how many maps I drew, no matter how much data I crunched—none of it has brought me any closer to finding the nexus. At least we are finally all together. Palace joined in on what we should do next.

"We need to find the others," Palace said. "Robert is still missing."

Dr Roberts was still somewhere in the tunnels.

Soleil Oupary

WHEN SOLIEL FINALLY rose up from the ground, rings of concentric circles cracked the concrete underneath her. My mind flashed back to the Silver Cannabis rearing back on his birch-like hind legs. It then hammered his feet on the ground. I remember feeling shock waves rush through the cement. It was a memory that was still fresh in my head; I remember how I staggered and struggled to maintain my footing and tripped. But I got back up, mostly unhurt.

"These quakes aren't natural...." I muttered unable to believe what I was saying. Of course, everyone arched an eyebrow at me. But I knew that what I just said made perfect sense. Palace shrugged.

"Enlighten me."

"These Centaurs that are hunting us in this cave are creating them. I've seen these beasts before, if you inspect the Novae Emblem, you'll see them there. Look at these hoof prints, this is the locus where the Silver Cannabis stomped on the ground. The waves of concrete around it are coming directly from that hoof print. What we are witnessing is something that's entirely beyond the scope of science. It's supernatural."

Palace squinted his eyes while his forehead stressed a bit as he thought to himself. That's the craziest thing I've ever said before. I'm the one who believed in evidence, facts and hard cold numbers. And yet, none of those explained why the quakes occurred. Soliel looked over to me, I had a feeling she was about to reveal the story she told due to the serious look in her eyes.

"That's not all. The Silver Cannabis or something similar to it was there when the cave in the arctic collapsed." She paused. "—and that. That was there too. It's where I found the Novae Emblem. It was buried in a case made of ice. Maybe the Centaur also caused the avalanche in the cave? That necklace Esabelle's wearing is a key to all the doorways in the universe. A key to this reality and the next."

Esabelle scratched at her neck. "Ow! It's burning!"

I looked over to Esabelle scratching underneath the chain of the necklace. Then I noticed it glowing and blinking red. Esabelle grabbed at the chain and tried to rip it off. We all heard the sound of crackling flesh as it seared further down into her skin. Callum ran behind her and tried to undo the magnetic clasp, in the process, his fingers briefly touched hers; the air around them swiftly changed. Its smell. Its taste. There was no darkness in the clouds, no wind or rain. Callum and Esabelle held the locket with unease and were transported somewhere outside of the tunnels. Lush leaves swayed in the wind.

Callum still felt the intense heat of the necklace buried in his fist. Something was moving fast through the valley, getting closer, shimmering as it gained speed. Silver streaks that gleamed in the sun were all that they could make out. Then it stopped on directly on the hill above them, it was a huge silver skinned warrior. They watched him brandish two heavy weapons in both of his enormous hands. One was a weapon that had twin blades with serrated edges and wicked curves on each blade while the other was a long broad sword. Callum and Esabelle stood next to each other not knowing whether to panic or cry for help. The warrior stared directly at them.

"What do you think he wants?" Callum whispered out of the corner of his mouth.

Esabelle shrugged. "I'm more worried about how the hell do we get out of this place?"

The fearsome figure took a step closer to them, making Callum nervous; more nervous than usual. They searched hastily for the "hazy doorway of return." Esabelle panicked as much as Callum; squeezing his arm. Callum's eyes darted away from the Warrior and focused on Esabelle. They both took a few shuffling steps back, as they attempted to figure out a plan.

"Why do these weird things keep happening to me? I thought I was wasting my life as a prosecutor. But now, I could get used to having less unexpected adventures."

They both walked further away as silently as they could. For the first time since Esabelle met Callum, she didn't just pretend to listen to him. She found something else about him intriguing as well. Here was a man who had awesome wit, but terrible self-confidence. But this was a thought that could wait for later, as when she looked to where the Warrior was standing; she was terrified to discover that he wasn't there anymore.

"Look. He's gone!" she said..

Callum did not spot the Warrior any longer. Esabelle's necklace burned so hot, a wisp of white smoke billowed from her neck. She clawed, pulled and tore at the necklace which had a piece of the Novae Emblem that was burning and leaving long red scars deep in her skin. Callum barely caught her before she collapsed

"Hey are you okay?" Callum asked a light headed Esabelle worriedly. She nodded her head but he was convinced.

The darkness of the tunnels once again surrounded them. Everyone was standing right where they remembered them. A slight, yet barely detectable tremor vibrated under their feet.

Soliel Oupary

HE DIDN'T BELIEVE IT. Could you blame him? I mean Centaurs causing seismic activity? Palace was willing to entertain most theories, *but this*? This he would have to see to believe. I looked at him and he tapped me on my shoulder. I saw the bewildered look in his eyes.

"I know what this sounds like. But this monster is real. I've seen it. I've seen the Silver Cannabis tear someone apart."

He looked at me surprised. I was the rare person whom he trusted at their word. I meant what I said no matter how farfetched. No matter how crazy it all seemed, he knew I would tell the truth.

"We can't stand around here much longer. The beast will come after us and when he finds us, he'll kill us all!" Callum reasoned. "Standing here just makes it easier for him to take us all out."

I got defensive. "No, we can't yet until we've found everyone who's lost in the tunnels. How would you feel if we just left you? How would you feel to be abandoned here in the dark alone?

No one answered. Everyone agreed with her. They wanted to search for the others. Robert hadn't even tried to contact Ashley since I've found the survivors of the train crash. I waved my arm to signal it was time to move out and they all quickly followed behind me. We continued down further in the long dark tunnel. At the end there was a strange hazy opening, with a terrifying blinding light in the center. The others had no problem keeping up, they were all motivated by the same goal and that was not to be decimated by the Centaur. The all too familiar thudding of footsteps began sounding behind me. There wasn't much time as I approached the opening, feeling along its blurry edges. I wasted no time and climbed through.

"Wait? You're not actually going to go in there are you?" Palace asked.

I didn't miss a beat. "I'm not going to wait on anyone to help save my friend's lives."

He released a deep sigh. The strangers I had met and the others on the Archaeology team all followed my lead. One by one, they crouched down and squeezed through the hole in the wall. The smell of death hits us without warning. I clutched my stomach and fell into a coughing fit when I saw Paula sprawled out on the ground. Paula's eyes were milky white; her body had already gone cold. How could we have left her here for so long? I couldn't help feeling responsible somehow.

I felt like it was my fault these bad things are happening to my classmates and my Drs. Knowing it was pointless, I felt along Paula's neck to feel if she had a pulse. None. The sweetest girl you could ever have met is now dead. My heart sank, but we had no choice, we had to leave her there all alone. The tunnel was covered with dried blood all over its rounded walls. Callum held on to Esabelle. Ashley covered her nose. There were two trails of blood visible.

"Who's the other person?" I asked.

"George," I said. "I knew Robert had gone and separated the team to find where you all were."

I heard more voices echoing further down the tunnel. I was absolutely fascinated how hyper aware I had become. I heard the voices again, so loud I could feel it them on my skin. This time I ran forward without saying much. Everyone hurried after me, afraid to be left alone again in these dreadful tunnels.

"Dr! Curtis!" I shouted.

A pair of men were standing in the corridor. They twisted around when they heard my shouts, relieve washed over their faces at seeing us alive. Robert grabbed his brother Palace and we thought they were going to hug, but instead, he braced him for what he discovered.

"The symbols," Robert said, his voice nearly gone, "They're the same symbols on the necklace. The Silver Cannabis and the necklace are one and the same..."

Soliel grabbed Robert's shoulder. "We found a way out."

"There's a doorway we can all go through."

"*Don't you dare.*" Robert warned.

It was too late; I had already made up my mind. It was just like last time everyone had climbed through the portal, except Curtis, Robert Dr Michaels and I waited for a moment before slipping all the way through.

"Be careful. The Centaur is still out there. I'm afraid leaving you alone for any amount of time is a big mistake," he warned.

At that moment I was yanked out by something powerful. Its grip was like a vice, as it grabbed me by the neck, choking me while I dangled in the air. Its searing red eyes descended closer to my face. I kicked and struggled to get gulp of air but failed. The creature stood his ground; his drool was dribbling a hot crimson red down his chin. He parted his lips and spoke.

"Lunati..." he breathed, his voice made her blood boil right to her bones."How did you escape to here...to this time?"

I felt myself losing consciousness. My legs and arms felt paralyzed as Silver Cannabis fixed his jaws around my neck. *This was it.* I thought.

A sudden noise from the tunnels distracted Silver Cannabis and he raised his head from my neck to see a terrified Pablo standing there. He was transfixed on the silvered skin Centaur, strangling me in his fist. Silver Cannabis spun around and hurled my limp body against the wall. The concrete shattered as the Centaur stomped on the ground and chased Pablo further down into the tunnel depths. I was half-conscious, I barely recall getting to my feet. I staggered a few times and finally made it to the blurry hole floating in the middle of the wall and fell backwards through it.

It took me a few seconds to come to. To make matters worse, when I dusted off my knees and stood up, I had no clue where I was. I stood alone on a platform; the only sound was that of the shifting rocks. Hundreds of pathways formed a maze, stretching out in every direction. It was so horrifying, and yet, it was real. I couldn't breathe. I was too scared to move. Terrified, I reluctantly took a step.

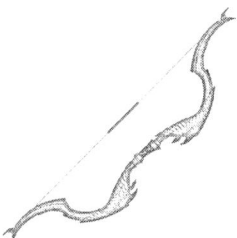

Chapter 7

Soleil Oupary

I wondered how I got here. To one side of me was a monster and on the other was a maze. What did the beast call me again? When he spoke and breathed against my neck, my body nearly melted in his grasp. How could that thing even exist? This is the center of New York—the capital of the world— Centaurs from far-off dimensions only belong in fantasy novels. No matter how hard I tried, I couldn't recall the memories buried deep within my mind, I still couldn't envision having anything to do with that beast. Then it finally came to me, the word the creature whispered in my ear.

Lunati…

Is there a part of me that I don't know? Some deep dark secret that I've repressed? Being normal isn't something I necessarily aspire to, but this was far out there even for me. It seemed certain events, out of my control, are now all aligning in place. I never wanted to be anyone. Not in the spotlight. Not anything. And yet, all my life I've been pursued by a secret history. A faded legacy so ancient it began before time itself. Here I thought my biggest worry would be writing a lengthy dissertation matter given many weeks I've put into this research.

None of that mattered now. The only hope I have left is to somehow survive. Murky shadows danced all around me like ghosts. My skin prickled when a sudden flash of the creature—the blood thirsty Centaur— came to the front of my mind.

"Get a hold of yourself, Soleil!" I muttered under my breath.

My shoes were sopping wet and made loud slopping noises with each step I too down the maze. It had long corridor doors with smooth pathways, the color of gunmetal and seemed to continue out to infinity. I didn't know what frightened me more, being alone are being lost. My dark hair was slick with sweat and stuck to the back of my neck and all I wanted to do was go home and take a long hot shower. But that was just wishful thinking, the reality was, I had to keep moving forward away from the Centaur. As I took a few steps, I focused deeply on the name Lunati, I knew I've heard it someplace else before.

Memories of cold air stinging my lungs flashed through my brain. It was suddenly clear to me, I heard that name when I was in the ice cave at Foxe Basin. I started to see a pattern that I hadn't noticed before. The Lunati of my dreams, if that's what you call them, was a young woman who looked exactly like me. Except she had elegance about her, almost as if she floated on rose scented air. And if things got ugly, she could handle her own in a fight. Of course, I leaned towards the logical. The last thing I would ever want to believe is a prophecy.

I began to think about Shoba, if only she was here. Even if she didn't know exactly what to say, she always had a way to make me smile or laugh and forget about my problems—at least for little while. To forget for a little while would mean the world to me.

My thoughts drifted back to the reality. How long can I survive the dark? In this place the air had no taste and no smell. Instead, it was like inhaling a choking vapor to which there is no escape. Despite all this, I felt is something worse than fear. Worry. How can I know that I'm not part of a great nefarious scheme that risks every human life on this earth? *Listen to yourself, Soleil.* I thought. Why I just go home to the quiet life I've made? I don't want to experience any more death, and I no longer care about discovery or adventure. Sure I'm not the first twenty something year old who found herself in the midst of a life crisis. But how many twenty-year-olds could say they live the double life in two worlds at the same time? That can definitely change things?

Oddly enough, I've never felt human anyhow. I can't remember the last time I thought I belonged. No matter how much I wanted it to be, something hidden deep inside me wanted to come out. Maybe that was truly the worst part. Even though I think I'm above the darker half of my psyche, with how things have played out in the tunnels. I'm not sure that's true. Given the chance, I'm sure Ashley would want to study the inside of my head. I know she would desire to figure out what secrets were hidden inside it. If she was anything, she was curious, maybe I needed her help after all. We both have questions about Nubara...

Callum Morrissey

THIS IS MY THIRD LEFT TURN. *Dammit!* Thought Callum. Everything just looks the same. It all started when I walked through that door. What choice did I have? It was either walk through the door or be eaten alive. What if I didn't take that train that day? What if instead I just took a taxi down twelve Avenue? Or, the glass? Any of those choices would lead me to somewhere anywhere but here.

Okay, so maybe the deposition I had planned for this afternoon wasn't of any great importance. I do hundreds of those a week. Not that I'm some great lawyer or anything. Still, I can't see how my time is better spent being lost with no hope of being found. Let's take a few steps back. You know, think about this for second. These tunnels are far from ordinary. The man eating creature pretty much erased all doubt.

As a lawyer, I see seedy types all the time. I spend hours digging for the truth and looking criminals in the eye. You might say criminals are monsters in a way, monsters that wear human faces. Anyways, all this is beside the point, which is when the hell am I going to get out of this place? Although I can't put my finger on it, there's something about these winding pathways. I'm not sure why, but I feel like I've been here before. Honestly, that doesn't make any sense, I'm lucky if I leave the Upper West Side. I've done nothing but take the train all my life. But never have I ever gone down this far down. With that being said, I'm not sure how to describe it but if it unleashes memories somewhere in my head. I remember this place, the way a child remembers a dream.

The visuals of place and time are so concrete, but the reasoning behind those visions are murky at best. What is it about this place? I'm no scientist, but you don't need an astrophysicist to see that what's happening down here is extraterrestrial. Don't ask me why, but being lost like this got me thinking about someone who up until now I couldn't stand; Esabelle. Maybe it was just my gentleman nature to care, but I would be lying if I said I didn't wonder if she was safe. If by chance she had someone with her, there's no doubt she would be barking orders. After all, it is Esabelle.

There's nothing I can want more than to finally understand what was causing those quakes. Not because I'm enchanted by the thought of solving a mystery, but because that would mean this adventure I've found myself on will be finally be over. Done. Finito! Until then, I'll just keep taking the next left.

"Hello?" I called. "Anyone out there?"

Ashley Boylan

THIS IS FANTASTIC!" I said with excitement. I know. I know. Everyone else thinks I'm just too obsessed with finding out the secret behind Nubara. It's just we're this close! According to my calculations, the quakes have been occurring three and a half minutes apart. Seismic activity that is contracted with less time between tremors can only mean the source is to be found somewhere here in this labyrinth. I'm sure the rest of the gang was here, by my side, they'd just go, "Yeah, okay Ashley." and roll their eyes.

Not that I care about that anyway. Being awkward and a savant with numbers was kind of my thing. Dr. Robert Michaels would know exactly where my excitement came from. Just imagine if you had been studying a legend for nearly a decade of your life. On top of that, think about how many times people have dismissed your research believing it to be an absolute waste of time. Wouldn't that make you want to prove your naysayers wrong? Although it easy to understand how stories of Centaurs and legacies of kings from a world long gone might not be appealing to those who only see the world as it is.

To the skeptics I would say, isn't that how all mystery's start? The only way to unravel a tightly woven riddle is to pull it apart one string at a time. Most people couldn't do the job I do, because most people don't care. For them, good enough is enough. Status quo is just fine. It's harder to find answers that accept things as they are. I guess that's why it's hard for me to find anyone who understands me. Someone who's just as upset about something. Maybe it has something to do with abstract numbers or the universe. Yet, I have never met anyone so passionate about something that burns like a fire in their heart.

Callum Morrissey

ABRUPTLY, OUT OF THE distance on my right, I heard something that sounds like the pitter patter of soft footfalls. I whirled around, swinging my flashlight in all directions. I inhaled deep breaths, attempting to calm my beating heart. Most people think I'm fearless, but that's far from truth, I get scared....alot. Especially of beasts with superhuman strength and the ability to rip me apart. I shrugged out of my flannel shirt and tied it around my waist. Then I crouched down and grabbed the pen I've been hiding in the back of my boot.

Think you're just going to ambush me? Think again. I thought.

Instead of waiting for the noise to approach me, I gripped the pen in offensive position with my elbow out at chest level and charged full speed ahead. My flashlight spun and caused a strobe light effect across the walls.

"What are you waiting for? Show your face," I shouted.

"Woah! Woah! Woah!"

Someone cried out, and I stopped in my tracks. The first thing I saw was tendrils of fiery red hair. "Esabelle?"

"Who else did you think it was?" Esabelle asked, gasping for air to calm her nerves.

I shrugged. "Well, you never know. I'm sorry for that back there, but I had to be sure."

"— *and* sure of what exactly?"

"Esabelle, trust me. I would never do that on purpose."

I'm sure deep down Esabelle knew because she smirked and punched me in the shoulder.

"Any read on what this place actually is?" she asked.

The truth was I really didn't know. Everything down here was a mystery to me.

"If I had to take a guess," I said. " From what I recall of the legends, the royalty on Nubara had built these mazes like fortresses to protect the most precious possessions."

Esabelle merely kindly nodded. It's no stretch, like everyone else, she just gotten exhausted with the entire ordeal.

"They have got to be somewhere," Esabelle said.

"I'm pretty sure all of us are somewhere in this maze. It's not like we had much choice in the matter, with the Centaur and all…"

The maze? Wasn't there something about the maze? Upon inspecting it again, with much more scrutiny, it did appear familiar to me. But I'm not sure why. It's like that feeling of déjà vu. That sense that I've seen this place before but I just can't tell where or when.

"Don't you feel that?" I asked turning my back to Esabelle and gazing upon the pocked maze walls. The walls lining the pathway made sharp edged geometrical turns. Certainly, that means that they are older than that of Paleolithic architecture. However, there was more but I just didn't say.

Esabelle rested her hand on my shoulder. "Find something?"

"Not yet but I'm curious to know the dates of when this structure was erected."

She widened her eyes at me.

"Excuse me, is this accident talking to the numbers queen?"

I tilted my head and flashed a weak smile.

"Yeah, no kidding. As much as I hate to admit it, I'm baffled. You can make a lot of educated guesses about the place. About what century it was built in or, millennia. However, none of that answers the big question."

"Which is…?" Esabelle waited for me to respond.

I coughed into my hand and then continued to stare at the wall.

"When was it built? And why?"

Palace Michaels

"BROTHER, COME HAVE a look."

I gestured for my brother Robert to come over to where I stood.

"These markings… I've seen them before," I snapped my fingers trying to jog my memory. "Aren't these the same as the photographs in the Encyclopedia of Nubara?"

Robert inspected the drawings too. I could tell by the expression on his face he remembered these drawings in great detail. If there's anything that my brother and I had in common, we shared a photographic memory.

"The mystery only gets bigger and bigger," Robert muttered focused on the images before him. "This place is less like a maze and more like a temple with many wrong turns. You see, these drawings are usually etched in reference to something. I can only assume at the end of this, we'll find this labyrinth was built for someone of prominence."

This whole thing almost started to feel too real. It's one thing when you look up information in a textbook or write research on the topic, but Robert and I were living it in the present moment. I felt my eyes straining, overwhelmed by the shroud of darkness.

"If there's one thing that worries me, these legends aren't fantasy stories," Robert said. "The civilization of Nubara is one of war and bloodshed, lest we not forget that."

"You're saying that these drawings here could be depicting something brutal, perhaps? Foretelling something that could happen?" I asked.

Robert scratched his chin, considering his reply.

I guess anyone on the outside looking in may wonder why anyone would be interested in discovering the truth of the warring long-lost planet. To that, I can only answer; you could dismiss the entirety of anthropology by asking such questions.

"No one can know for sure what we'll find at the end of this. But what I do know is that there is going to be a fight before it's all over. I would imagine that these people want their civilization to stay a secret, the last thing they need are humans exposing their world and ruining not only their power structure, but also their way of life."

I guess it's not all that strange. We humans are also a territorial bunch. We, like our borders, our nations and states are entirely arbitrarily drawn countries. So why wouldn't it be the same for the people to borrow? Or, their leaders anyway? And if that was the case, how can we be surprised if they don't want us here?

"Wait a minute!" Robert looked up, his eyes scanning higher on the wall. Obviously, something captured his attention.

I simply looked over his shoulder. "Are you going to clue me in?"

"Look," Robert pointed. "Do you recognize anything familiar?"

I squinted my eyes, which were already exhausted from having been strained for several hours, and focused on the quarter sized engraving on the wall.

"The Novae Emblem…"

Seeing the Emblem itself did surprise me, but then I had an epiphany about something else.

"Did you just say this mural was in exactly all daisies and roses?" I asked.

Robert sighed. It wasn't a sigh of frustration, but sigh of fear.

"You just have to point out, don't you Palace?"

Robert threw me a sidelong glare.

I raise my hands up in protest. "Hey, I'm just pointing out the obvious."

The obvious was something neither of us wanted to contemplate. The Novae Emblem still had mysterious powers none of us have yet cracked. Who knows what we would find? It could be as simple as a harmless relic of the legacy gone past. Or, a piece of a highly destructive force that we have yet to discover has existed. What we read in a book is one thing, but what we actually know is another. This was certainly one of those moments where we really could use the brilliance of Ashley.

Robert and I just stood there thinking, shoulder to shoulder, trying to sort out all the possibilities.

Soliel Oupary

A BRIGHT LIGHT SPILLED across my face. I threw my hands up to cover my eyes.

"Ouch!" I said, I wasn't expecting light in this damp, dark cave.

"My intention certainly wasn't to blind you..." I heard a husky familiar voice say.

The silhouetted figure turned the flashlight onto his face, and once I saw those burning sapphire eyes, I felt at ease.

"Is Dr Michaels with you?" I asked.

"He's not far," he replied.

For a few seconds I held my hand to my chest, I was so relieved to see my Palace standing there— alive. I think at this point everyone was sick of avoiding the obvious, which was that we are stuck here and there was no telling when we would get out. One of my shoe laces got stuck under the heel of my sneaker and when I started to reach for the lace, Palace beat me to it.

He waved his hand. "No worries, I got it."

This sort of thing felt alien to me, being doted upon. I can't wholly deny that I have a twinge of "modern sensibilities." The cynic in me asked *did he really just get down and tie my shoes?* No matter what I thought, I avoided opening my mouth and confirming my sometimes heartless nature. While Palace fiddled with the laces between his thumb and forefinger, he stole a few glances up at me. I half smiled, trying my best to seem charming. None of this came naturally to me, being cute with a guy everyone admired. Sure, I'm not a total idiot but sometimes being smart doesn't make you more desirable.

"You're doing it again," Palace said knotting the lace.

"What do you mean?"

He pointed at my head. "Stop letting that do all the thinking."

"Okaayyy..."

I stifled the urge to roll my eyes.

"What were you doing wandering around here on your own?"

"Wandering?" I raised a brow. "Would you prefer I walk around on a leash?"

Palace laughed from his chest. "This must come easy to you. I mean pushing people away."

"— It's an art," I replied.

He turned away chuckling and flashing is perfect teeth. My only hope was my affection wasn't quite so obvious. Socially awkward doesn't even describe it. I don't know anything about how to hold a conversation or captivate an entire room. It just seemed it came so easy to guys like Palace. When you look at his face, there is something so pleasing about it. I can't tell if it's his unruly auburn hair or the way he just looked like he never had a care in the world. Like I said, it's like you aren't even human. *The bastard!* When I look at him, there's no way I compare.

"Did you come through on your own?"

I nodded. "Yeah, just barely. That thing. The Centaur almost killed me. I thought for second there that I was going to die."

Palace pulled me into his embrace and hugged me gently.

"That's impossible, Soleil. You are one of the strongest people here."

Well, when you put it that way.

"I like to talk to Robert," I said changing the subject entirely.

Palace plopped the flashlight in the palm of my hand.

"He's standing just right there."

As I left Palace's side, I gave him a few more furtive glances, before he can catch me. Robert stood in a low crouch and was staring at the wall.

"So, you noticed the engravings too?" I asked.

"They're interesting aren't they?" He said "Palace and I spoke just before he found you wandering here on the pathway. We don't know what they mean without a cipher to translate them. However, what's most interesting is what you find near the top."

That's when I turn and gazed at the wall. At first, I had no idea to what he was referring to, then I saw it, an engraving just like the Emblem I found carved in the ice. The Novae Emblem haunted me no matter where I went. It was no different from an all seeing eye watching me from across the room. Without knowing his purpose, I can only fear what it would have in store for me. Especially, now that I'm the prophecy girl.

"I didn't say that would scare you," he said realizing the graveness of the situation.

I laughed. "I started being scared a long time ago."

I left Robert to return Palace's flashlight. I also just really needed time to think. Don't ask me about what, because I didn't know. The spotlight expanded in a ghostly white ring the closer I walked to Palace. He simply held his hand out expectantly.

"Thanks for that," he said.

"Why is everything you say so vague?" I teased.

He laughed. "Why do you need every detail explained?"

I didn't even bother making a comeback.

He nudged me on my shoulder. "Thanks for checking in on Robert."

"Think nothing of it..."

"Although I know everyone in our class thinks I was raised by wolves," I mused sarcastically. "I actually do have a family. Well, I did."

Of course that last statement had Palace staring intriguingly at me, I want to go ahead and clear the air. There's so little I hate more than being seen as a victim.

"What I was trying to say is that I used to be close to my parents. But they're gone now, and now it's just me and my brother."

I could tell my Dr knew I purposely avoided explaining what happened to my parents. I dislike that everything was going as far it did, but I didn't want the mood to change. No one likes to hear about your dead parents.

"Yeah, my brother and I are pretty close," Palace said. "The truth is I haven't really seen my parents in months. I love them, I just get too busy."

"That's not so strange really, like I said, I have an older brother. His name is Rex, I guess you could say we're kind of estranged. I don't see him all the time or much at all anymore. Ever since our parents passed away, he kind of drifted through his own life. He's not in school. He's not anything. He gets drunk and fights but he's still my brother, and I still love him."

"Do you mind if I ask?"

"It's not a crime to be curious. They passed away during an earthquake."

After that, both Robert & Palace didn't say a word. Unlike most people, I knew they relished the gritty details. Anytime the topic of my parents came up, naturally people want to know exactly how they died. Worse even, they want to know how I found their bodies strewn on the ground, crumpled and lifeless. They want me to describe the bloodstains soaking their clothing, but not Robert, he already knew enough.

Callum Morrissey

IT'S HOPELESS. Truly hopeless. I have been walking this path and haven't seen anyone yet. How far do I have to go before I finally just give up? *The darkness is getting to me.* Thought Callum. I don't even feel like myself anymore. Not that was saying much. Still, even though I don't have any sort of perfect life or perfect job, but it was my life and my job. Maybe this whole thing is some kind of purgatory. Maybe I've done something wrong like send an innocent man to prison or overlook a client, even lose one case too many. I closed my eyes and adjusted my coat since I was feeling a little warm. Suddenly, my knee twisted in the wrong direction, and I fall backwards frightened as I look up into the darkness frantically trying to find something to grab on to. I felt myself sliding back into a whole, grabbing onto the edge for my life. I knew I shouldn't look down, but I did it any ways and see elongated razor sharp spikes at the bottom waiting for me to fall so that they can impale me.

"Is anyone out there? God, somebody help me!" I shouted, "Please!"

I could barely hear the sound of the scuffling footsteps over my racing heart; they were heading straight towards me. Fear gripped me yet again but once I saw the spotlight, swaying across the floor, I knew it had to be the Drs. I felt my hands losing their grip and for some idiotic reason I looked down again. I was kicking my dangling feet which sent a sudden surge of vertigo through me. Everything was spinning and it wouldn't stop.

"Don't let go!" Curtis screamed.

Does he really think I'm trying to let go?

Curtis and Dr Michaels came scurrying down the pathway, reaching out frantically for my hand.

"Over here, Callum. Over here," Dr Michaels demanded.

"If I let go I'll fall."

"Don't worry, you're in good hands."

Within moments, my fingers were losing their grip and I started to slowly descend towards the spikes below me. I clenched my eyes shut expecting the worst. I hoped the end would come fast and painless, this wasn't how I imagined I would die. Then, Curtis and Dr Michael put all their combined weight into their final struggle and heaved me back onto solid ground.

Panting, Curtis helped me to my feet. "How the hell did you get yourself down there?"

"It's dark down here; I can't see a thing… I took a wrong step," I replied rubbing the sharp ache in my leg.

"Are you the only guys here?"

"Not by a long shot," Curtis said finally catching his breath. "Just about everyone is here."

It was almost like a reunion, seeing us all together again. Approaching from the dark, I saw Ashley still looking lively as ever while pocketing her flashlight in her bag. She dropped her bag at her feet and leaned on the giant wall behind us. Dr. Robert smiled at her. It took everyone a short while to gather near the back end of the pathway. By the look on Dr Palace Michaels, you knew a long conversation about the mural he and his brother saw would soon be necessary. Then Ashley stood up from the wall, and noticed it wasn't a wall at all.

Her mouth slowly parted. She only pointed and gasped. While her back was turned, Curtis pointed too just to mock her. I craned my neck out to examine what had left her speechless.

"Anybody got an idea what the hell this is?" Curtis asked finally being serious.

Callum replied, "By the looks of it, it's just one big giant door..."

Ashley quickly turned. "Wrong!"

"C'mon, guys. Think. It's obvious to a trained observer; this is more than just a door."

Ashley moved up quickly inspecting the engravings along the lining of the blue door. On both sides, an etching of a three-pronged trident could be prominently seen. Surrounding the engraving were intricately drawn pictures of water life sketched in pure gold. Doctor Robert stepped through the crowd to inspect the engravings more closely.

"No," he continued. "It's easy to make that mistake, comparing it to Atlantis, but this is definitely something else." Ashley sort of scowled, hating to be wrong. No doubt the detailing was unusual. Perhaps, the engravings weren't what she thought at all. However, a pattern formed on the doors, that much was obvious. Right to the point where many were losing interest, Ashley gripped Palace hard on his arm.

"That's it!" She shrieked.

Palace shook his head. "What's it?"

Ashley slapped her forehead. "The patterns should have been obvious to anyone who studied the legend of Nubara. What we're looking at is the actual doorway. The entrance to the kingdom of Nubara itself."

"You mean we already left New York? How is that so?" Esabelle asked. A strange cold blue shuddered through me. It just seemed up until this point we had too little time to be prepared and too many questions unanswered.

"This is officially insane..." Curtis muttered.

"Well, if you consider the fact that—"

Out of nowhere, a fast and loud clanking sound echoed behind us. The deafening noise was followed frighteningly by a low soft guttural howl. Concrete debris crashed to the ground around us, engulfing us all in a cloud of dust. We began to scatter like rats scurrying for cover, and saw the all too familiar Centaur that chased us in the tunnels. We all stampeded towards the castle gate doors. We could hear the loud sound of the concrete being crushed under the beast's weight. I screamed for Robert's attention.

"We need a plan and I mean really fast."

The colossal beast was right behind us on the walkway. Esabelle handed her purse to Callum and then struggled to open the doors on her own. She was pulling so hard that her whole body was trembling, desperate for a miracle. Just then, my necklace flew from around her neck and we all watched as it soared through the air afraid that it would shatter. Strangely enough, it landed in the lock of the doorway.

Click!

We all looked at each other in shock as the door creaked slightly open. While everyone else looked at it in awe, I put things back in perspective.

"Stop standing around. Go. Go now!"

Chapter 8

Soliel Oupary

"Soliel get in!" Ashley screamed.

I glanced at the open doorway as I tried to raise my aching body from the damp ground. Behind me, Silver Cannabis was edging closer and closer, ready to make a second charge. The creature's thick pearly-grey skin shimmered in the dim fading light. Pain exploded through my knees as I bolted in Ashley's direction. Ashley screamed again.

"Come on!"

My shoes were making a squashing sound as I ran as fast as my water logged legs could carry me. The Centaur was close behind me I could hear his hooves clopping loudly and increasing in speed. He was now chasing me at full galloping speed. I slide towards the door using all my momentum to slide through it. A pair of hands reached out pulled me into the darkness and then slammed the door; engulfing me in darkness.

Feebly, I stretched out my arms to get my bearings back on course. *What if I'm trapped?* I thought. *What if I'll never leave?* Without warning something gripped my forearm so tightly I couldn't move it. My eyes widened but still I couldn't see a thing in the darkness.

"Ashley, are you out there?" I asked. "Is it you?"

The intimidating blackness surrounded me. I was at a total loss of my senses. A sharp, almost commanding strength nearly pulled me to the ground.

A voice spoke.

"I'm here."

"I'm here, too." Another chimed.

Although I couldn't see their faces, I was relieved to hear their voices again.

The sound of footsteps trailing off made me cry out.

"Don't leave me!"

I heard a click and then a blinding light shone in my face. Ashley moved the light under her chin and the shadows outlined the features of her face. She tilted the light toward me. I waved at her and smiled.

"Still standing..." I said.

She whirled around and familiar faces appeared as the light chased the darkness away. Callum, Robert, Palace, Pablo, Curtis and Ashley & Esabelle of course. My heart slows, and I let out a sigh. I'm just glad to see everyone alive.

"Now what?" Callum asked.

The others fiddled with their flashlights, flicking them on one after the other. Instantly, I started walking without hesitating this time. Callum looked at me and said, "Are you all right?"

The truth is, the question was too big to answer. Part of me was left behind in the tunnels along with all the dead bodies we left along the way. There's a strange feeling I had that something new was starting at this very moment. Ashley unfurled her fingers from around the flashlight. You could feel the tension in the room was thick. Everybody looked afraid, they all were breathing heavily and thankful to have escaped. At this point, I was so scared to make any noise even a yelp. Palace clenched his fingers on my shoulder.

"It's going to be okay, Soliel. Don't worry."

The thing was I wasn't even worried. Not about my life necessarily. What kept my mind running and winding was the rush of fear sending shivers throughout my body. I have seen the Centaur ripping away the lives of both the conductor and Pablo's ex-girlfriend. It wasn't only that we were stuck here. It was that we also didn't know why.

Ashley spoke. "So, what are we going to do now?"

Callum shrugged. "I'm not sure really, it's not like we have a map of the place." I was trying to release the nervous tension out of my body when we heard a thunderous bang in the wall behind us. Then suddenly, something heavy slammed into the door. We knew the only thing it could be was the Centaur, Silver Cannabis. Silver vapors whirled all around us. I knew it was far from over and that the worst part was actually just the beginning.

I shook my head, confused of how I could have known anything. "None of that really makes any sense," I said.

I didn't even have the energy to nod my head. I slumped up against the wall, trying to relax and then Ashley came in. She didn't need to see any details. She knew exactly what I was feeling. Partly, I felt like I was flying backwards unable to control the events happening around me. Like every other time in my life, I was completely out of control. Everyone else seemed to be doing pretty good. Palace and I held hands.

"Maybe its best that we separate, you know." He pointed at all of us. "We're not going to get anywhere standing around like this."

If this conversation we were currently having had been about a walk in the park or heading up the class, then maybe I would have agreed with him, but how are we going to know which direction to take?

"Why is this even happening in the first place?" I asked, flapping my arms like a two year old throwing a temper tamper fit. I was simply tired of going along with everything so far.

For hours, we've been shuffling through the tunnels with no clear direction. "How would this be any different?"

Palace maneuvered between the divided group of people. He tottered right above me and then crouched down. He gazed at me widely with those intimidating baby blue eyes. I hesitated a moment to say a few words, but I was afraid they would come out in a jumble of incoherent mutter, so I decided not to speak. Palace contemplated a moment and then addressed me.

"You can't give up now, Soliel. I know that's exactly what you're feeling."

I held my breath, still afraid to speak. By sitting like I did, there would be no way for any of us to move forward.

"But, you saw that thing back there, hauling dead bodies of our friends. Tell me, how is this all related to the Nubara? How is this all interconnected?" I knew I hadn't been particularly reasonable. I looked up at Palace, searching for answers. If one of the most brilliant scientific minds couldn't give me a clear answer, then who could?

Palace rustled his fingers through my hair and then tapped my forehead.

"Getting a bit heavy for you there," he tapped again. "Let me enlighten you."

I flattened my back and listened.

"These creatures are older than shadows. Older than time itself. Remnants of history collected in the dustbin of the universe." Palace shuffled nearer. "There are some things not of this world that none of us will truly understand."

Was it really my fault that things were happening? Is that why everyone stood around twiddling their thumbs waiting on me to act?

"So, did you guys decide you want to do?"

Truthfully, I've run out of options. Last thing I needed to do was make a ripple between the group. After another bout of eerie silence, I backed up off the wall. There was no doubt something lurked behind us.

"How exactly are we going to do this? Who's going to choose who goes with whom?"

At first Palace wasn't sure what I meant. "It's not rocket science, Soliel. The real question is how will we all be grouped? Which path are we going to take?"

Ashley glanced at me. That haywire look she had in her eyes reminded me of my friend Shoba. Undeniably, I needed her more than ever right now.

Curtis' face was starting to flush, there was no doubt he was becoming impatient. It almost seemed like his eyes would pop out of his head at any moment.

"Could we *get on* with it already? If no one chooses, I'll choose for everybody."

Palace stepped back, raising his arms and shoulders.

"Have at it…"

We all clustered together waiting for our name to be called.

"Okay," he pointed. "Callum, Dr. Roberts, Soliel and Ashley—"

Curtis's voice squeaked on Ashley's name.

"Ashley?"

Ashley cupped her hand over the light to control its beam.

Curtis simply rolled his eyes. He moved along the walls feeling it with his hands. Ashley separated from the rest of us, examining the ground with her flashlight. She had a dim view of some strange swirling etches scrawled on the walls. Her skin began prickling and she immediately dug her hand in her pocket. Oblivious to the rest of us, she jerked something out of her pocket. It took me a few moments to realize what the quick flashes that appeared and disappeared were, and then I realized, she was snapping pictures. *Who would want to take photos of this?*

"Amazing," she exclaimed. Her eyes lit up in ways I've never seen before. Pablo staggered over to us ad looked at us with a bewildered expression on his face. I took his trembling hand but he immediately jerked his fingers from mine.

"I don't know who you people are. You're crazy!"

The sad part was, he wasn't wrong. We're scientists, and honestly, it's in our very nature to be crazy—we seem to revel in the fact.

"Just admit it, Pablo." I said. "You're one of us now."

Pablo formed his lips into a scowl and kept moving past me. Completely ignoring me.

Robert stood silent, peering off into the darkness; deep in thought. He held his hand to his chin and then placed them thoughtfully over his mouth. He nodded as if agreeing to something. He really wished everyone would call him Robert like Soleil did but old habits die hard.

"What's on your mind?" I asked.

"Well, the thing is, I know we're close. But how does the Arctic connect with the Centaur that is hunting us in the tunnels?"

Curtis looked thoughtful. "Clearly, there's someplace we're forgetting to look and now, for whatever reason, were standing here waiting for those answers to just fall into our lap…"

Curtis shook his head. "It doesn't make sense to me? Does it make sense to you?"

Robert was still unsure about how to pinpoint exactly why these two locations, the Arctic and the tunnels were connected. He finally stopped scratching his chin, and lowered his hand to his side. Pablo didn't seem to be handling the situation very well; he had one last drop in his flask and was looking inside it, sloshing it around in its corners. He then took his last swig and wiped his mouth with the back of his hand. He was stressing out, but could you blame him? He just had gotten out of a possible life sentence, and now, he was practically sentenced to wander underneath the New York City subway. He just stayed in his own corner and didn't care to acknowledge us. As far as he was concerned, he was just stuck with us but we weren't exactly his friends.

Not interested in pushing the matter any further, I just left him alone. So did everyone else. He mainly kept to himself anyway, staying near the shadows with his hands in his pockets. When I lost my parents, I had the same sort of discomfort as well. I had the same sort of urge to isolate myself from others. Most people, who haven't lost someone can't really understand what it's like. There's this hole that stays with you, and it never fills up. It's hard when you lose a part of your life that you thought would be there forever.

He sighed, looking defeated. When I looked at him, I had to take a deep breath. Suddenly, I was shocked at Esabelle, who hadn't said a word since we went through the door, she just pranced around pacing from one end to the other. Her body language was very restrained, resting her wrists comfortably behind her back.

Even when Callum addressed her, she didn't answer or reply. I guess that while pacing she couldn't help but be aware that the both of us were somehow connected to all of this. She tugged at her hem, tying it slightly to keep it from dragging on the damp floor.

Curtis shifted further away. "I'm splitting. If you're interested in coming with—well, let's go." Everyone's gaze fixed on Curtis' back. Ashley soon followed after. Esabelle and Callum broke off.

Palace and I exchanged looks while the others dwindled into the darkness. I had the sudden realization that figuratively, and literally, we stood in the middle of the road. He startled me when he took my hand, but once he had a hold of it, I didn't dare let go. Instantly we walked together, hand-in-hand, we were both curious and horrified by what we might find. The thumping sound still echoed behind us. I could hear the primal guttural moans of the Silver Cannabis, thrashing at the door. I fumbled a few more of my steps, walking fast but still staying by Palace's side as we all neared the fork in the road, each of us, had gone our separate ways.

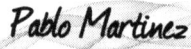

Pablo Martinez

WAS I TO BLAME FOR TAMARA'S DEATH? I insisted on coming down here. I insisted on following Tamara down to the tunnels. No doubt I hated her for what she did. Pablo threw his head back, hold off the choking feeling in his throat. But then he lurched forward, with his flashlight streaking across the floor, trying to dampen down the stirring of helplessness. Thoughts raced in his head, and he couldn't switch them off. He had gone too deep now, too aware that the world wasn't what he thought. The low-level lighting made his vision blurry. Each of his infrequent steps scuffled and dragged. Pablo wriggled his stiffly aching shoulders.

What could I do now? His life may not have been over, but neither was it fulfilled. No prison time, sure. But who did he have to come home to? It's obvious—at least to him—that there are secret pairings, hiding in plain sight among the group. There's this thing that he couldn't quite attain—love.

Everyone had some tiny taste of it. He could see it in the way Soliel looked at her Palace. He detected it between Callum and the red-headed woman...*what's her name again?* Thought Pablo.

"There are definitely some very intense feelings being hidden, but not from me. I'm not old, but I was young once and I know what young love is like. Worse, I've felt the pain of young heartbreak as well. Either way, to feel something for someone, anyone is literally one of the few pleasures in this God forsaken world." Muttered quietly to himself.

Ashley Boylan

THE SMELL STARTED GETTING TO ME. Of course, how exactly can I expect a tunnel that resembled a sewer to smell? Like roses? The thing is though, to me, this black and gray place held a gorgeous mystery. I stopped in my tracks, feeling like the luckiest girl alive. I kept the entire ordeal impersonal. I just kept my eye on the pathway in front of me. As horrific as the encounter was, the Silver Cannabis changed everything. I mean I actually got to see it face-to-face instead of as an etching on a jewel. I knew the Dr, who stood right by me, felt something too.

My pulse quickened when something caught my eye. I stumbled over Dr Robert, making my way to what I saw. Dr Michaels had described moments like these—moments when you stumble upon a great mystery, something that could very well change the world. Dr Michaels was and is extraordinarily focused as I am but that didn't mean he still could be captivated by a truly one of a kind discovery. With each clue, oddly the less we solved.

This indefinable mystery revolving around the strange and inexplicable legend of Nubara changed our lives in many ways much beyond our control. I slid the camera strap over my shoulder. My flashlight pierced the blue foggy haze swirling all around. No clue how long we'd be holed up down here. Honestly, I'm just too preoccupied to care.

"Dr," I strained my eyes in the dark. "If we see the Silver Cannabis that means all the things we've been studying are true, right?" Without breaking stride, Dr Michaels answered me.

"First of all Ms. Boylan call me Robert."

The possibilities are what intrigued me the most. What would a discovery like this mean for humanity? How would the average Joe react? Knowing that there were ancient kings who existed before the start of the entire universe. It's truly interesting to think about. I spent my entire childhood crunching data and reading the numbers, but *this*... This isn't something that's easily quantified. Believe me, coming from me, that's a pretty big deal! There have been so few breakthroughs that I've witnessed in person. Even during my graduate courses, the labs were never enough. Instead, we were analyzing and researching from a very different place. We didn't have much hand on experience, certainly not like this.

"You've got your head in the right place, Ms. Boylan. But who am I kidding? You've proven that many times over the course of your thesis work," Robert said.

He smiled at me. Then patted me softly on my shoulder. Robert was one of those Drs who wanted to see his students out there, working in the field.

"It's definitely a question that begs to be answered." I said, grinning slightly. Robert always had us chasing for answers. He never was an easy one to understand. I recognized one of the words on the floor as I was crouched down studying the edges. There was something there, possibly a silhouette but definitely something. Dropping closer, I thought I could see it. My eyes glinted with curiosity and puzzlement and I was eager to show Robert what I found.

Callum Morrissey

I DON'T KNOW HOW SHE DID IT, thought Callum. I just can't understand how she could walk full speed ahead as if the putrefying stink didn't overwhelm her. Esabelle ignored it of course, like she always did. I still can't understand how she could simply ignore the stagnant smell of water. For a second, she circled round and fixated her glare on my leg. *What was she looking for?* I didn't know. She slowly released the flashlight and plopped it in my hand. After pointing at the cut on my leg, she spoke.

"You're bleeding, no seriously. Just look down at your leg," she told me.

I swept the light down to examine the cut. Blood splattered a river down my pale leg. Esabelle peered closer. She looked at me for a second, and then lowered her eyes. I couldn't help it; I gazed longingly at the red hair swept across her face. A soft rustle sounded as she pulled a willowy silk scarf from her neck.

"What are you doing?"

"Be quiet," she said.

I stifled a yelp as she blew on the bright red cut and tied the scarf around my leg and knotted it as if she were wrapping a birthday gift. My legs began to give out but just as I was falling backwards, Esabelle caught me and held me steady. At that moment our eyes locked and I'm sure I had a dead fish look on my face, but I couldn't help it when she smiled at me. The woman was purely infectious. She had a simple way of making me want to get to know her regardless of how different we were. She leaned in closer, then she stared directly at me. I tried my best to avoid her glare. Esabelle blinked, poking me in my wound.

She pointed back. "What do you think that was?"

"What what was?"

I think she clapped her hands but I couldn't see anything clearly in the darkness.

"Come on, you know exactly what I'm talking about. The flash we had. The spark. Whatever you call it!"

She had a certain quality about her voice, tired and generally unamused.

"Don't you remember that place? The field?" she asked. Truthfully, a part of me was too afraid to consider it. I also have to acknowledge paranormal time paradoxes and brain added visions, otherwise known as hallucinations. My life as a lawyer wasn't exactly easy, but my life as a lawyer and a part of some big grand prophecy was much crazier than anything else I've seen.

Figuring I remained cryptic long enough, I confirmed the same.

"What do you think the warrior from our vision means?" I said, wrestling my hair back with my hand. She considered it, she was just as clueless as me. I'm not sure what answer I was looking for. *How would she possibly know?*

"I'm not sure. I think it has less to do with this place and more to do with us—all of us, "she spoke quietly.

At once, I stop and lowered my eyes. Esabelle held out her hand and looked at me. She smiled despite herself. Her eyes studying me under that curtain of fiery red hair. She was the most beautiful sight I've ever seen. It's far too early to make anything of it, especially with Esabelle. Not sure how she did it, but she had a hold on me of the likes that thought I could never feel again. There are some times when you have to take notice as fate whispers sweet nothings in your ear. And this time, fate was screaming at me at the top of her lungs. For the first time, Esabelle didn't look completely appalled to be near me.

"I have a feeling we will meet the warrior again," I said, starting forward.

She didn't quite ignore me, but she didn't look at me either. Esabelle took small hopping steps while looking down at the amulet around her neck. She traced her fingers along the metal casing and pulled it up to show it to me.

"I don't know. Soleil gave me this necklace, hoping that I could keep it protected—keep it safe." a hint of panic reverberated as she spoke. "I'm not sure if I can."

"Does that have anything to do with the legend?"

She nodded.

"That monster we saw back there, the Centaur, it's the same one on this necklace."

She held it up for me in the palm of her hand. I didn't pick it up, but I felt along the surface. The luminescent whorl reflected under the light. At first, I found nothing, but after I leaned in for a closer look, I could see the tiny markings. They were barely noticeable, but there was an image of Silver Cannabis etched in stone.

"I'm not sure if I'm cut out for that responsibility anymore."

We emerged out of the dark and I took a seat next to her. When I was close enough, I slowly stretched my arm out and settled it around her shoulder and pulled her close to me to comfort her. Everything was happening so fast that it was hard to catch my breath.

Curtis Anderson

NO ONE WOULD BELIEVE WHAT I FOUND said Curtis to himself. My usual vacant expression withered from my face. At least, this time it made sense. Everyone around me, including Soleil, Ashley and even our Drs seemed to get severely thrilled by even the slightest things. It was certainly no small frustration of mine. *I mean how do you think I feel?* It's not easy being the consummate skeptic. Unlike Soleil, I don't suffer lucid visions about Greek mythology, but I have my uses.

Usually, I took out my frustration in the lab, analyzing near indecipherable data. Of course, Ashley and I would end up arguing about it. She would crunch numbers in her head and somehow prove me wrong. Although, at some point I would get tired of arguing, this always made her ego swell even bigger. Somehow, I've been able to remain impressively logical about all this. This time was different. This time I thundered down the pathway, my arms extended to control my speed. It didn't help that I couldn't breathe and was constantly hacking up thick wet phlegm from my throat. The only trouble was: *Who would even believe me?* I've been the rational one for so long that they probably would just roll their eyes. My feet splashed through the puddles on the corroded pathway. Once I tracked them down, I'll tell them about the doors.

It was a race against time. As I took a few more steps, I was startled by a mysterious shadow that seemed to float in the dark.

"Hello?" I called.

The shadow spun around immediately when it sensed my presence. I stopped and waved my arms which instantly was clear to me that wasn't such a good idea, as many more figures rushed from the shadow directly towards me, and I couldn't tell whether it was one of my colleagues or a Centaur that would love nothing more than to eat me alive.

"Curtis!" I hear a voice. "It's me Soleil." A wave of relief washed through my entire body when I heard her voice.

Beyond the cheery platitudes, I said what I needed to say.

"Where is everybody?"

Soliel looked back at me casually. "Some of them are heading back to the main door—why?" She shrugged.

She straightened up under my tight grip.

"Would you mind letting go?"

It took a second to get a nasty cough out of my heaving chest.

"Tell everyone to follow me. I have something to show them."

Soleil raised her brow and gave me an amused, but serious look. We all walked together, nearly hitting each other as we made our way towards back to the entrance. When we arrived, everyone else already was there and waiting.

"Go ahead, tell them what you're going to tell me," Soleil said.

I nodded, holding up a single finger. And after I finished wheezing, I told him what I had found.

"I found the doorway."

"Where does that lead?"

Overtaken by coughing and the phlegm in the back of my throat, I tried to speak again.

"Trust me, it's better you see for yourself."

I wasn't too excited about running again. Despite my slow moving efforts, everyone followed me. When we stopped, I slumped over and pointed.

"Right there," I wheezed.

Soleil wandered further to investigate the set of massive cobalt doors. I'm sure she wondered whether she was brave enough to open them and see what's inside. She was never one to be patient, I elbowed my way past her.

"Get out of the way. Just let me do it…"

A group of us took each other's hands and began walking forward. I cleared my sore throat and then followed everybody inside. Soleil heard noises across the group, but stopped rigid in her steps when she saw what was inside. Shelves upon shelves of gleaming objects glinted about against the wall. I can't say for sure what I was looking at, but reading the expression on Soleil face that she knew. Our eyes darted around the room. It appeared we had wandered into an armory; there were mysterious weapons of all sorts.

"Where do you think all this came from?" Palace asked. "What do you think they're for?"

Robert inched his way toward a broadsword glowing under the bright eerie lights. He gripped it with both hands and swung it, being careful not to lop off his own head.

"Murdering enemies...I presume," Robert replied.

Esabelle and Callum glanced at one another, slightly anxious, recognizing that was the same one they saw in their vision.

Half joking I said, "Maybe we're all getting ready for war."

Soleil completely ignored me. Her eyes zoned in on one weapon, the blue glow of it reflected on her stunned face. The prospect of actually touching it and holding its crackling power in her hand frightened her.

"I think you're getting a little too close, Soleil," Palace said. Soleil didn't pause, she only stretched out her hand and grabbed it, careful to only curl her fingers around the string.

"OW!"

Then she yelped and quickly dropped it on the floor. It was obvious that touching it was a risky undertaking to which none of us saw any good coming from. Soleil sucked her finger, pulled it from her mouth and gazed curiously at the wound. Ashley ran to her side and looked down at the arrow, which was still crackling and whizzing with that strange blue energy. That blue electricity would probably seriously hurt anyone else in this room. But I couldn't stop staring at it.

"That did the damage right there," I said pointing at the blood-stained pin on the arrow.

Despite the pain Soleil felt in her hand, she still remained curious about its origins. This time it wasn't about how such a weapon even existed or even where it came from, it was something else. We had gone to an entirely new place and with what we know now; this had gone far beyond scientific labs and well into the realm of the supernatural. Ashley, being true to her nature, delved deep into her pockets and took out her camera again. We could hear the clicks snap at all angles of the room. She moved forward, utterly transfixed, snapping pictures as she went.

But it is doubtful, just like the rest of us, that she understood what she found. After a few more seconds, she stopped with a sudden fascination. The rest of us warily followed her. Behind all the weapons, was another hidden doorway? Even at this point, I thought it would be a good idea to leave well enough alone, but Ashley thought different and gripped the door handle. She held it for moment and then tugged. We all were careful to stay out of her way. After pulling for a few more minutes, she paused briefly and then pulled some more, but the door wouldn't budge.

Ashley slapped her sides and yelled at us in frustration. "Well, you just gonna stand there or what?" All the guys looked at each other, then walked purposefully towards Ashley and grabbed the handle of the door. We gave one another reassuring look as we prepared to pull open the door.

"Ready?" Robert asked.

"Ready as we'll ever be," I mumbled.

"One. Two. Three?"

Callum staggered back and released the door handle, letting the other guys pull his weight. He walked backwards towards the scattered weapons on the wall and stopped next to Esabelle.

"Strength was never my strong suit anyway..." he said.

I SHOVED MY HANDS in his pockets and cast my eyes downwards as the other guys still attempted to pry open the door. Esabelle noticed something between her and my feet and immediately bent down to get a closer look. She reached out and touched it, feeling it with her hand and then picked it up dangling it in the air. She was holding two bracelets that were silver and gleaming with open clasps. So naturally she had to try it on. The clasp pinched as it tightened around her wrist. I didn't have particular fondness for jewelry, but I swallowed my pride for her. She strapped hers on her right wrist, and I strapped mine on my left. Being this close, I felt more connected than ever.

"All right, I think I've had enough," I said. We tried to get the bracelets off of our wrist, but neither of them could be unclasped.

"That's not normal," Esabelle replied.

Palace leaned over a neatly displayed a case of lightweight blades. They had a high metal sheen and sharp curved tip with serrated edges. They reminded him of blades that he had seen before, but only in texts of course. The handle was made of a smooth curvature and nearly everything else was exactly the same as the Sai blades. It finally sank in, this room he was standing in had more history than he's ever studied in his life.

Behind him he heard sharp gasping breaths. Ashley and a group of guys stepped back from the doors; open and welcoming them inside. We were speechless, the room was lined with gold trim on the corners and the floor and a velvet rug stretched all the way to the back of the chamber. Soleil moved ahead, she seemed to be drawn further and further inside, almost as if something called to her. She needed to know more about Nubara. She wanted answers. She wanted to face him. She knew that this might be the last chance she had.

Eventually, the rest of us slipped behind her, no less shocked about what we saw. The mysteries didn't add up, they just kept on coming. I struggled to put into words the grandiosity of the fixtures and the chandeliers hanging from the ceiling. And then, I realized my sense of fear exceeded my sense of awe. Soleil, had gotten much too far ahead and then slowed down to wait for the rest of us. An uncomfortable mixture of astonishment and terror settled in my chest and made my heart hammer. Ashley finally broke the silence with a barely audible quavering voice, it was the first time anyone had seen her having trouble speaking, but it was something that finally was on all our minds.

"Where the hell are we?"

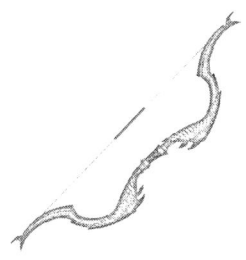

Chapter 9

Soleil Oupary

You would think at this point and after everything that we've been through, I would simply want to collapse. It's been an hour since any of us had any rest, and I completely lost the color in my face. However, this nightmare I have found myself in was far from over. When I walked about halfway of though the room, I was overcome by a stab of agonizing pain that throbbed throughout my legs. The source of pain originated from my scars. I fell to my knees and scrapped the palms of my hands on the floor. My skin turned deathly pale and dark circles formed under my eyes.

"What's happening?" I screamed. Palace nearly grabbed me right there and then but I stopped him before he got too close.

"Soleil let me help you!"

He tried again but waved him off.

"Whatever is happening to me, the last thing I need is someone else's death on my hands."

Finally, he backed away. My eyes were gaunt and red-rimmed; they had sunk so low, I thought they would fall out of my face. I stayed hunched over. My temperature was rising and sweat was starting to pool down my back as every muscle was convulsing in my body. Then, as quickly as it happened, it stopped and I felt my skin cooling down. The surge of intense pain subsided and I was back to normal, at least as normal as I can be. I coughed a few times, collected myself and rose up from the ground.

I had everyone turned around as I lifted my shirt up to look at the harsh ugly looking scar that ran like a snake along my side; it vanished before my eyes. *How could this happen?* I thought. For the past month, I've been recuperating from the collapse in the cave. The pain of the ice ripping through my rib cage is something I'll never forget. It never fully healed due to its location but now, I was completely healed. Palace came to my aid again.

"Are you sure you're alright?"

Yeah, I think it was just a spell."

Of course, I wouldn't tell him the truth. He never would understand. I let my shirt flop back down to my waist. I was still in disbelief, after living with the pain for so long, I found it strange to finally be set free. Everyone else was unaware of the fact that, somehow, I felt entirely on my own. Who else could understand what it's really like to be me? When I looked a bit closer at my hand, a glowing aura emanated from the tips of my fingers.

Immediately, I stuck them in my pockets. The weirdest part of it all was, I felt like a stranger in my own life. I shut my eyes briefly, took a breath and pulled my hand up from my pockets. We also stood a bit closer now. Even so, I still felt entirely alone. So far, I had these weird connections with total strangers and other colleagues in my group. None of what they experienced came close to what was happening to me.

There is a definite confusion in the air. I can hear it in Ashley's voice. "And this place is supposed to be what exactly?" Ashley muffled.

We all turned to look at Ashley. The fantastic, yet garish nature was becoming increasingly difficult to ignore. For group of so called scientists, we didn't have the slightest clue what to do next. When the group moved further, a crunch sounded from the ground. Ashley was the only one who bothered look down first. Crushed glass, so finely smashed, it deeply embedded the soles of her shoes. Ashley took a deep breath. Her eyes trailed along the pathway of broken glass all the way to what looked like a shattered cage.

"Whatever was in there, they sure didn't want it to coming out..." Esabelle muttered. That's exactly the problem wasn't it? Monsters running amok, getting loose and starting a rampage where they don't belong. Curtis looked as though he was about ready to pull out his hair.

"What is it now?" He straightened his hand across his face. "And we expect to be running away from other supernatural beasties. You know your garden variety vampires and werewolves?"

Maybe, he could come up with the plan with much less sarcasm. Perhaps, that was hoping too much, the latter was just too instinctual for him. My attention shifted back to Ashley. She was focusing her attention to the broken glass.

The pieces looked like a thousand jigsaw puzzle parts. Her thoughts turned in her mind as she thought hard and lowered her hand onto a shard. She thumbed around the edges, trying to see how the small pieces would fit with the larger glass case.

"Ugh!"

Apparently, she was no less a klutz than I was. Like me, a fragment pricked her finger. Ashley recoiled and pulled her hands toward her face.

Callum shook his head. "The message should be loud and clear by now. Don't touch."

Maybe as a lawyer he didn't understand, that as a scientist, curiosity was second nature. Instead of focusing on the pain, Ashley seemed to be turning over the larger questions in her mind. In that moment, visions flashed through her head. A woman stood before her draped in white cloth. *Who is she? Where am I?* The only problem was it looked exactly like her, as if she was looking at herself in a mirror. She hunched her shoulders and a woman held out her hand to Ashley. *None of this makes any sense.* Ashley thought. Although everything was occurring in her mind, it felt nothing like a dream. Instead, it felt like it was the first time she was truly awake. The white cloth dragged along the floor. The mysterious woman wore a rosemary garland in her hair and when she spoke she murmured something that Ashley couldn't hear.

"I can't hear you?"

Ashley looked at the woman who strangely looked like her and stepped forward fearlessly to inspect her doppelganger. She simply figured she had been up too long, and all this was a sign that she needed to go home. She looked again at the woman's cloth and a liquid seeped to the surface. Ashley had to blink a few times to be sure of what she saw. She concentrated, watching it drip onto the floor and form a pool. She noticed its dark red color and raised her eyebrows. Ashley continued forward, curious to ask it more questions. She needed to know who exactly this doppelganger was.

"Don't be afraid."

Still, the woman did not respond. With all the commotion, she retreated further back and Ashley followed. The woman moved back faster, and Ashley ran after her. We both ran in the same direction.

Darkness faded away, the bright white surroundings shifted and transformed into a lush forest. The sounds of nature echoed through the trees, and primal creatures lurked out of sight. There was silence for a moment before Ashley realized where she was.

"Is this what Soleil was talking about?"

When she looked around, she had convinced herself that she and Soleil had visions of this same place. She recalled vividly how Soleil described a saltwater taste in the air. After inhaling a deep breath, the air was nothing like she never experienced before. Her body seemed wider somehow, and her mind processed information much more clearly. Never in her life had she been so wonderfully aware of all the senses that she felt them in this moment. I turned, hearing a noise coming from the trees.

I dove straight to the ground for cover. Two voices spoke in a language that was foreign to my ears. Instinctively, I stayed out of sight hoping to learn something from their body language. These people wore cloth wrapped snugly around their bodies like Romans in a forgotten era. I stepped forward cautiously, lowering myself further. I closed my eyes and lie there, listening to them speak It took a moment for my brain to register, but suddenly I understood the words they were saying.

"It's been breached," a man with coal dark hair said.

The other nodded." This world has been opened to the next. It will be a matter of time before the humans find out about this place," a woman with red hair scowled. The expressions on her face were stressed and urgent, it was obvious she feared something was to come. For whatever reason, my pulse quickened and a painful throbbing went off in my head. My nerves tightened as well. I threw my hands up, pressing them deeply into my temples and held a stifled a scream. The searing pain felt like acid was dissolving the soft tissue in my head. I fell back on the ground, looking up at the sky above me.

When my squirming ceased, I kept very still not knowing what to expect next. I swallowed hard clutching leaves of grass in my fist. Once again, I felt myself going under, falling with no place to land. I don't know how long I'll be suspended like this with nothing to hold on to and nowhere to stand. All I know is, that if I make it, I can finally say I'm sorry. I can finally tell Soleil she was right. My body fell back on the ground, and I snapped upright. When I glanced down, I realized that Soleil was holding my hand.

"You blacked out there for a second," Soleil said. "Gave us all scare."

Not wasting any time, I looked into Soleil's eyes desperate to tell her about the forest and the girl who looked exactly like me.

Soleil looked at my hand. "Ashley, don't you think you're holding on a little too tight? It's okay we're not going to leave you."

A few minutes later, when the deliriousness stopped, I thought it would best to head back.

Callum Morrissey

WE BOTH STUDIED the intricate detailing of the bracelets on our wrists. They were a little tight, but not especially painful. I thought. With my impatience, I tried to remove it again. Esabelle followed suit. Combined we yanked and tugged and then yanked and tugged some more. The shimmering bangles didn't budge, they steadily remaining on our wrists. Immediately, Esabelle leaned in close.

"How do you get this thing off?"

To be honest, what happened to us was no stranger than anything else that happened thus far. Still, it explained why the bracelets called us, sought us out. Once the initial shock dissipated, we struggled to pull them off again. Tired of doing the same thing and expecting different results, I suggested something.

"How about you take mine, and I take yours?"

Esabelle turned to me in the midst of her pulling.

She shrugged. "Worth a shot…"

We moved sluggishly, and then took each other's hand. At least for a few moments, we stared into each others eyes. Just like last time, there is absolutely no pretense, our guards were both down. And then, a slicing noise hissed through air. We both looked at our arms, searching for the source of the sound. It took us a second to see it clearly, two razor-sharp blades protruded out of our bracelets. We jumped in a nervous impulse, looking utterly bewildered. But with the sudden movement of us releasing each others hand, the blades hissed again and disappeared. My nerves twisted inside me, they were just about ready to send me into convulsions. Esabelle eyed the bracelet again.

"Now, how do you explain that?" She asked wide-eyed with incomprehension.

I shook my head. "It's probably best to stay far, maybe even an arm's length, away from each other," I reasoned. Esabelle stepped up, cocking her head with a glazed look in her eyes. That just wasn't going to happen. She reached out again and took my hand without asking.

"Let's try this once more," she said.

Of course, I obliged her. And just like before, the blades forced themselves out as we touched hands. For whatever reason, when we touched these bracelets became deadly weapons. I couldn't help but think that just a few days ago, we were total strangers. *So, why is it that we have this eerie connection? Why are forces pulling us together?* I never met anyone in my life who in some small way I felt understood. We released each other again. And then nothing but silence came between us. I scratched my throat, and quickly yanked my hand away once I realized how easily the bracelet could rip out my neck.

I couldn't help but be worried that all the visions that I've seen so far we're foreshadowing something violent that might happen in another world full of sharp weapons, large and broad swords. Esabelle proceeded to meet up with the rest the group.

"We can't tell anyone about this. They won't understand they'll just freak out."

When Esabelle answered, she was careful to avoid touching my hand. "I've got nothing to say if you don't."

I nodded my head relieved. A tremendous weight had been lifted off my shoulders. Too much demanded our attention, and lethal bracelets weren't at the top of the list.

We both wanted nothing more than to just get out of this place. The others were still concerned with helping Ashley off of the floor. We stood and hovered along with them, inching ourselves closer, standing just about shoulder to shoulder. I still wore a shocked expression on my face, careful not to entwine our fingers. Esabelle moved back a little and I jumped when I felt her hand rubbing my shoulder. Esabelle may not have shown it, she wasn't as vulnerable as I was, but deep down inside her something stirred too. She couldn't say it. It was still much too early. However, for me, this relationship—or whatever you call this thing we have—had much improved since a few days ago when she used to punch me in the shoulder without warning.

A vast improvement over the strong-willed girl I met yelling on the train. We both went through a great many transformations up to this point. *Who knows?* Maybe this was supposed to happen all along. With everything that's happened, I wanted to find out which it really was. I wanted to know, ultimately, what these visions meant for me. For so long, my life has been a long trip where I didn't understand my existence.

In that second, we held each other's gaze. I've never felt more content, as though I had a purpose. She rose up, bumping her shoulder next to mine. I honestly couldn't be sure if that was by accident or if it was some genius orchestrated plan. Without warning, Palace walked between the two of us. We straightened up immediately and refocused our attention back to Ashley. However, I knew inside we were astonished by our true feelings. And yet, there she stood, only so many inches away. I drew a slow breath. We all helped Ashley rise to her feet. Esabelle rushed over to see is she was okay.

No matter what, I would be unwilling to leave her. I extended my arm, and Esabelle took it, slowly interlocking it with hers. The two of us are powerful enough together. She and I were no longer simply Callum and Esabelle, when we touched, the two of us made something cosmic, something timeless. We winded through the group, glancing at each other as we shoved. No one else took notice, but I did. The two of us have become one.

Everyone was kind of scurrying around doing their own thing now. Robert picked up the camera that Ashley dropped. He did a quick spin, and looked lost in thought, he was probably thinking how this information has gone woefully undocumented. Robert then proceeded to walk away from the group taking pictures of the glass that shattered on the floor. He wandered around quickly tapping the button on the camera. He looked up, lowering the camera from his eye line. He had been working his whole life for this moment.

He stood in the chamber of Nubara and for a full minute, he focused and unfocused the lens capturing the shining gold details in the ornate jewel chandelier that dazzled above him. No one else really took notice. Palace was too busy consoling Soleil and Ashley. He needed to make sure they were going to be alright. I'm sure Curtis, with his usual sad sack attitude, thought of nothing but how to find his way back to the surface. Pablo stood alone, far away from the group, interested only in himself.

He thanked his lucky stars that he hadn't died back there in the tunnel. I watched him pull the flask from his pocket and take another swig.

Eventually, I hoped he would be okay. There's no way to prepare for this sort of thing. With all of us together, the only choice we had was to figure it out. Finally, when everything sort of settled down, I felt that I had a chance to speak with Esabelle again. My throat constricted, feeling tense about what she was going to say. *Get a grip Callum!* Maybe I'm not as much a coward as I thought I was. It could be just that I'm just wired differently.

Realizing this, I stopped hesitating and grasped her hand. As soon as our fingers touched, we tumbled backwards and fell on the plush carpet. My heart was gushing, and I felt it circulating all over. The heat burned so intensely, my fingers almost went numb. Esabelle glanced at me but didn't say a word. She didn't have to because I knew it scorched the insides of her too. As we lay there on the floor, holding each other's hand, our blood radiated limitless energy. I turned to her, unable to bear it. Esabelle shivered. She looked otherworldly, almost regal. The scarlet color of her hair intensified to a brightly red hue. This whole time, I was unable take my eyes off her. I even felt the blood burning in the cut on my leg. It was all too much to handle. My stomach twisted in knots, but I didn't care.

Somehow, we both opened our own portals of energy; we shared a complex spirit that only we could understand. Red lines of energy crisscrossed all over our bodies, that only we could see. At the point where I held her hands, the temperature ran so high, and an orange glowing light emanated from our grasp. The slow process of us finding one another was over. Sure, if someone told me that I would meet a woman who apparently just happened to have supernatural powers and lived in New York, I never would have believed them. Finally, we released one another's hand.

"I finally feel like I'm cooling down," Esabelle said.

Although the heat had dissipated and was no longer rushing through me, I still a blinding intensity surging all over. I couldn't stop thinking about what this would mean for our lives once we got out of this place. I couldn't stop thinking about what the larger picture meant; what our destinies meant.

Destiny.

Now, I finally had one.

"That's funny, I feel like I'm burning up," I said. Esabelle flashed me a sarcastic scowl, then erupted a deep guttural laugh. At this point it didn't matter whether we were no longer touching, the connection was still there. Now, it would stay there forever. I cracked a smile. Esabelle was glowing but that didn't stop her from punching me in the arm. We both nodded to each other. To avoid looking too obvious, we decided to not smile at each other so wide. It was hard but we did it, we drifted apart to the opposite sides of the chamber. Esabelle glided through almost as if she floated on air, her blue dress scintillating under the warm chandelier light.

She took on a heavenly quality that was too hard to describe. It was greater than how beautiful she looked or how strong she was bigger; much bigger than any of that. The legend of Nubara, something I didn't even know existed until the last few hours ago, actually saved my life. Excluding the bloodthirsty and flesh eating Centaur, that just complicated things. Even though my life just got a hell of a lot weirder, this is the first time I've ever felt normal. Because at the end of the day everything comes down to being accepted for whom you are. For that, I felt grateful. And there were a lot of reasons why we could be more rational. A lot of reasons why we should forget our feelings, but I only needed one reason to forget about the rest. That reason was Esabelle. I shifted my glance across the room and saw her staring into my dark eyes. I've never met a woman who would have that kind of effect on me. A woman who distracted me completely. I was fired up and ready to take on the world. Even though I wanted to tell everybody in the room, I didn't say a word.

"SHE'S GOOD," I SAID. I moved back a few inches to give Ashley some room to walk. She gave me no indication that she would fall over and collapse again.

"Like she said, okay. I don't need you guys hovering over me," Ashley chimed in.

Ashley didn't want to get an argument about the kindness of her friends looking out for her, but I could tell she was feeling smothered.

That's when I took a stand. "We should focus on how to get out of this place now. Agreed?"

Curtis nodded. "That's all I've ever been saying."

It was only then that I wondered, *maybe that will never be possible*. I mean who knows whatever was in that cave could have been like us, trying to escape. And with that, I thought, maybe I may never see Shoba ever again. As my thoughts started getting heavier and heavier, I took a deep breath and just simply tried to relax. What we all needed to focus on right now is what we can do at the moment.

"So what's the plan?" Ashley asked.

I shrugged. "There's got to be something in here that we can use, something has to be a clue. So, here's what I'm thinking, why don't we split off and look around the chamber and if one of us finds something we'll let each other know."

"Sounds good enough to me," Ashley said.

It wasn't just the standing around that I found annoying, it was the hopelessness that wore on me. Nubara's chamber had too much to look at. Way too much. On the upper part of the walls, the curved outermost part had a dull sheen. You could tell these were used in battles fought eons ago. I adjusted my view to the bookcase lined up against the wall. Hundreds of books centuries old, and weighing a ton were stacked with their spines forward and begging to be grabbed.

I let my curiosity lead me as I felt my fingers along the edge of the book and felt the aged indention of the letters on the title. After I pulled my hand away, dust collected on my fingertips. I squinted my eyes and read the title.

"*The History of Forgotten Kings…*" I read. Wanting to know more, I grasped the book and staggered back a few steps. I tried to balance myself under its weight and once I got my footing, I immediately rifled through the pages. I turned, hacking a cough and feeling the dust tickle my nose. The page I landed on had a picture of two people standing together wearing a white cloth draped around their bodies. I frowned not sure how any of this information could help me at all. At first without really noticing, I saw something in the picture out of the corner of my eye. An Emblem, like the one on the necklace I had given to Esabelle, it was cleverly hidden behind the figures on the page.

"It's there too!"

What was the meaning of the symbol? I've been seeing it everywhere. Ever since the Arctic, staring at the same symbol on the necklace and now on this page. What I really wanted now, was answers. *Why me? Why was I so special? I'm just a girl whose parents died and has a brother she never talks to*. I tried my best to calm down. *Stop getting so angry*, I told myself as I slammed the book on the floor. Everyone in the room shot me a glance when they heard the noise.

I've had enough. I was finished. Done. Right at that moment, I felt something pricking me like a million needles searing all the way up my hand. The Novae Emblem drew itself and traced a tattoo on my arm. I've seen the same Emblem in the jewel and now in the old book. I blinked my eyes. A faint throbbing pulsed against them. Everyone rushed towards me.

"Soleil!" Ashley shouted. "Move your hands. Let me see."

The first thing I did was cup my hands over my eyes. I tried to enter the ache of the swelling in my head. You couldn't imagine what the pain felt like, even if I told it to you. When at last I moved my hands, everyone gasped, which increase the amount of fear that I was previously feeling.

"What? What is it?"

Esabelle looked at me as if I were walking death itself. She pointed her finger.

"Soleil, you really do need to look at yourself, its —your eyes."

She moved down, trying to look at me from a different angle. I felt like a lab rat, feeling the pressure of all the staring eyes. Even though I didn't like this much attention, at least something was happening. Seconds later, a furious gale rushed into the chamber. It pushed open another hidden door. I more felt than heard a presence calling me inside the room. I had no choice I walked towards the room.

Everyone else watched as I walked closer to the door of the light shining from inside. I felt as though I was caught in a trance, I could hear Palace calling my name.

"Soleil, don't go in there!"

Palace followed after me, but when he tried to touch my tattooed arm an invisible force blew him back. Each of my steps was careful, slow and deliberate. Ashley waited to see what would happen. With each inch, they all held in their breath. I had no choice but to keep moving forward, keep walking towards the blinding blue light. When I finally walked inside the room, it was brimming with enormous riches of all kinds, diamonds, jewels and precious stones were stacked from the floor all the way to the vaulted ceiling. Everyone else followed behind me.

"Holy…" Curtis cursed. He stood with his mouth agape, but who could blame him, especially at this time standing in front of an infinite amount priceless jewels. "I'll catch up with you guys." He waved his hand and dug through a pile of gold coins, stuffing them in his pockets.

Callum saw a ring made of pure gold with a sapphire stone placed squarely in the middle. Robert and Palace held items and were examining them carefully in their hands. Ashley had her camera that she dropped and started snapping pictures. Pablo, not having gone too far, was fascinated by just how much wealth was accumulated in this treasure room. As everyone staked their claim of the treasures, my body had a mind of its own. Palace still followed me closely, and I stopped. On the back wall, hidden behind a trove of more jewels, an enormous portrait mirror hung. Palace had seen that picture before, but not like this. Inside the portrait mirror, a face stared back at us. The reflection of Omegaura, the rumored Princess of Nubara, she had eyes that roamed across the interior of the room.

"Wait, is she looking at us?"

She had the perfect skin that glistened like fresh dew after a rain. She had a jewel affixed in her elaborately pinned up hair. The picture seemed so real, that although I could not be sure, it blinked at me. Call me crazy, but I was pretty sure that frickin picture just blinked.

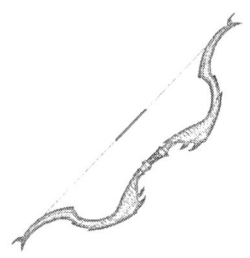

Chapter 10

Curtis Anderson

"You're in the way, Curtis. I can't see anything." Ashley sneered.

I leaned back purposely to block Ashley's view.

"The anticipation is killing me. I've got to see!"

For me, everyone's voices drowned out as I focused my attention on the portrait in front of me. The tight smile drawn across Omegaura's face made her hard to read. I felt a twinge deep in my body when I stared directly into her eyes.

Ashley tilted her head to the left, as if that would help her gather more information. Robert, the residing expert on all things Nubara, had to make his own judgments for himself.

"We are in the presence of history that goes as far back several millenniums," Robert said.

Callum moved himself to the front. He saw the rest of us taken back by the gravitas of the moment and raised his brows.

"I hate to be that guy, but can anyone explain to me why this is important? And what it means?"

Ashley nodded in his direction and prepared to serve up a long winded answer to his questions

"Callum, could you be anymore forgetful? We are standing right in front of royalty. Don't you remember the legend Soleil spoke about? Well, Omegaura is the Queen…no Princess of the Kingdom of Nubara."

Pablo stared, unblinking. "I've never seen anyone like her."

What he really meant was; he hadn't seen anything as astonishingly beautiful, but didn't want to appear as though he didn't care or respect her. Palace felt his hand along the picture frame searching for any kind of clue. Maybe something in the room will give him a sign of how to escape back to the surface. My eyes followed

Ashley as she openly tried to find key points of interest in the room. Not far from where we all were gathered in front of the portrait, a single leather bound book lay on a marble pedestal.

The spine in the cover was adorned with gold detailing just like those on the castle doors. Ashley swept her hand across the cover and pulled it away slightly when she noticed that her entire hand was covered in a thick layer of dust. After a moment of hesitation, she just continued rubbing away the thick layer of dust until the Golden lettering serviced.

"Queen Marietta of Nubara…" Robert read aloud while gently lifting the book out of her hand. He then attempted to read the title himself.

"No matter how hard I focus or squint my eyes, everything I read looks like gibberish," he said.

Ashley grabbed the book back, took a deep breath and read the title again. Nothing seemed wrong or out of place.

She shook her head. "I'm reading it just fine, it's a diary." I walked over to where Robert was standing, I was eager to see if I could read the title, or if it was only Ashley who could. To my surprise, I could read it too. I also understood the words.

"What's happening to me?"

"It's all right," Palace told her. "Just don't panic."

"Well, if you can read the title, why wouldn't you just read what's in the book?"

And here I thought Omegaura's constantly had her eye on me. No one needs to tell me how crazy that sounded. I already knew. So, presumably, I'm either out of my mind or there is more to this than meets the eye. I have a hard enough time standing in front of a crowd, which is exactly why I didn't like her constantly watching me with her eyes. While Ashley flipped through the pages of the diary, I made her aware that the painting possibly was watching her too.

"I feel it too, believe me it's not just you". That painting was omitting a strange energy, making me wonder if there was something more to it. Ashley nodded at me, recognizing the eerie feeling that the Princess's painting spread throughout the room. We both sensed her gaze, and while everyone watched from a safe distance, I approached the painting. I touched its center only to find that the middle had a smooth finish, like that of glass. I broke away abruptly.

"This is a mirror," I exclaimed.

"Why is everyone getting so worked up over a mirror?" Pablo asked.

Without missing a beat, Ashley gave Pablo a sideways glare.

"Are you sure you don't see anything surprising about it? The mirror I mean. Nothing at all?" She asked raising her voice in frustration.

He tried to look harder and see if he missed anything. Then he finally figured it out.

"But am I the only one who noticed that there are no reflections in the mirror?"

Leave it to Pablo to point out something that no one else noticed. He was right. The Princess stood gracefully in the mirror but I didn't withdraw my hand from the center of the mirror. The cold glass and the arched frame sort of gave the mirror a similar appearance to a French window. At least that was the best way I could describe it. The mirror had no damage not a single scratch or crack. When I tested the center with a single finger it rippled this time, as if I were running my hands through a calm body of water.

Callum Morrissey

AFTER A FEW SECONDS, I tried to break my way through the crowd. I scrambled so fast I collided right into Esabelle, the person I wanted to avoid the most. Esabelle unraveled my arm from around her. We got caught in a tangle and both of us sheepishly hesitated to utter words.

I shrugged. "So…"

"…so," she answered observing my body language. Immediately, we both felt that awkward connection. It seemed that the more we avoided it, the more noticeable it became. Esabelle casted her eyes down, focusing her gaze on my coat sleeve. Then she raised her voice. "That mirror is pretty strange, huh?" she asked.

"No kidding," I replied in my manly Callum tone. Well I spoke slightly lower to seem disinterested, but I doubt it worked.

Esabelle puckered her mouth and nodded. "I bet this will have a lot of repercussions somehow. In other words, you might call that awkward."

All I could think about is how we made a mistake. But truthfully, I didn't feel that way at all. Part of me liked the tension, the sweaty palms, the feverish nerves...

And even though my mind encouraged me to just run away, I felt frozen standing there staring at Esabelle. It would be impossible to hide our feelings now, not after embracing each other passionately in our visions.

"Well, I best be off then," I replied hoping to salvage what little dignity I had left. Even without them noticing, the gap between us narrowed. Whatever logical reasons we told ourselves, it didn't matter. What happened in the valley couldn't be reasoned away.

Ashley Boylan

EVERYONE REMAINED STANDING, ready to hear what I had to say. As I held the diary in my hand, the first thing that surprised me was its heft; the weight of it. I held the history of the universe in my hands, a part of me considered that maybe I don't want to know the answers. Perhaps, I should stop while I'm ahead, but that part of me isn't the real Ashley. The real Ashley asked questions and found the answers. As I rifled through the pages, I started to get the impression that this diary was written in emotional distress.

"Are you going to start?" Curtis asked.

I swallowed hard and then read the first word from the page.

"Bloodshed," I said.

Everyone looked at each other around the room incomplete contrast to how we all stood when we first saw the painting.

"Blood... Shed..." Curtis repeated.

Palace gestured away, signaling me to continue. So then, I read a page from her diary aloud:

I shall ever be guided by the nameless Gods who protect my reign over Nubara. With each passing day, I discover new traitors up to their old tricks. I have been told the people call me the "Heartless Queen although I am a Princess." To rule is a cruel fate to all those who seek it. One needs cold reasoning to make the tough decisions. To decide which a child lives or dies. One cannot deny their station.

However, for what I am certain, I rather am respected and loved. And once the people understand this, then they will no longer wonder how I can ration their water in favor of keeping mine full. They must know why I've granted the Centaur's to do whatever is necessary to keep order. Even if it means taking the lives of the young and of the old. How can I be blamed? I am but fulfilling my duty to Nubara as their Princess...

When I stopped reading, I knew everyone's perception of the Princess changed.

"What a heartless woman!" Esabelle said first.

"What's not to like? She's a murdering greedy sociopath and we're standing in her kingdom...." Curtis said sarcastically.

I tried to ignore it, but I started feeling pain. Regardless, I pushed through it and read some more pages out loud.

The creation of Nubara is somewhat shrouded in mystery. People don't understand how small we are compared to the world. Nubara was birthed in the creation of fire and made of something not created of the universe. It is an undiscovered entity altogether. Its creation goes back to a history that's never been recorded, but only remembered through generations of the enlightened peoples.

Soon after, I looked into Soleil's eyes. I recalled the vision she told me about being chased down and running for her life. To hear these words from their ruler, only gave her clarity of just what sort of evil we are up against. Then suddenly, my vision started to get blurry and an aching nausea infiltrated the nerves in my head.

Oh, no! Not again. I thought.

The last thing I needed right now was to pass out. *Don't faint, Ashley. Don't faint, Ashley.* I repeated to myself under my breath. Then the light started to flash all around me, and I felt dizzy. The room grew terrifyingly dark and all I wanted me to do was close my eyes. I felt a sudden drain of energy where all I wanted to do was to sleep. No matter how hard I tried to hold on, I felt my consciousness slipping further and further. I felt as though I stood at a long road to which I could never reach the end. Then it hit me, and I was powerless to fight it. I took a step forward, everyone gasped and then I crumpled to the floor.

Soleil Oupary

ASHLEY," I YELLED as I shoved" hard on her shoulder, trying to wake her up. She didn't react.

"We need to do something," I said, pulling Palace to the side. We couldn't let what happened before happen again. I tried to think of how we could get something to wake her up.

Palace rubbed my shoulder, as a cold fear washed over me. An epiphany propelled me to grab his arm.

Everyone helped to lift her up and carry her over to a nearby French chaise positioned against the wall. I headed off to a secluded area so I could best remember the well water in the castle.

Palace called to me. "Soleil, don't go too far."

I glanced behind my back as Palace ran towards me. His hair fell in front of his brow, almost obscuring his eyes in dark shadows. The way he rushed towards me just made my heart flutter, like it could almost fly right out of my chest. Why was it is that every time Palace stood at my side, my imagination always got the best of me? I would sometimes see him as larger than life hero.

"Shall we?" he asked.

I nodded and we both left to the greater parts of the castle. Whenever, we stood side by side, I never felt quite adequate. In fact, the opposite really. I felt quite undignified. If you looked at him, standing there, Palace always had his sleeves rolled up, as if he could solve any problem. I didn't really remember everything from my visions. A lot of what I did was just filling in the blanks

"Each passing hour feels like we're never going to leave this place," I said as we walked into the main hall.

"It's too early to make any predictions."

"... Just stating the obvious," I replied.

Both of us strode past the main staircase were we noticed a sizable atrium. When we walked through it, we could see a well stocked pantry with everything that anyone's taste buds would desire. Before I retrieved the water, I asked Palace something.

"Why are you always so sure you know the answers?"

Palace wasn't quite sure how to respond to this.

"Well, Soleil, everyone can't wallow in misery at every first opportunity we get..." he teased while pulling open the pantry door. Moments later, after searching for the food leftovers, I noticed there wasn't anything for Ashley to safely drink.

I couldn't pinpoint exactly where I saw the well near the castle; I just knew it couldn't be far. I tried hard to concentrate on where it was. Then touched Palace's shoulder and he nodded.

"It's got to be behind the atrium."

When we walked through the atrium, a well covered in dark green peat moss was directly in front of us.

Esabelle Matthews

IS IT POSSIBLE THAT I *could have been here in another life?* I asked myself. I unraveled my red hair bun on my head. Just like Ashley, I didn't feel entirely new to this place. Neither did Soleil. So then how did the three of us all coincidentally share the same experience? There has to be a reasonable answer to our connection to each other in this world.

Since Soleil and Palace were gone, the rest of the group was busy taking care of Ashley, so I had time to roam around unsupervised. If I had let them know where I was going, they may have stopped me. And I had already gotten tired of just sitting around. I couldn't really tell you what room I'm was in, I just knew that it was the one far from the group. After being attacked with talent, I just needed space. Some time to think. But what I ended up doing instead was walk aimlessly in the hidden wings of the Nubara estate. Everything had either gold or precious jewels lining even the most mundane objects, such as a toothbrush or a paddle brush that was lying around. Up until now, most of my focus has been on Callum Morrissey.

"Water," I said. "She needs water."

I thought more about it. *Is it so bad?* Before I met him, I just seemed to be a vagabond in my own life. I had no real direction, and I didn't really care. I've never imagined I would fall so hard for somebody. What's going to be even harder is I don't know if there's hope for the two of us.

Curtis rolled his eyes. "Why would anyone need a mirror this big anyway?" Callum didn't even respond. He glanced over at Ashley still lying there. She was out like a light.

"What do you think the mirror is used for?" Callum asked.

"Are you saying you don't think the mirror is used as a mirror?"

"I'm saying everything about this just doesn't feel right. The last time Ashley fainted, she predicted the coming of the giant Centaur. It's not a stretch that this latest episode might be foreshadowing something we just don't see—yet." Curtis said, taking a seat right in front of Omegaura's mirror. Why can't everyone see that we're stuck in some sort of time-warp? At least, that would be my guess. How can we discover a castle in the middle of downtown New York City if there isn't some sort of rift in reality?

I slammed to the floor as the ground rattled underneath our feet.

"What the hell?" Curtis shouted.

I tried to find something to cover my head, to protect me from flying projectiles that could knock me unconscious. The entire room rumbled and we both had a shocked look in our eyes. Then I turned my attention to the mirror. Warbling glass rippled in the middle and it moved from rigid to wavy but stopped just as fast as it started.

I slowly stood up after being hunkered down on the floor. Curtis crawled from underneath an ornately carved table. Both of us whirled around to catch our balance. Our heads and our insides spun and after a few moments, we finally found our bearings and focused our attention on the mirror in the center of the room.

"Wait, you don't think..." I asked rubbing the back of my bruised head.

Curtis ignored me this time to inspect the glass in the mirror.

"It's almost as if it's not glass at all, but something else," he said at a whisper.

I examined the floor and saw something barely perceptible, but not invisible. A hairline crack traveled all the way from my loafers in a zig-zag pattern and continued down underneath the mirror. Maybe it was just our adrenaline pumping, or maybe it was something else, but Curtis and I simultaneously came to the same exact conclusion.

"It's the locus!" Curtis shouted, grabbing hold of my shoulders. "This is where the quakes are coming from. *Right here.*"

Soleil Oupary

"BE CAREFUL, YOU DON'T WANT to fall down," Palace warned, as I slowly made my way towards the well. For old time's sake, I crouched down and picked up a handful of stones. The last time I skipped stones I must have been four years old. Anticipating the sound of gushing water, I wrenched my arm back just above the peat moss covered edge of the worn down well and after a short spin, I tossed my first rock. I fully expected to hear it plunge and plot against the surface of the water, but I didn't hear any sound at all. I thought this was odd so I approached the edge of the well, and peered deep into the darkness.

Nothing. I saw nothing at all.

For whatever reason an adrenaline induced madness overcame me.

"Why isn't there water in there?"

Palace quickly came by and approached me, holding his hands up in the air. "Don't you think you're overreacting a little bit?"

I staggered backwards, unable to breathe.

"I'm trying to understand what's going on, Soleil. If you keep acting like this I can't help you," he said.

At this point I didn't even want to hear any arguments. I just wanted something to work out for me, for once. I wanted to do something that will help people, people like Ashley.

"No one's asking you to stay," I snapped. "I don't mind being here all alone. It's not like you haven't left me alone before. Or don't you remember? And how you abandoned me in the hospital after the accident in the Arctic."

Palace didn't budge. No matter how hard it was to push him away. He wasn't going anywhere.

"Please, don't get mad. This isn't what I wanted at all. Soleil you're one of my best students. I'll do whatever it takes to win your trust back. The archaeological team and I just had a different mindset, we we're trying to figure out the source of the quakes. Please understand I don't think the research is more important than your life."

I wasn't able to hide the tears that were coming down my face. Before I could wipe them away with the back of my hand, Palace smudged them away with his thumb.

Esabelle Matthews

WHEN I TOOK ANOTHER TURN out of the bedroom, I noticed a small crack in the wall behind the bookcase. Given how strangely aligned the bookcase was to the wall, I figured I should inspect it to satisfy my curiosity? *If I do this then Callum's nickname for me will be true, Little Miss Mousey Pants...hmm should I anyways? Well who am I kidding Esabelle just do it.* Once I stood before the small opening, it felt a light breeze blowing against my face. I used all my strength to push the bookcase in the opposite direction. The sound of the bookcase scraping the floor made me a little uneasy. Clearly, someone had tried to hide this room. In the room there isn't much but a couch with the cover shrouded over it, some few loose electrical wires and many piles of magazines. Then I noticed an elongated object posted up against the wall.

Without wasting time, I quickly made my way towards it to see what it is. A small podium made of a fine wood. I'm not a sleuth of any sort nor am I like Ashley, but I still cab make a rather keen observation; something on the podium is missing. I lowered my hand over the small etchings; they were just like the kind in Queen Marietta's end and identical to the engravings on the walls in the maze. And, of course, I can't read a thing.

"*Figures...*" I cursed under my breath.

I dug my hand in my pocket and fished out my cell phone. I held it at face level and started snapping pictures. I knew I wouldn't understand what the messages on the podium meant, but I know Ashley will.

Ashley Boylan

I'M SURROUNDED BY TWILIGHT. It's not quite heaven or hell, but an entirely different state of being. Without knowing where I was, the first thing I considered was that I was dead, even my surroundings were strange; I couldn't quite call what I was standing in a room. It was more like an endless vast plain stretching to some invisible infinity. Being naturally me, I needed to get to the bottom of it. As I was about to take my first step, the light brightened in the room. There was no doubt that I would soon find some answers. The silhouette of a blinding white figure appeared before me and walked in my direction. However, I didn't feel a twinge of fear, anxiety nor the need to run.

"Do not fear me. For I am not your enemy..." a strange woman's voice said.

This strange woman's voice and the diaphanous gown she wore overwhelmed me with calm.

"You seek answers to questions you did not ask," she said, her tone soft like mist.

For a minute there, my voice was unable to escape my throat. Every nerve in my body buzzed. My senses became supercharged and everything tasted sweet and savory, an odd combination that I've never tasted before.

My heart beat so slow that I thought it would stop. When I extended my arms, I felt a clunk of something cold surrounding me. I outstretched my hands again and realized I was encased in a glass shell.

"Why do you have me trapped in here?"

"You're free to go whenever you choose…"

I was still very aware that there was no way of me getting out the glass shell I was in. All the energies inside me felt balanced and I didn't know whether to thank this woman or be angry with her for trapping me in here like this.

"My name is Ashley. And I don't belong here, do you understand?"

The feather soft voice didn't immediately answer.

"Listen to me," I raised my voice. "You can't keep me here. I'm not like you. I have a home out there."

The silhouetted woman pressed the palm of her hand against my glass case.

"I am a force not of nature. I am your destiny. We cannot deny what you are, not forever," she spoke.

Destiny?

I've waited all my life to discover something like this and to understand the mysteries of the world both big and small. But I could not fulfill what the specter wished of me. These visions never seemed to end and each day made me feel colder. Even though neither of us wished to obey the other, I had a mutual respect for the woman I didn't know. Now she leaned in close to the glass, and the two of us locked eyes. Then I finally asked the question plaguing my mind.

"Tell me your name?"

I stared into her arresting eyes.

"I am the Auracle."

Soliel Oupary

MY CHEEKS WERE STILL WET from my tears but at least my eyes stopped leaking. This is the closest I've ever been to Palace. He hovered over me with a curious expression on his face. *Will she hate me now forever? Will she forgive me for my mistakes?* I know it's silly to think, but his emotions were so easy to read. When I held onto his neck, I feel pangs, deep aches where I thought my feelings were dead inside. Yet, I'm feeling so much now and I'm scared to know if the he was too.

"I feel like I have a fever," I muffled against Palace's chest. He gently grasped my chin, resting his face against mine.

"No, no, believe me. I know what you mean. I feel like I'm burning up too."

I honestly didn't know how to continue the conversation. Each time my cheek pressed against his upper chest, I felt mesmerized by his warmth. Even more alarming, he hypnotized me with his kind eyes.

I pursed my lips. "We better get back with everyone else and check on Ashley too."

"So this little talk we had," Palace whispered against my ear. "Didn't mean anything?"

What does he mean? Is he trying to say it's different this time?

"No!" Then I realized I made a mistake. "I— I— mean no it's not the same as all the other times. I'm sorry if I sound so incoherent. It's just things like this have never been an issue for me before."

Palace arched a brow. "Things like what?"

I felt embarrassed; I couldn't even look him in the eyes. "Yeah, sorry. I'm not even sure what I meant."

Palace stepped in my path and wouldn't let me pass. I could tell by his stance that he had something serious to say. I gulped, worried that all of my stupid words and all of my stupid klutz mannerisms only scared him away.

"You look radiant."

I heard him say it but I couldn't believe the words. My first instinct was to run. *Run now!*

"Palace, I've got to get out of here—" I started to say until he interrupted me.

"I'd rather you stay here with me."

He leaned in close, first wetting my ear with his mouth and then pushing his lips against mine. I couldn't think. I couldn't feel. I couldn't breathe. I simply closed my eyes. Until...

"HELP ME!"

I heard screams from somewhere but I couldn't pinpoint from where or from whom. A soft muffled noise echoed in my direction. The noise banged out again and then I saw someone trapped in what looked like a glass bubble. A girl? Is that a woman? Ashley?

In an almost out-of-body like experience, I rushed in Ashley's direction. She was crying out with red rimmed eyes, hoping someone would rescue her. I raised my arm and pressed my palm against the glass. At last, I spoke her name.

"*Auracle.*"

FOR SOME REASON, I saw a book from the corner of my eye. The same one Ashley read, Queen Marietta's diary. I wasn't too sure what possessed me to pick it up, but I did. Just as before, the language looked like nothing but gibberish that I didn't understand. I cracked it open one more time, and while rifling through its pages, saw a bunch of pages ripped out of the book. *Maybe they're scattered somewhere around this place?*

I heard some rustling on the couch. Slowly but surely, a groggy Ashley woke up from her long slumber. The first thing I did was come down to check on her to see if everything was okay.

"You took quite a spill," I told her.

Although Ashley was awake, she had a distant look in her eyes.

I tapped her on her shoulder. "Hey girl, you alright?"

Ashley moved effortlessly out of the chair and darted over to Soleil. I simply stared dumbfounded, I had no clue what was going on. She moved like she didn't faint in front of the group just a few hours ago. Everyone shifted their attention to Soleil huddled next to Palace.

Ashley said one word. "Lunati."

And then she repeated it again and again. "Lunati. Lunati. Lunati. Lunati!"

"Stop it! Stop it now!" Soleil screamed.

Soleil looked like she was caught in a trance and that the two of them were telepathically going at each other's throats. In that moment, Soleil snapped out of her fugue state and become self-aware again. She looked around frantic, unsure of what just happened to her. Her brow glistened as if she awoke from some hellish nightmare. I finished going around the room, searching for the different pages and I held them all in my hand. I shuffled them in the best order I could and placed them in the diary. I saw Ashley sitting over there alone; almost catatonic.

"Ash, you gotta sec?" I asked her.

She only looked at me. I handed her the book and the pages, out of order of course. I was hoping that she could make some kind of sense of them. Ashley snatched the book out of my hand without saying a word and shuffled the pages in the proper order.

BAM!

She slammed the book in both her hands. The book opened itself all on its own and a bright blinding light forced us to shield our eyes. When the light finally weakened, a flickering image stood before Ashley. The woman pointed out her hand, pointed at all of us as if gesturing that we were next.

"Why have you summoned me? You will now know the wrath of Queen Marietta!"

Chapter 11

Soliel Oupary

Even though we all suffered frightening moments, nothing compared to the terror we experienced now. All of us looked stricken, with wide-eyed expressions on our faces. We didn't know whether to be afraid or intrigued. Just a few hours back, Queen Marietta gazed at us lifeless and cold from a picture frame. I was still having trouble accepting that the entire situation was real.

"Hold up guys, don't you think you're getting a little too close?" Callum asked.

Of course, Ashley's own curiosity got the best of her. *How else could you explain the image of a long-lost queen appearing out of thin air?* Ashley knew the technology behind this could not be explained away with a logical or scientific reason. She was pretty certain of that.

I watched her pull her hand out from her pockets, not exactly the best idea she's ever had. The rest of us held our breath as she waved her arms through the image of Queen Marietta.

It rippled like water and a snowy distortion made us all realize that what we stared at was only a hologram. Ashley stepped back with the rest of the group, dazed and confused. Queen Marietta's hologram flashed again as we all looked straight at her.

"Why have you disturbed me?" she asked her voice bitter and frail.

We stood silently in the gloom of her presence, until I finally found the courage to speak.

"How... How is it that you can come alive with the pages of the book?"

Immediately after I finished speaking, Queen Marietta twisted her head around. She gritted her teeth after inhaling a gulp of air.

"Please don't talk like that."

I shook my head not really understanding. "Like what?"

Queen Marietta seethed, fixing those piercing cold blue eyes on us

"I hope you have a good reason for disturbing me like this?" She asked. "Nubara is not just some shifting rock hurtling through the void of the universe. At one point in time, it was the lifeblood of all distant life forms, the beating heart. And I ruled, doing what's best for the people, even if they hated me for it."

"Where is everyone? Have you made contact with the rest of your people?" Palace asked.

Queen Marietta didn't answer, and simply continued her story.

"The Isle of Nubara was born from a choice made by King. The King of Nibris. The Atlantians lived under a black cloud, a shadow and a cosmic nightmare. Very few knew of this dark time in history, a time that was known as the Greys..."

I slipped my hand through Palace's arm, but he didn't seem to notice. It's not that I expected him to. To be honest, it was more of a nervous reaction standing next to him just made me feel safe. Robert looked anxious. The knuckles of his fingers were stark white as he dug into the pockets of his coat. What should have been an awesome moment of discovery, evolved into something much more sinister. It was obvious to all of us that we had to see the bigger picture. We no longer had a choice in the matter, so we listened some more.

"The King of Nibris had a weakness for the Atlantians. He was forced to stop an ancient feud between the Greys. They planned to make a better life for themselves by usurping control of the planet from the Atlantians. The Greys devoured everything in their path, and they set their sights on your Earth. This is why the King had to stop them. The King of Atlantis discovered his daughter had fallen in love with one of the forbidden peoples—the Atlantians. Enraged, he sought to destroy the Queen's bond and cut her off from the rest of her civilization. And so, she disappeared... never to be seen again."

Ashley and I looked at each other, bewildered. By the time Queen Marietta had finished the first half of her story, it made us both uneasy, but we both continued to listen closely. There's something about her story that spoke right to us. My body went very still, and the blur of my memories started to make sense. I shuddered at the thought of being a part of that cosmic life force. Especially now that I know that I am Lunati.

Is there something there? I asked myself. Sure enough, we all had a clear view that something inside us with special.

Only one important question was left.

Why?

During the Queen's speech, I noticed Esabelle throwing glances at Callum. Her hand drifted up to her neck. But she no longer wore the locket. Instead, I spotted it dangling around Callum's neck, at least half of it was. Callum tugged at the small half-broken artifact, struggling to truly understand its purpose. It's not that I was opposed to these two growing closer, which was the least of my worries.

The bigger problem was that we needed to focus on finding where the other half of the necklace had disappeared to and not being killed in the process as well.

After unhooking my arm from Palace's, I pointed at the necklace around Callum's neck.

"The rest of it," I started. "Where is it?"

Esabelle gave Callum a direct look before turning away from us both.

Callum settled his hands back at his sides.

"The beast. That thing we saw in the tunnels…"

I stifled the urge to roll my eyes. "You have to be so cryptic about account. Believe me; all of us are aware that there are creatures on this planet that make us question our own reality."

Callum shrugged his shoulders pitifully.

"What I'm trying to say is that Silver Cannabis wears the other half on his neck."

"A part of me feels like we're just waiting for a mistake to happen," Esabelle whispered. "There's something we overlooked. I just know it."

"Don't say that," Callum reassured her. "Maybe just this once. Good things are bound to come our way. I just *feel* it."

Esabelle then realized something…"Wait, the Centaur is pretty strong right?" Callum looked over at her, his brow lifted and he looked puzzled as to what Esabelle was trying to bring to the surface. "Yeah, so what?"

Esabelle then spoke and what she said made me freeze and think. "Well it could have killed all of us without a problem then why all this cat & mouse game unless it wanted to lead us here to this place."

Suddenly there was a sound of a crash which caused the group to step back; caught by surprise. Jagged shards of glass rained down from above. It sounded like thunder struck the center of the room and a cloud of black dust billowed in the air, forcing us all apart in the blinding confusion.

Esabelle Matthews

"WHAT'S HAPPENED?" I screamed not knowing whether anyone could hear me through the suffocating black smog. As I worked my way through the middle of the dust cloud, a pair of yellow eyes floated right in front of me. A hoof stamped in the middle of the old book, disrupting Queen Marietta's holographic message.

Without knowing what to do, I just looked up at the Centaur with an embarrassed smile. The beast focused on me with a hostile glare. Not a word was spoken between us. At his back, Palace and Robert made a mad dash to the weapons room while I kept the hulking creature distracted.

C'mon, I need someone to do something. I thought, panicking.

I could feel Silver Cannabis's hot breath against my neck. "I love that look."

I turned away.

"Don't. Look. At me!" He shouted.

I could hear crystal shards crunching underneath his hooves as I slowly turned to return his gaze once more.

He grinned. "Yes, that's more like it. I like the sight of fear almost as much as the sight of blood."

I stumbled back and a half-smile spread across my face. "If you really like the sight of blood so much. Maybe you'll like the sight of your own!" I hollered.

Seconds later, Palace and Robert emerged with a mace and a long sword. Before Robert could even take a swing, the Silver Cannabis struck him to the ground, knocking the air right out of his lungs. Neither of them got close enough to even nick his tough pale silver skin. The Centaur clambered over them both and rushed straight for Callum. Callum brushed off the fragments of dust and glass from the sleeves of his shirt, he didn't notice that he stood in the middle of a stampede, until it was too late. The Centaur noticed the half of the Novae pendent chained around Callum's neck.

Glancing everywhere, Callum looked for the best place to run. Time seemed to pass at a heart-stopping speed.

"Why are you standing there like an idiot?" Esabelle screamed at Callum.

After a couple of seconds, I watched Esabelle run in his direction. Free flowing red hair madly swirled above her shoulders.

Esabelle called out to him. "Give me your hand! Now!"

Callum outstretched his arm as quickly as possible. Esabelle nodded as they interlocked their fingers. They felt the familiar connection immediately surge through their bodies, the same fire that burned through them as they stood in the dream realm. They felt that raw power inside them grow as the Centaur lunged at them, his horns ready to skewer them both. Just as before, the strange protection apparatus triggered. Two blades forced out of the bracelet moments before Callum and Esabelle were trampled to the ground.

Dropping down to his knees, Silver Cannabis bellowed due to the searing pain of the swords. He hissed then spit as his attention focused on all of us in the room.

"I've survived more than a thousand lifetimes that I could never fear death," the beast grunted. Understand this…"

Silver Cannabis paused, looked down at the bleeding gash in its stomach. Bloody drops dribbled down his torso and splashed onto the pristine marble floor.

"…I will seek my revenge."

A fear settled into us again, my mouth had gone dry. Charging forth, the Centaur galloped at full speed out of the main chamber and back into the winding maze from which it came. The glow of the moon reflected off of his silver skin as he disappeared into night.

"I thought you two were goners…" Curtis said.

Esabelle exhaled a deep breath. "I can't say you're exactly wrong."

Pablo couldn't keep his eyes off of their bracelets.

"That's definitely not normal..."

"Has anything we've seen so far been normal?" Callum asked.

"He's got a point," I replied.

After the beast scuttled away, we all helped Robert to his feet. He grabbed the walkie-talkie that fell from his pocket. There was a break of static, and then the deafening noise of feedback pierced our ears.

"Is that thing still working?" Curtis asked.

Palace moved out ahead, holding his hand up to signal for the rest of us to just keep quiet.

"C...ome in.... C...ome in. Can anyone read me? Are there any survivors of the Train 12G crash."

Palace smacked the bottom of his hand against the battery pack, desperately trying to strengthen the reception.

"Please come in," he held the receiver to his lips. "We're survivors. We broke out of the car and got in the...I don't know... some abandoned tunnels."

None of us really knew if the authorities on the other end could actually hear us.

"You gotta hurry. The battery is weak. We're losing the signal!" Robert warned.

"Who...r..e....we...talking to?" the voice on the other end crackled.

"My dear Dr. Michaels. I am John Courbet one of the biggest benefactors of Rolling Hills University. When I heard your team had gotten lost, I called in a few favors...got some of the best excavation crews in the city. I just wanted you to know the tunnel has been breached. Just sit tight, help will be down there to get you out soon."

The rush of relief passed through us all. I looked to the ceiling and spotted bits of the foundation still crumbing in total shambles.

"This doesn't look good," Curtis whispered in my ear.

"Not just that," I replied. "We've got only one way out so far and it's over there."

We both looked through the shadowy doorway where the Centaur escaped.

Esabelle elbowed Callum in his side. "Maybe you're right. Maybe we're finally due some good."

She forced a smile still feeling quite a mess. Courbet's voice came out loud and clear. It sounded like he stood with us in the room.

"So, what's the plan? We just stand here and wait?"

"Whatever you do, don't move. We'll have tracers pinpointing your radio signal. Be ready kiddos, pretty soon you're going home!"

I wrapped my coat around me tightly. I noticed Queen Marietta's book lying under a strewn of glass and debris, a blue light still flickered faintly.

Is the hologram still playing? I wondered. I hopped down closer to the floor. Then I tugged on its tattered edges, allowing the message to replay.

"The truth is right in front of your eyes…"

Queen Marietta's voice sort of warbled as the ghostly imaged flickered in and out. Dust stuck to the tips of my fingers. The tone of the queen's voice possessed a strong note of caution.

"You will know the Nubarian among you by looking for the marks."

She then looked down and two blazing stripes, like healed over scars, glowed on the back of her hands.

"If they see these marks, they will find you. They will hurt you," she finished.

Her distorted voice weakened growing softer by the second. Until finally, the faint image just flickered out and didn't return. All I had left was simply a musty old book. I shifted my position, glancing back at Ashley. She pulled her hands from her pockets so I could better see.

"No one's going to believe any of this. You know that right?" Ashley said.

"It must stay quiet, Ash. We can't tell anyone. We don't know who else may know of the prophecy or who else may want us dead…"

A dire look flashed a through Ashley eyes as she heeded my warning and avoided mentioning another word about it. Caught by a sudden confirmation I was really not of this world, it made me more aware of the oddness of my friends in the room. I just stood quietly staring at Palace's rough hands.

Nope, no bright blue scars.

It made me feel frustrated that Ashley and I were so alone, then for whatever reason, my attention returned to Esabelle & Callum. They were standing together, but very careful not to touch hands. I'm pretty sure they weren't even I aware that I was looking at them. For a second, I could see something blue, but faint glowing on each one of their hands.

Why is only one of their hands glowing? I wondered. I made my way towards them; I had to know whether they had changed as much as I had.

Callum looked at me warily when I stepped up in front of them. And yet, somehow he kind of understood what I wanted.

"It's the markings, isn't it?" he asked.

I tilted my head. "How did you know?"

Esabelle answered for him. "He can't explain it, neither can I — it's just that there's just this odd connection between us all."

The scars on their hands still piqued my interest. Again I wondered why they didn't have scars just like mine. Or, at least, what the different scars meant.

"Take his hand," I told Esabelle.

"Is this some kind of joke, because I mean. We need to be serious."

I sighed. "I am. Just do as I ask…please."

Callum & Esabelle looked twice at each other before gripping their hands. They both craned their necks back avoiding the sharp blades that jutted out of the bracelets in a bizarre turn, instead of three glowing scars tracing along their hands, a single scar zigzagged across where their hands touched. It all made sense to me now, they had a unique connection unlike anything that Ashley or I had experienced.

Everyone else only stared at us, probably having seen enough insanely weird and utterly unexplainable behavior that they couldn't take it anymore.

"Excuse me," Curtis interrupted in the middle of everyone's astonishment. "Am I missing something here or did I just see evidence that my classmates are actually aliens."

"That's not funny, Curtis," Ashley rolled her eyes.

"Who said I'm kidding?"

Robert didn't want the arguing to go on any further.

"We're almost out of here. Let's just stay calm until they come and get us. That means just keep it quiet Curtis."

Palace moved up from behind us.

"That thing may come back to finish us off at any minute."

He swung the sword he had previously found in a downward slash, it produced a high pitched whistle as it sliced through the air, there was no telling how sharp the blade was, its smooth edges glinted underneath the dark evening light.

"We all need to get something from the Armory to protect us. Something's going to go down. You know it. I know it. And I don't know about you, but I'm sick of waiting for the worst to happen. Time to get prepared."

Palace was right. It's no secret now that we've got bad guys of enormous size who would like nothing more than to hunt us down and peel the flesh from our bones. A part of me felt worried about what I could do? *How can we fight an ancient warrior with thousands of years of training?* I thought.

"What I just said goes for you especially Soliel, remember, you've got some kind of link to royalty...what was the word?"

As Palace tried to remember the words, he snapped his fingers.

"Lunati," I replied.

"Exactly."

He then lifted up the weapon that he clutched in his hands. The shimmering light reflected on my face as he raised the bow and arrow.

"Now, tell me. Do you know how to use this thing?"

Chapter 12

Soleil Oupary

The bow had a zig-zag design with a crisscrossing pattern that ran down the smooth wooden handle. A strange pride burned within me when I aimed it, I pretended that I had a Centaur in my sights. The bow's curve had a beautiful symmetry. No doubt who ever fashioned this bow was a fine craftsman. As soon as I looked up from my bow, I couldn't help but notice Esabelle and Callum gazing deep into each other's eyes.

Clearly, they'd been really embracing this "kismet" thing. Becoming closer and letting the power take over them both.

Ashley whispered in my ear. "Why don't those to just go get a room, huh?"

A snapping noise came from her walkie talkie receiver.

"Grab it!" I told her, trying to help her pick up the phone before the signal died. An adrenaline rush jolted up through all of us. We readied our weapons in our hands, ready strike at first notice.

Palace climbed the old stairs up to the balcony over the entrance of the main chamber. None of us followed him. I moved quickly and pressed my back up to the left wall. Ashley stayed in the center while Robert watched the palace gates from the ground. We had to be sure that whoever entered the room, man or beast; we were prepared to take it down. I took a deep breath, shaking my head in disbelief. If the Silver Cannabis returned, it would chase me down and eat me alive.

We all had the room carefully surrounded. We split into two teams and let the two "love birds, Callum and Esabelle, share a post together. I stood next to Ashley. We nodded to each other. Ashley knew I had her back. Whatever we had between us, was now water under the bridge. Since we were only hours from being rescued, I had to put the past behind us.

"I don't have any hard feelings if you don't," I said.

She smiled. "It's already forgotten."

Callum & Esabelle took the first steps toward the exit of the main chamber that led back into the maze. There was always the chance that we could get into a several encounters while waiting for our rescuers. Courbet had to be tracing us now, but who knows how long it would take for him to get here. My eyes adjust to the darkness as I grabbed an arrow with a trembling hand. I could hear my heart pounding in my chest as I followed the two of them closer to the exit of the room.

Callum Morrissey

WATCHING THE BLADE glide out of my bracelet never got old. Before I left the main chamber, I looked at everyone's faces; they all had smudges of dust and grime smeared all over. Soliel had a face like stone. You would think that she had held a bow and arrow like this before. Slowly and cautiously, Esabelle and I walked through the Armory with our hands interlocked and our arms outstretched. If anything came running at us, they would slice themselves on the tip of our blades.

"Esabelle, you and I are meant for something. Even if we don't yet know what it is," he said.

"No one doubts that. But I honestly don't want to know more. If I could go back, I would erase everything I know. I don't even want to know the truth," Esabelle confessed.

"I don't blame you, but what we want and what will happen is out of our control."

I stood close enough to Esabelle that I could see the tinge of yellow in her eyes. It looked something like shifting flames. Truthfully, I didn't want to struggle through this without her.

Soliel Oupary

I RUBBED MY ACHING ARMS and lowered my bow. Ashley stumbled up at my side. She brushed some dirt off my back.

"You're still a little dusted up from the chaos."

Chaos.

Ashley described it perfectly. After pushing the hair out of my eyes, I answered.

"Please don't tell anyone else about this."

"My lips are sealed," Ashley said after placing her hand gently on my shoulder.

"I just didn't know who to tell. It's complicated enough that I know that only you could understand me."

Ashley shrugged. "Understand what?"

"I don't know. It's something I saw. It's like trying to remember a scene from a movie, but it's not a movie, Ash. This is my life."

Ashley noticed that I was inhaling air too quickly.

"It's okay, I'm here. And you know I'm not going anywhere."

She parted her lips as if she had something more to say. She kept her eyes on me to let me know that she was listening.

"It's happening. Again, I mean. The visions. I—I saw this girl. But she was trapped in this cage. And it's crazy because she looks just like you."

Ashley raised a brow. "Like me?"

I nodded.

"And she was in a lot of pain. She wore this white tunic and looked powerful, but at that moment afraid."

Ashley interest waned. I could tell she was thinking. Connecting the dots all on her own. She did this anytime she neared a theory and wanted to map out it's plausibility in her head. No matter how much we've been through, Ashley could never fail to let her scientist roots take over.

"I've seen her too," Ashley said. "The woman in the cage spoke to me. She called me something. I'm not sure I remember. She gave me this look. More like a glare with dark red eyes. I wanted to turn away, but they were impossible to avoid...I know what you're thinking. Ashley & her made up theories again. But I saw it!"

Ashley had no idea how relieved I felt, it almost made me wish I had told her sooner, instead of keeping these visions to myself.

Every terror I had imagined, Ashley had imagined too. We steadily watched one another, waiting for our turn to pass through the main chamber door. The legend stopped being these stories we studied in our anthropology books & had now become our reality. Our team waited outside of the palace gates. Everything seemed to take on a gloom and cold demeanor. I hoped Courbet would find us first before anything else had the chance to. Suddenly, a heavy sound thundered towards us.

"W-wait. W-wait," I stuttered.

I didn't need to see it, I knew what was headed for us, and glints of silver could be seen shimmering close to the ceiling. It grinned at me, the Silver Cannabis sneered as he galloped towards our group, thumping with loud banging steps. Callum & Esabelle were standing in front of everyone else to put up the first line of defense. Their hands glowed and the blue light spread across each of their bodies. The electric energy absorbed through their skin, giving off a faint blue light. I gasped watching it seep into both Callum and Esabelle's eyes. Blue flickering orbs flashed wildly on their faces.

Grinning, Callum waved the Centaur forward. Daring him to charge.

"If you really want us so bad, we're waiting,"

The Silver Cannabis roared through the shadows, clashing in our path. He bent down, and attempted to grab the power duo down, swinging at them with his massive shoulders. It smelled what it wanted dangling around Callum's neck. The beast rotated towards Callum's face and widened its jaws. He snapped hard, cracking his teeth on the mystical blade and missed Callum's neck by mere inches. Esabelle & Callum fell, releasing their hold, which caused their blades to instantly retract.

The Silver Cannabis hovered above them as Esabelle & Callum scrambled on the ground.

"You must think this is a joke," the Centaur spat. "Believe me, I will crush your bones into dust and devour what remains…"

He then lowered his jaw to retrieve the Novae Emblem from Callum's neck. Hot drool dripped down onto their faces. The hulking creature skidded to halt when a blinding light torpedoed towards his chest. Silver Cannabis reared up wildly on his hind legs. A plume of smoke cleared where Ashley stood. She grasped a flare gun in her unsteady hands. The beast struggled through the chaos of smoke, trying to regain his senses.

He paused to regain his focus on getting the Novae Emblem. Callum took a hold of Esabelle's hand. The Silver Cannabis shirked back, he made no attempt to hide his desperation to exterminate the group like vermin. He knew that if he didn't find a way to escape, he would continue to be surrounded and outmatched. When Callum and Esabelle's blades forced themselves free, I noticed that Silver Cannabis tilted his head and looking strangely at the blades. Although I wasn't sure, it seemed as though he recognized them from somewhere.

"You thieves! There is no way you can wield the power of the dual blades. Those are only supposed to be wielded by Lantis!"

The beast then charged forward, shoving his hulking body right into Ashley. Ashley slammed down fast; she didn't have a chance to react. The Silver Cannabis stood over her body as he slammed down, inches away from her face. Thinking quickly, Ashley rolled over and grabbed the flare gun again. When she lifted the barrel up, she immediately pulled the trigger.

Click. Click.

Nothing! She had run out of flares that's when panic set in as Silver Cannabis grinned with a dark blood hungry look in his eyes. Curtis slid across the floor with his hand stretched out to Ashley.

"Take my hand!" Curtis shouted.

He screamed for Ashley to move as quickly as she could. Ashley fumbled forward on her elbows grabbing for Curtis hand. Curtis pulled with all his strength; teeth gritted trying to push Ashley to the other side of the maze wall. The Silver Cannabis wasn't really interested in those two anyway. Something still drew him to both Esabelle and Callum.

The beast stiffened his pugnacious jaw. "Which one is it? Which one of you is calling him back from the dead?"

Neither Esabelle nor Callum understood what made him so enraged. However, as long as they stay connected holding their hands the beast could not harm a hair on their heads. The Silver Cannabis hunched his back, snapping at the two of them and slamming his front feet to the ground. No matter what, he could not tear the two apart. Nor did he know which had resurrected the power of Lantis.

"He can't hurt us!" Esabelle shouted, as she and Callum made their way back towards the group. "He can try to scare us, but as long as we are holding hands, he can't hurt us. Quick, get behind us!"

The monster stepped back, shrugging his filthy looking coat, wanting to crush everything in his path. Caught on the opposite side of the room with his brother, they took a deep breath and bolted straight towards the group that was safely shielded by Esabelle & Callum.

Sensing blood, the beast charged at them immediately. Palace tried to dodge to his right before the Silver Cannabis could flatten him, at the same time; Robert pulled out a gun and shot Silver Cannabis in the chest.

A high-voltage current struck in the center of the Centaur's heart. An enormous surge of electricity forced his thick muscles into a rigid standstill but it didn't last long. It only amplified the Centaur's rage and he charged straight for Robert, at the last second, Palace pushed his brother out of the way and towards the safety of the group. The impact sent Palace flying backwards and he landed hard on his back knocking the wind out of him. As he attempted to stand to his feet, the Silver Cannabis hurled his body into the wall, a loud cracking noise exploded in his ears. Palace cradled his arm with his left hand; lifting it an inch shot intense pain through each part of his body.

The beast backed away still suffering from the effects of the shock. I moved in close to Palace, attempting to pull him by the shoulder.

"Don't," he muttered. "It's broken."

I couldn't immediately tell until I looked at the awkward jack-knife position of his arm. Palace was powerless in the face of relentless pain. The pearlescent skin of the Silver Cannabis glowed eerily in the moonlight. It glowered at Palace who was slumped over and barely conscious; leaning against the wall. Again he struck his hooves on the ground, ready to forge a destructive death charge. He pulled a sword free from its sheath ready to hack down anything in his way.

Palace accepted his fate; he turned and faced the Silver Cannabis as it charged in his direction. Its muscles flexed as it rushed forward at an unstoppable speed. He struggled to look up at the sound of something cutting through the air. Arrows! They sliced through the air soaring right for the beleaguered beast. Palace spun around and saw me standing there with the bow and arrow in my hands. I came forward, completely at full attention.

"You want to get to him. You'll have to get through me first..." I said ready to shoot a few more rounds.

"God," I heard Palace holler from behind as his free arm braced his leg. My eyes caught something sticking out from his calf.

"Next time be careful where you aim that thing." Palace said gruffly, pulling at the arrow that pierced his leg. My face turned pale, knowing I had shot him when I only wanted to keep him safe from the enemy. I dropped my weapon fast, and heard it clang to the floor behind me. I locked on to Palace's leg, he shot a painful look at me. Then I ripped a piece of his shirt.

"I just want to apologize before hand," I told him.

Palace gave me a confused look, fearing what I might do next.

Without a warning, I pulled the arrow from his leg. A geyser of blood shot out of his leg before I could securely tie a make shift tourniquet around his wound.

"I'm sorry," I said. The sound of the others struggling with the beast continued all around us. Most of my other classmates' bodies lay strewn around the maze pathway. The Silver Cannabis held his huge sword high, leaned back and wound up to take another swing. Pablo was standing way to close and Silver Cannabis swung it at him. We all stood in horror at what just happened. Pablo's eyes didn't move, nor did his lips. He just stood there with a shocked look on his face and took a few mindless steps backwards; reluctant to utter a word.

Robert called out to him. "You alright? Say something."

When Pablo attempted to open his mouth to speak, a spray of red mist spewed onto the dark floor. His knees collapsed first, followed by his head rolling on the ground. Pablo's body crashed backwards pooling blood on the floor.

"Pablo!" I screamed so hard it rang in my ears. The grotesque Centaur expected no other threat. He had bitterness in his eyes that spelled a hatred for all things human. But why kill Pablo? Why hurt anyone? Callum tugged at his locket. He must have felt responsible for the death of our friend. All of us did. The beasts deep dark eyes locked back on me. He straightened his arm and lifted his gleaming sword above his head.

"How much more blood must I spill?" The Centaur shouted, flicking the tip of his blade to slake off the blood. "If you wish it, I will spill every last drop to keep you from getting in my way."

The savage then turned to me, his fingers tightening around the handle of his sword. He had a scowl on his face that observed me from afar. The smell of freshly spilt blood still reeked in the air. If he wanted to come after me, I didn't move from his path. He would have to give it a shot.

Do his worst.

The Centaur didn't budge, he just stood his ground. In the end, I lifted my sword, feeling a combination of fear and but rage. I had seen the dark truth of the existence of Nubara and I could not imagine allowing this madness to continue any longer.

"If you want to see me dead, what are you waiting for?" I said taunting him.

This sickening smile spread across half of the Centaur's face.

"I thought you would never ask, Lunati…"

"What the hell do you think you're doing?" Palace asked while struggling to keep hold of his arm. "Soliel, listen to me. This is not a game. If he comes too close, he could kill you."

I was paying no attention to Palace. I was focusing on gathering all of my hate, anger and pain. Now, I needed it to unleash it on the animal smiling before me. Unlike before, I didn't let the fear rattle my nerves, I pulled the bow back, ready to release and fire. Something inside me found the strength to stand and face the Silver Cannabis as the lunatic tried to stampede me into the ground.

An intense burning pain traveled from my wrist to the tips of my fingers. The blue scar that Ashley and I share started glowing so hot and bright. I looked down not sure what was happening. Palace was too shocked to say what he was thinking, but I could see it written all over his face.

Soleil that's impossible! Soleil…what are you? He must have thought.

In Queen Marietta's holographic diary, she never mentioned what the scars mean. I didn't know what to think either, to be freaked out or feel like I had everything under control. A drop of blood dripped freely from my finger. Just as it had when I first picked up the bow. I only tried my best to grin and bear the pain. While I wiped the blood off on my jacket, the Centaur spoke to me.

"Lunati," he said twisting his mouth into a smile. "I will kill you."

I knew that the beast would show me no mercy. Rest assured that I will show him exactly the same.

He swung down at my head by I dodged back before he could slice my neck. I held my hand out to all the others in the room. Telling them not to interfere. Ashley, Callum and Esabelle waited on the near the maze walls gazing helplessly as I tried to get a clear shot at the beast.

"If he kills her, we're done for…" Esabelle said.

"Don't worry, Soleil knows what she's doing. Trust her," Ashley replied.

A dark blue splash of energy emitted across my face in waves, I shook my head trying to regain my focus. Another flash, a vision of the strange world I witnessed seemed to be there; right in front of me.

Why am I seeing these things? I wondered losing my focus and lowering my bow. I blinked hard trying to stop the visions from violently flashing in my head. After a split second, I went crashing onto the ground. My bow and arrow was knocked out of my hands.

You are more than what you seem.

I heard.

The fight does not end here.

I heard again.

While the visions flashed madly in my head, Callum & Esabelle raced towards me. My head was spinning and I could barely process where I was or what was happening. Callum & Esabelle were attempting to manhandle the beast with no success. The Silver Cannabis loomed over them both, swinging his heavy sword in wild circles. Callum launched himself at the monster, pulling him back from its deadly stance over me.

Before the Centaur hit the ground, he calmly doubled back underneath the twilight darkness. He dropped down over Callum, grabbed him by the back of his jacket and thrust him high into the air.

"Callum!" Esabelle screamed. She immediately rushed towards the beast, pummeling him with her fists until the Centaur turned fast and stomped on Esabelle hard. He kicked Esabelle across the corridor and set his sights on the shining reflection of the locket that glimmered in his eyes. He drifted towards its direction. It was at that moment that Callum realized what he wanted. It made sense now; the Centaur had a link to the Novae Emblem locket. It beckoned him to hunt it down no matter what stood in its way. The Silver Cannabis moved his exhausted body and stormed to Callum's side. With the edge of his sword, he slowly slid it underneath the chain of the necklace, then with his other hand; he tugged it free from Callum's neck.

Callum reached for it, grasping at it desperately. "Give that back!"

In a low voice, the beast spoke to Callum with a wicked smile on its face.

"You should be dead for taking what you stole. What do you think that thieves should not be punished? I have a mind to end this...right here...right now..."

The beast then leaned up, unfastened his strap pack and dropped the locket inside.

Nobody realized just how out of it I was. An extreme throbbing kept pulsating in my head.

All the pictures that I was having trouble recalling were flashing through my brain. I saw Queen Marietta telling us about her world. Then there were images of Ashley rocking back and forth in a cage. All of these images I saw were the same ones that I've experienced on my journey here. The last image that flickered through my mind was that of Palace. It's was as if he was standing right there, holding me in his arms and leaning in to kiss me.

I gazed up and I stared at the beast's deep set yellow eyes with flecks of red. The shimmery gray skin on his back looked slimy to the touch, but felt rough hewn like the texture of sand paper. I didn't want to hesitate any longer; I knew I had to do something, even if I couldn't see past by nose.

"Lunati…"

He called to me.

"Can you hear me, Lunati? We meet again even if you wear a different face…"

When I opened my eyes again, I no longer found myself in the maze. My body floated freely in this dark black space as if I were gliding through a void.

Come on, Soleil! You have to get a hold of yourself. What you're doing right now is hallucinating.

I had managed to get lost in the whirlwind of my own emotions. Without really knowing what caused this, I thought I must have gone into some sort of shock. My body was in such utter agony, that now I felt like I deserved this pain. Am I feeling this way because of Pablo? Because of what happened to the train conductor? Their deaths were a mistake. Even so, all of my loaded emotions boiled up at the surface no matter how hard or how deeply I tried to bury them. The guilt of not being there to save them still lingered. No matter what, whether I knew it was impossible to save them or not.

Even though I couldn't see it, I could feel a pair of hands wrapping around my neck. I had to snap out of it, my life depended on it. The tight grip choked me up and brought me back to consciousness. I heard a loud shriek. Callum shoved the Silver Cannabis in the gut to stop him from suffocating me. By the frightened expression on

Callum's face, I could tell that he did not have a plan. The beast raised his blood smeared sword in the air with both hands.

He whirled around and pulled it back before lunging it near Callum's chest, aiming right for his heart. Just before impact, the sword fell free from his large hands and dropped, clanging onto the ground. His glinting eyes moved down, and he caught sight of my arrow sticking out of his bleeding chest. A vibration of shudders shot through the Centaur's body. Callum took Esabelle's hand and raced in the opposite direction. The glossy grey skin of the Silver Cannabis transformed into dark black as that of a cloud shrouded night sky. His grey face resembled that of a ghost.

With his good arm, Palace ripped the bag free from being slung around the beast's shoulder.

"Pretty sure, if you're dead…you won't be needing this anymore," he said.

The Centaur collapsed on his side, the shimmering silver glow was no longer present over his skin. We watched Palace empty the contents of the satchel in his backpack and had caught the locket before it got buried. He inspected it to be sure that it was still intact. Callum sighed; relieved that he hadn't lost it, especially, after he made the promise to keep it safe for Soleil.

The Silver Cannabis lay on the ground trembling for a few more moments until it finally stopped moving entirely. The heat in his body had already gone from burning hot to freezing cold to the touch. Soleil's breath hitched in her throat when she realized the worst of it had finally ended. Curtis angled the flashlight upwards as we all stood crowded together in the depths of the maze.

"Well," he spoke waiting a little to say the rest. "Is it over?"

Soleil Oupary

IT TOOK NINE HOURS for the transit authorities to find us. We were so far beneath the old tunnels that they couldn't believe they even were built that far. The winding confusion and darkness had now become nothing more than a distant memory. None of us really knew how to handle being rescued. We'd seen so much that we were still figuring out how to deal with it all. This was true for me, at least.

Sirens blared all around and the high pitched noise pierced my ears. Who could I tell about the Centaur? The Princess from Atlantis? A King from of a different planet? And honestly, who would believe me. Sparkles of sweat glistened all over my body. The threat of the Centaur ripping me a part may have ended, but I'd only been left with more questions. I wanted to know what this new world meant for all of us who have a connection to Nubara. Ashley and I saw a vision of something much worse than an ancient beast. We saw the beginning of a war between our planet and a race as old as the cosmos. That means we have to be ready, all of us; for what was bound to come next.

Of course, when the transit authorities had dug us out, they asked us a bunch of questions. All of us got interrogated one by one. They told us that they just wanted to get our statements before rushing us all to the hospital to check for our injuries.

Robert stepped in the way of the transit office eager to ask me questions.

"It's been extremely rough for all of us; do you think you can give us a minute to process it before probing us carelessly with your questions?"

The officer just raised his hands and stepped back to give me some room.

"I swear these men can be absolute vultures," he told me rubbing me on the shoulder.

"It's no surprise they want to know what happened down there. Why we got trapped for so long?"

"Maybe so, but there's a time and a place for everything. When people survive a trauma like we just had, we need a moment to regain our bearings and realize that we just barely escaped with our lives."

I only nodded. There wasn't any way I could be sure I could tell anyone what happened. Robert withdrew his hand from my shoulder as he took a short walk to the ambulance parked right next to us. Palace had already been strapped safely in a gurney. With his arm broken and his leg injured, he couldn't wait around too long. He gasped trying to adjust himself comfortably.

"We'll meet you at the hospital," I said.

Palace shook his head. "Don't. Come with me."

He held out his hand waiting for me to take it. The two med techs in the back looked after his broken arm. I took his hand, and then sat at his side as we both rode silently to Rolling Hills Medical.

"You're lucky."

I turned my head and stared at the doctor.

"What do you mean I asked?"

"You're lucky that you're not as badly injured as your friends. It looks like you all survived hell…"

The hospital room had people coming and going from everywhere. Patients being wheeled off to surgery, family visitors standing at the bedside of their loved ones, but no one came for me. My classmates rested in hospital beds not far. A nurse came around and smiled at me.

"Soleil Oupary," she stated. "I have a visitor who has come to see you."

A visitor? I wondered.

Could it be my brother?

I hadn't seen my brother in so long. If I saw him now, I would just break. The nurse only smiled without saying a further word. My eyes widened when I recognized the visitor's face.

"Shoba!" I shouted then cupped my hand over my mouth.

"Please remember to keep you voice low," the nurse reminded me in a friendly tone.

"I thought you flew back to England? What about your grandmother? Is she—?"

Shoba stopped me right there.

"She's fine. Well, fine for now, when I heard you went missing, I couldn't leave it to chance, so I got a flight out as soon as I could."

God knows how much I missed her; I wanted to tell her all about what's happened. However, I kept most of the wild stories to myself. I didn't want to scare her off. The last thing I wanted right now was to look like a crazy person with deluded visions. Shoba didn't need to know about ancient Queens or prophecies….at least not right now.

"Dr Michaels looked banged up. When are you going to fill me in on what happened down in the subway? I mean it looks like—" Shoba started to ask, but I interrupted her before she could finish.

"A train crash. We got in a really bad train crash, by some dumb luck we survived. Don't tell me how. It's just as much as a mystery to me as it is to you."

"Goodness, Soleil. I'm really sorry. Some part of me feels like I'm a little responsible for this. Leaving you like I did."

I parted my lips as if I was going to say something, but I only paused trying to piece together my thoughts.

"You're here now," I replied. "That's all that matters."

Shoba glanced over at Callum & Esabelle chatting closely in the corner. Callum got up and then sat back down with two paper cups filled with water. He handed one to Esabelle.

"So, what's the story with those two? Isn't that the same woman you met on the train? She's getting awfully close to that guy."

"…Ow!" Shoba shrieked after I pinched her shoulders.

"C'mon you just got here, you're not seriously going to turn into a gossip queen are you?"

She laughed. "Someone must. We all know you're too good to get your hands 'dirty,' so to speak."

I pinched her again, truly Shoba had no clue. I've gotten my hands dirty enough for the both of us. I've gotten my hands filthy enough for a lifetime.

"How is Palace?" I asked.

"Sleeping. They put him on some pretty heavy drugs. Not surprising, considering that if they had given him a prescription, I might ask if he'll pass me some. What you think?"

Just like the Shoba Ali I remember, I didn't think it was possible for her to get anymore shameless. She just never cared what anyone thought.

"Well, given everything that's happened, remind me why anyone rides the train again?" Shoba asked.

I couldn't hold my laughter in any longer and I'm sure that's exactly what she wanted. Everything in my life has changed. No longer did I hope to just get a position after I finished my grad classes. None of that seemed to matter at all. All that mattered was protecting the locket and understanding our connection to the past of Nubara.

Something else was definitely coming and it wanted many of us dead. Queen Marietta wouldn't rest until she found out who the intruders were. She'd likely want to know how we got access into their world.

It's the same reason why the Silver Cannabis desired nothing more than to see us ground up into dust. They didn't want us revealing their secrets. Little did they know, we hadn't really discovered much yet, but that wouldn't stop them anyhow? To the rulers of Nubara, all of us were a threat and they wanted kill us to keep their world a secret.

The nurse came striding back into the room. I mostly just lay their motionless. I wanted only to rest. The smile on her face disappeared, and I knew it must have been bad.

"Is something the matter?" I asked.

"We're going to need your assistance," the nurse answered.

I did overhear Callum saying something, and this must have involved the same thing but I let the nurse finish asking anyway.

"We have quite a few bodies downstairs that were discovered when we rescued you all from the tunnels. We've been asking everyone in your group to come and help identify them."

Shoba met my eyes with a sorrowful look. She knew it wasn't something I was ready for.

"Do you need me to go with you? Just ask and I'll be there," she said.

"It's okay, I'll be fine," I told her.

"I realize this isn't easy for you. The memories are still very fresh," the Medical Examiner said.

"I'm James Oldham. I'm investigating your case. After we pulled you guys out, the transit authority went digging deeper to see if there were any other survivors on the runaway train."

I'm not really in the mood to stare at dead bodies, but is anyone? I just knew, I had to get through it eventually. James Oldham had a head of gray hair and a long mustache. His dark toned beard could have used a little more trimming.

There were three bodies laying on the three gurneys. I swallowed hard, knowing that no investigation would find who was behind these murders. Not unless they found the Centaur at the scene of the crime. *Would they find his body?* I wondered. *What would they think?* Seeing a Centaur in real life away from the Greek fairy tale and the books would just sound absolutely crazy. If they did find it, I would be relieved. No longer would I be forced to hide what I knew of the truth. That these evils do exist and they are lurking among us.

Oldham just stared at me, listening for my word.

"Just tell me when you're ready and we'll begin."

And then I looked at him with affirmation.

"I'm ready," I said.

The other cadaver room techs wheeled the black leather bags right under the washed out halogen lighting. They held the zipper close in their hands. Oldham nodded, and the tech pulled the zipper slowly up until the body's face and chest were revealed. The body's mouth hung open. Oldham pointed at it.

"Do you recognize this person?" he asked.

I didn't really recognize him, I only briefly knew him. It was Henrik, the train conductor who got sideswiped while all of us made a mad dash for the maze.

"Yes, this man was the man driving our train."

"Why don't you tell me a little bit about how he died?" Oldham asked.

It was at this point, that I had no other choice but to lie.

"It's like I've already said before, you know in all of those written statement about everyone that died on the train. We wandered a little further out to look for help, when we couldn't find any help we then waited where you found us."

Oldham stared at me and I didn't know whether he thought I was telling the truth or not.

"Well, can you at least confirm you saw this man on the train before it collided with the electric rail?"

"Yes, I saw him when I boarded the subway car. That's all. After that, I never saw him again…until now," I replied.

The Medical Examiner didn't push the matter. Oldham could see though, that it was a touchy subject that begged to be investigated some more. The med tech led us both to the next body lying prostrate in the body bag. What clued me into the person's identity was that the top of the bag lay very flat. There was another low zipping noise that sounded resonated throughout the room.

"The transit authorities told me that when they found this body, they hadn't seen anything like it. This corpse is missing a head. So far, no one has found it."

When I looked down at the exposed body of Pablo, my gut started to roll violently and I tried my hardest to keep everything down. I couldn't believe what I had gotten myself into. Oldham knew I was hiding something and keeping the secret was making me sick.

"Now, tell me, Ms. Oupary. How does a man lose his head in a train accident?"

My breath rose to the top of my throat and that gagging sensation almost made me lose it. Yet I spoke.

"I don't know this man. He could have been sitting anywhere on the train. You can't really expect me to know where everyone was sitting. Can you? A girder could have slipped free when the train crashed. A piece of glass may have flown free from a broken window. Any number of possibilities may have happened. I'm not going to sit here and name them all."

"Fair enough, Ms. Oupary," Oldham replied.

Everything inside me was just telling me to run. To get out. Leave now. Each person he showed me, I knew, I talked to them face to face. Adrenaline exploded through my chest at the thought of another lie. Oldham stopped the med tech from leading us to the last body lying on the table.

"There was another that we found before this one. However, the body was so badly shredded there would be nothing left to identify. Luckily, we found an ID with a picture and a name." James Oldham held up the driver's license for me to clearly see.

"Know her? Did you see her on the train when she died?"

The driver's ID was that of Pablo's girlfriend who got ripped apart when we got separated in the tunnels. She was the first victim of the Centaur. The first one in our group who got killed by the beast.

"Haven't seen this woman in my life." I lied, again.

I had to keep it this way. I had to keep the truth hidden, to keep others from getting their lives tangled in the mess. The train crash just happened to make the perfect cover up for all of these unfortunate "accidents."

Oldham chuckled feeling a little duped.

"You know what's funny about all of these bodies I just showed you? Don't worry; we'll get to the last one in a minute. None of these bodies were found anywhere near the train wreckage. How can a victim of a train crash be discovered miles off from the scene of the disaster? Doesn't add up does it? Just doesn't make any sense."

"What do you want me to say," I asked. "When it happened I was pretty out of it myself. Who knows? Maybe some of them went to look for help."

"No way was this victim looking for help with the state her body is in. The severity of her injuries, such as they are, looks like someone gutted her with a lawn mower. Train crashes, hell, no sort crash can do that. I've got an inkling, you can call it a hunch or whatever you want to call it but there's more to this and I want you to tell me."

The words I wanted to say next strangled in the pit of my throat. Even if I wanted to say the truth, who's to say that this guy would believe me? And it's not like I wanted to lie. It's the complete opposite but I know by telling the truth I might take more lives than I'm trying to save.

"There's nothing I know." I replied still throwing him off intentionally.

He eyed me as we both made a straight path to the final body lying on the gurney.

He spoke. "Now, the transit authority has been double checking the security footage during that day to see if the identities match up. When they got back to me about this victim, can you guess what they said?"

"What?" I asked.

"They got back to me and said there's no record of this person anywhere. Not on the cameras and not on the train. How does someone who was not found anywhere in the train station somehow still become a victim in the train crash?"

I shrugged. "Maybe there was a side entrance. Maybe he was trying to steal a free ride. I mean, I really don't know."

This time I meant it. I had no idea who the last body could have been. Right now, I just wished they stop dragging this out and just show me the body already. Unless they were just fond of keeping me here and wasting my time. My heart finally began to settle down in my chest. When the med tech reached for the zipper to pull it down, it seemed like it moved much more slowly now. And when I saw the victim's face, it's like I woke up in a nightmare.

"You know him?"

I didn't even know how to answer that question. The body was of a man that should have been a beast. The dead body looking back at me had no shimmering silver skin or frightening yellow eyes. Instead, it was just the body of a man and nothing more.

Chapter 13

Soleil Oupary

"Sometimes I feel so helpless," I said. My eyes slowly gazed up to the clock hanging in the corner of the room. The psychiatrist just nodded. You could say everything had gone back to normal, at least sort of. Even so, not for one second did I feel at ease, nor did I feel in control.

"Ms. Oupary, is everything alright?"

I went silent and my mind went blank. Dr. Morris didn't say a word. He gave me as much time as he thought I needed. After all, how could he expect me to react, given what I'd experienced? I raked my fingers over my jeans, catching lint under my nails. Strangely, this calmed me. It's not like they could be totally honest anyway. No doubt the more I revealed about my life the more trouble I got myself in.

Dr. Morris eyed me seriously. "Soliel, it's never my place to interrupt during a session, but you look so lost."

"It's just that there's so little for me to reveal. Besides, this whole pouring out my heart thing never came to me easily, but I'm sure you hear these sort of stories all the time."

Then he appraised me with a stern look in his eyes. "Well, you must know that anything you say in this room will stay here forever. You're in a safe place. You have nothing to fear."

I fear the truth. Of course, he had no idea. But all I can do is keep this secret hidden.

"It started way before, getting trapped down there. I was chosen by my Dr for a special assignment along with a few my classmates. We got assigned to do a survey of a cave that was speculated to have some connection to the Legend of Nubara." That's right I said it.

The shrink looked at me with a blank stare, he hadn't heard of the legend at all. That was no surprise, of course. In fact, it made going through this whole thing that much easier to lie.

I folded my arms. "What exactly happens next?" I asked.

"There are no rules, Ms. Oupary. Right now I'm just taking an assessment to measure whether your experience in the subway warrants further sessions."

No, I can't let that happen. I can hardly bear the thought of spending further time in the spotlight. My tired eyes wandered while the doctor took a sip from his glass of water. It just didn't seem like a good idea to put any of us through this. Not right now.

Even though I haven't seen it yet, all of this must have been a breaking story on the news. I can see the headlines now: *Ivy League Students Spend Several Harrowing Hours in Abandoned Subway Tunnels. Who Is to Blame?*

Dr. Morris waited patiently for me to speak again.

"Everything was a blur; all I can remember is that there was lots of smoke billowing all around the train like a dark and endless shadow. Then the next thing we knew, it flew off the rails.

Then a moment of silence passed between us. He looked down, writing notes on the pad resting in his lap. It felt like time had slowed down. I turned my attention to the window only a half aware now. Snow melted off of the frames of the windows as winter snow covered much of the city. All of us were expected to give our own version of the events that happened in the tunnels. What did the police expect anyway?

Clearly, Oldham had his suspicions but why would he assume that there was any foul play? I heard the sound of a pen hitting paper. The pure silence ended when the therapist asked me a question.

"You're certainly a mystery, Ms. Oupary. Do you not think your survival story isn't worth telling?"

"Well, it's not interesting, and I'm just tired of telling it over and over again. I fear I'm beginning to sound like a broken record. We met a man who was some sort of crazy obsessive. When he spoke, it was mostly gibberish. But from what I could understand, he was trying to find some sort of 'treasure,'" I replied.

He then got up from his seat and placed his bag on his desk. A chill went through me and I started rubbing my shoulders. He took a seat behind his desk after glancing up at the clock.

"Well, I'm afraid that's all the time I have for you today. I want you to think about what I said. Given everything you've suffered, it's not unusual to go through a kind of post traumatic episode. Just understand, you're not alone and if you need to talk to anyone, schedule an appointment at my office."

Here's hoping I'll never have to come back here again. I thought. An hour was pretty much all I could stand.

Callum Morrissey

THE NOVAE EMBLEM shimmered in the palm of my hand. Sometimes I can't understand what possessed Soliel to allow me to take it. I hardly knew how to keep my life together, let alone keep watch over a precious legacy stone.

"What's that you're holding, Mr. Morrissey?" The therapist asked.

Immediately, I pocketed the locket in my breast pocket.

"Oh, that? Nothing," I replied patting down my blazer. I lowered my voice to keep from drawing attention to himself. All of us already agreed on how we would spend the story about what really happened to us in the tunnels. The therapist leaned forward to listen much more closely, gazing at the strange heavy bracelet on my wrist. There was only a few minutes left in the session.

"The train crashed. We got out. We looked for help. That's the story."

I couldn't let Soliel and everyone else down. Not after I felt like I've already found my place in the world. Who would have thought a lawyer down and out on his luck would discover that he was once a mythical warrior in another life. Now, I want to know how many more secrets are hidden inside me that I've yet to uncover.

The therapist didn't ask any more questions about what my bracelet was for, however he wanted to know how I found it.

"Is that a family heirloom?" he asked.

"It's nothing. It's just something I wear," I said.

The therapist then moved to a different subject entirely.

"Did you also see the psychotic man?" he asked.

At first, what he asked didn't register. *Psychotic man?* I thought. Perhaps, if he were talking about the psychotic man-beast. I would understand what he meant. Then I replied.

"Ah, yes." I started. "We were all kinda out of it actually, and then we heard screams coming from some other tunnels in the near distance. We soon found out there was this insane quack pot who had been living in the tunnels and wanted everyone to get off of his turf."

It didn't make any sense to even the therapist, but he wouldn't doubt me. It's against his job description. His only job is to listen to what I've got to say, nod his head and possibly write a prescription. If I'm lucky, it would be something strong. There's almost nothing I wouldn't give to forget that whole nightmare in those tunnels didn't happen.

"Why am I here again?" I crossed my legs at the ankle and tapped my foot on the floor. Everyone else may have tolerated this "therapy" that felt more like a back handed interrogation, but I wouldn't. I thought Esabelle.

Esabelle Matthews

THE THERAPIST SWALLOWED HARD.

"It's just I want to get a sense of how you're feeling about what you've been through recently," the therapist replied.

"How do you think I feel? Isn't it obvious?"

The therapist then raised a brow when looking down at my wrist. "That bracelet…"

"What about it?" I asked.

He just looked at me for a moment before answering my question.

"I've seen the exact same bracelet on another patient of mine."

Callum. He must have been talking about Callum. That didn't mean he would get any answers out of me.

"It's just something I wear because it matches with everything."

I shrugged flippantly, and didn't have any more to say.

The psychiatrist continued, "Am I to assume you've seen the psycho killer too?"

"No, I never saw the psycho killer, but I know he exists because I remember the screams. You don't forget when someone screams like that. I had no doubt that whoever the deranged man was, he wanted the woman dead."

The psychiatrist seemed confused. Then he shifted a few files in his hands.

"Woman? What woman? I've only read a few names. The women who survived the train crash are a part of a very short list," he stated.

Honestly, I just said whatever I thought would sound believable. I only parroted the same story I had rehearsed with everyone else. The shrink walked stiffly away from where I sat. It's obvious he had had enough of talking to me. It's true; I've never been the easiest person to talk to. Still, it didn't matter, if we wanted to keep our secret of the real horrors hiding underneath the city, a guy like this wouldn't believe the truth if I said it anyway. It's not like he would believe that we saw a holographic projection of a Queen from a different planet, or a giant maze with a blood thirsty Centaur seeking that we all suffer and die horrific deaths. We had to hide the truth. We must.

Esabelle's mind went into the incident just before they were all found, right when the Silver Cannabis was put down.

Soliel Oupary

ESABELLE HAD BURIED her face in Callum's chest. The rest of us stood in a circle as the smoke cleared at the exit in the tunnel. I brushed my sweaty hair out of my face to make sure that I was seeing what I thought I saw. Ashley was the only one of us who didn't stand; she sat on the floor and rocked back and forth holding her knees. Palace rubbed my left shoulder.

"It's over now," he said. "The police will be down here soon I assume."

"Is it really over?" I asked. "Didn't you see what happened? We're connected to Nubara through a legacy that lasts several decades. This won't end tonight. This won't end tomorrow. This will follow us forever."

"Whatever comes, we will be able to handle it," Palace emphasized.

I wanted to see everything that happened through his eyes, but I just didn't know how.

Even though that was the truth, I still didn't believe it. We've been down in the dark so long I almost lost any hope that we would find the light. We knew that if we wanted to make it out of this with as few questions as possible, we would have to keep our stories straight. Esabelle's eyes were swimming in tears. What would the cops think when they saw a dead Centaur lying on the ground. The key now was to protect ourselves.

I saw Callum's eyes widen. He pointed, with a trembling arm at the dead beast lying in front of us.

"Hey guys, Um....you're going to want to come over here and look at this." he said, his voice rising with confusion. The group shifted to where Callum was pointing and hovered over the Silver Cannabis lying stiff in the middle of us.

"This isn't normal..." Esabelle said.

An eerie blue aura surrounded his entire body. I tried to rack my brain and understand what was going on. Slowly, the beast's enormous sinewy body shrank smaller and smaller into itself right before our eyes. Its hooves expanded into thin bones like that of a human. Its muscle extended over the bone which was followed by rapidly spreading skin. Its red eyes drained of its previous dark and menacing red and changed to an icy blue.

"But why?" Ashley finally spoke up after having kept silent for several hours. "Why is it changing into a human?"

None of us knew the answer to that question. But it couldn't have happened at a more opportune time. It would only be minutes until the cops came down and discovered us. The random evolution stopped. A muscled naked body of a nondescript dark haired man lay right at our feet. If you never saw what it was before, you would think nothing of it. *Except how do you explain a dead man without clothes far off from the subway crash?* I thought.

Robert crouched down right next to the now human body and turned it face up. The Dr. in him was dying to study the creature now human but the situation they were all in called for another solution.

"Here's my idea about how we should explain what happened."

We were all ears.

Robert continued. "After the crash there was a lot of commotion. Smoke. Fire. Screaming. Anyone can get shaken up in that kind of relentless chaos. We need to explain how we all found each other after search through the dead and unconscious passengers. Then we'll explain that Henrik corralled us all to climb out of the wreckage and use the emergency tunnels to get back to the higher levels."

"What emergency tunnels?" Esabelle asked wiping her eyes.

"The ones I just made up. Given that Henrik is...well," Robert paused and then continued. "There will be no else to refute the story."

"Then what do we say next?" Callum asked. "Aren't the cops going to be curious why we left the train wreckage? That would be the most logical place to wait for help at the scene of the accident."

"Yes, but who could blame us for wanting to take our chances after having waited and being trapped down here for so long. That's not suspicious at all," I retorted.

They all backed away from the body, and Palace spoke.

"We need to swear that we will keep what we've seen here to ourselves. Not only for the safety of the secrets that we now carry, but for the safety of every human on this planet."

Robert was right. The repercussion of what happened in the tunnels meant no person was safe. The world we lived in was different now. We had to acknowledge it whether we wanted to or not.

We heard the footsteps of the police heading our way. Hastily, I lowered my hand, expecting the others to do the same. One by one, my Drs and classmates lowered their arms. The lights from the police's searchlights traveled across our bodies and they swarmed us all at once.

After all of us had our sit down with the psychiatrist, the state investigators let us go. Luckily, all of our stories matched up, and none of the deaths could be attributed to any one of us. Then all of us went our separate ways. On my way out, I caught a glimpse of Callum reaching out to Esabelle's side.

Palace came up behind me and turned me around in his arms.

"Look, we survived it. Don't let this get to you Soliel. You've got bigger things on your plate to worry about. Promise me you'll take a couple days off. "

"I don't know why any of this is happening, and I can't stop it. A couple days off will not change that."

Palace looked at me. "Look, this is not yours to fight alone. I'll be with you every step of the way."

Then I looked up at him and saw him in a different light. The lives we had before, the Silver Cannabis had changed completely. I felt the softness of his hand against my cheek, and I became something other than myself. This time I didn't want to be Soliel, but I wanted to be with Palace, I wanted to be in his arms. In this moment, I had the feeling of déjà vu, like the time we spent in the tunnels and he had kissed me.

I just wanted to relive that feeling again; I spread my arms open and wrapped them around his neck. I pulled myself closer to him and we pressed our lips together. It felt exactly like it was the first time. Suddenly, Palace pulled away warily not sure of how to react. He glanced at me and followed Robert to his car.

I stood alone and looked to my left; Esabelle had rested her head on Callum's shoulder. Clearly, a lot has changed and not just for me, but for my classmates as well. The thought of returning to my regular routine didn't even seem possible to me. I edged back, and headed to the train station to take the train back to Rolling Hills University.

"HELLO?" I ANSWERED over the phone.

"We need you to come in."

It was late, and I was already sleeping when Palace called me. "What's happening?"

"Everyone's here. You need to be here too," he said.

Rubbing my eyes, I hit the light next to my nightstand. Whatever it was, it must have been important. I grabbed whatever I could in my hand and rushed out of the door.

Everyone was already there. Except me, of course. A fleet of vans with giant spotlights were all over the Michaels' residence. The press wanted to know more about the people who were the only survivors of the train crash. The general public was as stricken as we were. No one had ever seen that many people perish in such an accident before.

The thought of having to cross the line of journalists with their mics and cameras in my faces frightened me. I would have to tell the lies all over again. Many of them have been camped out here before we were even rescued. They waited it out to get the story first. There was a long silence before I finally made my presence known. I saw their faces spin around and look at me. Without missing a beat, they pounced on my position and forced their mics in my face.

I threw my hands in the air attempting to keep the lights from blinding me as I ran for the Palace's door. He embraced me in his arms, protecting before slamming the door behind me.

Then the two of us held each other, making all the others uncomfortable in the room.

"So…" Ashley interrupted the silence. "Robert told us all to stay here for the night. Now, we're here."

Palace released me, rubbing the back of his neck. I walked forward and took a seat on the chair.

Callum then spoke.

"How are we really going to move on from this? We can't go home. We can't walk anywhere without getting noticed. I just want my life back."

In a way, Callum spoke for all of us. All of us wanted to go back to our old lives, where no one cared who we were. Esabelle came over and grabbed Callum's hand.

"It will blow over. Something else will take the attention off of us," said.

Callum shook his head and didn't really know if he could believe that anything would change.

"There's something else," Palace interrupted. He walked to a desk right behind us and pulled out a drawer. None of us could see what he pulled out of it. What could he have been hiding? Did he take something with him out of the tunnels when we weren't looking? A small bag hung loosely in his grasp. There was something about it that I recognized, even if I couldn't quite yet put my finger on it. With one swipe, he cleared the table with his arm to make some room. But for what?

Palace emptied the contents of the bag on the table. That's when I noticed that the pouch he held in his hand did in fact belong to the Silver Cannabis. Silver and a Bronze locket fell in a tangle, scratching the table's glass surface.

"Where?" I asked. "Where did you find those?"

I didn't recognize the symbols on the front of the lockets; they didn't look anything like the one I saw on the locket that I gave to Callum. Esabelle moved closer to inspect it. Esabelle tapped the light on the front end of her cell phone and shone the light closer to the Emblems. Suddenly, a flash flew up and shone on the wall behind us. Palace stepped out of the way so we could all see what the picture was.

"It's…" Callum started. "A map?"

None of us knew what it was. Could this be the map to Queen Marietta's Island? Maybe it was for the planet of Nibiris? There really was no telling what it could be for.

Callum buried his hand in his pocket and then pulled out his cell phone. He angled it to capture the entire map for a picture.

A bright white light flashed briefly as he took a picture. Callum then sent us all a copy of the map. A few seconds later, I felt my phone vibrate in my pocket.

"There. Now, we all have a copy," he said sliding his phone back in his pocket.

"Guys," Esabelle said crouching underneath the table. "There's more…"

Everyone else knelt down too, looking at the picture of the map being cast on the floor. The second bronze locket had another piece of the map of the tunnels. Ashley moved hear hand along the tunnels shown on the map and realized that the very end on one path looked very similar to a path on the map on the wall.

Quickly, she snapped a photo, rose to her feet and placed her phone on the table. I followed, watching her open the file Callum sent us.

"Do you know where these two maps are leading us?" I asked.

Ashley fiddled some more with her phone adjusting the two photos, but I still didn't understand why.

"It's not that they're two different locations, they're actually the same location."

Everyone else stopped viewing the map on the floor and immediately stood. We all gazed at the map on Ashley's phone. Clearly, the lockets had a different purpose to keep the whereabouts of this mystery place a secret. But I felt especially confused. I turned my back away from the others. I could scarcely move my mouth when speaking, knowing that I had seen that map before.

I couldn't tell them. Not now. I needed to understand it more for myself. I had to know why the vision played out like a memory that had been implanted in my subconscious. There was obviously no way I could have traveled to that place, yet I felt like I've been there before. What if it had something to do with my connection to the Queen? No one else made any assumptions, because they didn't even understand where the map led to.

Robert & Palace moved next to each other with grave looking expressions on their faces.

"What these ancient beings want is to start an all-out war with us that spans much further than our own galaxy. This is what we are facing. It won't go away and we need to find out how we are going to protect ourselves from such a threat."

"This sounds like something from a really bad movie..." Ashley replied.

Palace walked over and then proceeded to pace in steady circles around where we sat. I could tell that he wished to know the meaning behind it too. He couldn't imagine having to be a part of the small group that was responsible for saving the entire human race from being eradicated. It looked like none of us would be sleeping soundly at night anytime soon. Instead, we would be spending the next few decades of our lives trying to keep the people of Nubara from wanting to destroy our way of life. A long legacy of hating humans has been their creed for a very long time.

Callum got up from his seat; he was feeling a little fed up with it all.

"It's not that any of us are under the impression that we're all just going to walk free from this. Let's stop walking on egg shells here. The tunnels have changed us forever. We found out about the truth about ourselves in ways we didn't even know exist. Who knows why I'm some sort of warrior? Who knows why Ashley's some type of Oracle? Or, why Esabelle and I are connected with the power of the bracelet?" Callum addressed us, hitting his hands on his sides.

Then Callum looked over at Soleil...."Let's not forget Soleil the Archer of Nubara past..."

It's obvious he was frustrated with trying reconciling who he was now and who he might have been in the past. Even stranger, is how he had found strength about to say whatever he felt? Only a few months ago, he had trouble looking anyone in the eye. It was almost like a complete change from day to night.

I was uncertain he had become this way because of the cross-dimensional revelations we witnessed or because of Esabelle. He wanted Esabelle to see that he had changed. That was the man on the train who rode home dejected and feeling like a professional failure. He had really changed.

Everyone in the room raised their voices after Callum finished his peace. Robert waved his hands trying to calm everyone else down, but the noise level erupted even more. All the while, I waited for a good moment to share my thoughts without being shouted over, I looked to Ashley. She had been weird this entire time and mostly keeping to herself.

Still, she didn't seem in any mood for really talking. Usually when I saw her like this, it was because she had gotten an idea in her head and she needed to work out how to go about proving it. Ashley reached her hand down in the middle of her laptop bag, jingling the latching buckle as she tried to get a hold of something. Tattered and ripped old pages were pulled free from inside and Ashley balanced Queen Marietta's giant journal in her hands.

Everyone else was still too busy pointing fingers and yelling at each other to notice. Finally, Ashley held the heavy diary high above the table, allowing it to fall from her hands onto the table. The book slammed down with a loud bang and forced everyone to turn around and pay attention.

"Now, that everyone's quiet..." Ashley said sarcastically. "I can tell you what I've found."

The entire room went silent and everyone listened.

"If we really want answers. Maybe we need to go to the source," Ashley said.

"How did you sneak out the diary? The police searched everyone?" I asked.

"What matters is that I did. And now, we can find some real answers about the map. All we have to do is ask about what we don't understand and about what's happening to us."

Ashley then straightened the book so it was facing her. Then she opened it. We all expected to see the likeness of Queen Marietta as Ashley ruffled through the pages. But nothing happened. Our eyes scanned the room surprised that this time the book didn't showcase the Queen's holographic recording. Ashley continued to thumb through the pages, looking for answers.

"Is there anything in there about there a map of different locations? Is there anything in there that is useful to us?" Robert asked.

"Give me a second alright, I'm looking..." she snapped.

Then, after propping her hand under the back of the book, Ashley turned hundreds of pages at a time until she reached the very end. There was something written there but the script was written backwards and upside down. Again, Ashley spun the book around so she could see it better.

"It's a little difficult to read. So, you're just going to have to give me a minute," she stated. With her finger, she traced the sentences and read them slowly aloud.

"...if there is a history of my people. It expands much greater than one book could ever bound. Our legacy must be recorded in such a way that shows much greater powers in the cosmos..."

"It sounds like gibberish. I don't understand a word," Callum said.

"It only sounds like that to you because you're not really paying attention," I replied. I was starting to lose my patience with Callum's attitude lately.

Callum didn't say anything else. He just continued to listen to Ashley speak.

"Yes, there's more than one book," she said somewhat low since she focused on deciphering the words.

"There are two. Two books and that map." Ashley turned and pointed to the map on her phone. It will lead us to where the second diary can be found. Inside that second book, we'll discover where to find the third."

Soleil Oupary

THREE BOOKS? I THOUGHT. Who knew what we would find inside them? I think I speak for the group when I say; I don't want to hear another revelation. There are still so many mysteries to learn about my past. Now, I don't even feel like the same person anymore. I just want to find out how to stop having these frightening visions. There's more that I need to know so I can control whatever powers I have. We only have so much time before something blows up in all of our faces. We must be smart about this.

We must be prepared.

Everyone sat in the room quietly. No one talked to each other, we were all self absorbed in our thoughts, letting reality sink in that there are two other diaries that the Queen used to hide the history that we all shared. It's going to be bigger than all of us soon. The consequences of what happened in the tunnels are going to have far reaching repercussions. It's only the beginning now and it's obvious, based on what we've seen so far, we're not that far from the end.

Palace then sat next to me and I looked him in his eyes.

"I just want my old life back..." I mumbled under my breath.

"We'll never get our old life back," Palace said.

They say time heals all wounds. Why do I feel like the pain has only intensified since then? Several months have passed and the winter snow has blanketed the entire city. The dying leaves on the ground have been scattered by the wind. Spring may have been on the horizon, but the world to me appears a colorless gray. I'm just having a hard time trying to build myself back up again. Palace offered to come over tonight.

We've been seeing each other more often now. I'm not sure what he sees in a brooding malcontent like myself. The thing is I want to change, I want to be my old self, but I just don't know how.

"You haven't said anything during dinner?" Palace said.

"That's true," I replied.

"Despite how much time has passed, I can't really get away from it. What happened to us I mean."

"We've gone over this already. There's no point to worry about the past or being afraid of the future. It's wasted energy, Soliel."

"I just keep thinking that there's so much more that we could do."

Palace nodded his head. He knew I implied something much greater. I didn't try to deny it. I've been obsessed with finding more answers lately.

"You mean the second diary. You want to follow the map to the second book," Palace replied.

I know the last thing that he wanted was to see me face-off with a life threatening danger again. The only thing he wanted was to simply move forward. He didn't think we had to forget, but we had to stop letting all the miserable events in the subway tunnels take over our lives.

"I just feel like it's my fault, that you're getting dragged into all of this," I said folding my arms.

"No one dragged me into anything, okay. I chose to be here. I knew the risks, and I'm here anyways."

A half smile spread across my cheek.

"If what you really want is to find that second book, then we can do that. There's nothing left to think about," Palace replied pulling me close into his side. I've never felt this safe in my life. Sometimes I thought what grew between us almost worked too well, and at any moment it could all collapse out from under me.

Callum Morrissey

I GAZED AT THE BRONZE LOCKET hanging from Esabelle's neck. Esabelle came down to my office, and I offered to give her a lift a home. What happened in the tunnels was a subject that we talked about often. Ashley, Palace, Dr. Michaels or even Soliel felt comfortable to talk about it out in the open like Esabelle and I.

"It feels like a freakish nightmare, but it also feels freeing in away," Esabelle said.

"How so?" I asked.

"Well, all of my life I thought I was kinda of a weird person and now, I know why."

I turned away and laughed. Automatically, Esabelle scooted her arm under mine. She was careful not to use her arm with the bracelet.

"You know, it's funny," I replied feeling like the luckiest man alive. "I was always afraid I would die living a normal life. That I would never do anything remarkable. And it always made me feel like no matter what I did, it would never be good enough."

"Ow!" I shouted.

Esabelle punched in my arm. To think at one point, we couldn't stand the sight of one another. Now, we were inseparable. I never could have imagined in my wildest dreams that I would find someone who could accept the kind of weirdness that I possessed. Of course, all it took to come this far in my love life was a beast from a parallel dimension. I often said that I didn't care about those annoying details. Esabelle saw that there was a much better Callum somewhere deep down in me. And in many ways she saved me, and there isn't anything in my life that I could have wanted more than that.

Dr. Richard Michaels

AFTER EVERYTHING THAT'S HAPPENED, I needed a change of scenery more than anything. I pretended like nothing happened and lecturing history courses at Rolling Hills University wasn't going to keep me sane. Not anymore. I had taken up working at the Museums of Natural History. There was a new excavation exhibit being put on display that has discovered ancient fossils in Indonesia. I've been most fortunate due to my lengthy resume; the Museum Director gave me a chance to take on the position of Head Curator of the newest Indonesian Historical Exhibit. That means I had access to all the art pieces that come through the museum. Even better, I had absolute control of how the floor plan and layout would be prepared. It was certainly something I've wanted to do but have kept so much of my attention on completing my research on the Nubara. It wasn't until Ashley had pointed it out to me that I realized I had let my obsession get the best of me.

I was obsessed with finding out where the other two diaries are. Soliel wanted nothing to do with any of it anymore. Palace has mostly been her support along the way. Just like Ashley, he wanted me to step away from the endless nights searching for any sort of clue. That's why now I'm finally following his advice and keeping my distance, before it drives me to dark places or darker places than I've already been to.

I have the history of the world right underneath my finger Tips. From the origin of man, to the tiniest insect and the rarest natural gems of the Earth. It was a nice reprieve. One I greatly needed, as I spent the entire fall locked up in my office trying to make subtle connections that I'm not even sure are there. The first order of business was preparing everything necessary to celebrate the annual Premier Winter Social.

A literal historic event celebrating its 110th year. My first thought was, *Galas, really? Aren't you the most respected and renowned emeritus of anthropology and polar molecular research in your entire department? What the hell are you doing throwing parties?* It's a legitimate question for sure. Believe me, I've asked them myself. Then, all of a sudden, I stopped caring about what other people thought and just did it anyway.

I knew I couldn't go on the way I was, not if I wanted to stay in good health. Plus, the best part of all of this was; that much of the exhibit pieces that I had unearthed myself during my lifetime of anthropological and bio-physics study. They simply called me one evening out of the blue and thought they would display my work. I thought about it for a moment and then...

I said, "Yes."

Chapter 14

"Hello." The voice spoke in an almost accusatory tone. The caller never addressed their name. I was standing on the subway waiting for Palace to meet up with me on the way to the Premier Winter Gala when I got the call.

"Hello," I responded a little unsure whether to keep talking or hang up.

"It's me. Rex."

After hearing that, I felt a terrible sickness course through my body. Sometimes you never think about these things until they hit you like a ton of bricks.

"Why are you calling me now?"

"Is now not a good time or something?"

Of course, it was a good time. Anytime was a good time when you haven't spoken to your brother in decades. I thought.

"What if I hadn't been home when you called me? What if I didn't have my cell phone?"

"Soliel, I don't understand what you're trying to say. Stop being hysterical."

The frost from the snowflakes that were falling chilled the back of my neck. It's just that long ago I figured my brother and I would never speak again. Not after what happened during that party. Not after what happened to my parents. The whole conversation was making my head hurt. I hopped off of the side walk and sat on the curb.

"Are you sitting now?" he asked. Almost as if he was watching me from somewhere nearby. As a kid, Rex had this weird sixth sense. He could tell how I was feeling or know what I was doing even when he wasn't there. It's was a nice feeling somehow, like I could never be alone. No matter how far apart or how many years passed us by. It was just the two of us again.

"Sis, I'm glad you're alive."

I didn't quite understand what he meant until I realized that the tunnel ordeal had been splashed repeatedly on the prime time news.

"I'm afraid that we left things on bad terms the last time we saw each other. I didn't want to make the mistake of not saying hello to you in all these years and something happens where I never get the chance again."

Us talking felt no less surreal.

"Are you still trying to understand the mysteries of universe?" he asked.

"If you're asking whether I'm still in grad school or not; the answer is yes."

"Can we meet up and catch up, like old times."

I felt extremely frustrated with how casual he phrased that. *Like old times?* I dug my hands into my pocket to hide my clenched fist. I had gotten so angry that it was manifesting into the deepest part of my psyche and adrenalizing my nerves. Whatever, animosity or grudges I felt for my brother, I had to let them go. The two of us were literally all that we had. The last two left of the Oupary family. Hating him would only make it worse and it would change the fact that—no matter what—we are still family.

Callum Morrissey

"IT'S TIME WE START taking our new found...powers seriously," I said after taking another sip of water.

"I mean we're all-powerful-beings for God sakes. It's time we started acting like it," I added.

Esabelle tilted her head at me. Without a word, she knocked our wrists together. I jumped back at the glinting metal forcing itself free from our bracelets. This time instead of being scared out of my wits, I couldn't hold in my own laughter.

Esabelle winked at me. "Hmm, something tells me I'm starting to get the hang of this."

She pushed me in the chest; separating us.

No doubt its weird having a chunk of metal clamped down hard on your wrists. If we wanted to get the hang of these things, we would have to try different tactics and see what fits. At least, that's the best plan I could think of.

That made Esabelle smile even wilder.

"Different tactics, huh?" she grinned.

Esabelle knocked me down hard on the floor. When I looked into her eyes, they were hard to read. She had the look like she could actually impale me or maybe even worse. I had serious doubts of what might happen next. Esabelle giggled hammering her wrist on top of mine again. This time she fell on top of me.

I looked up at her. "I guess this is what the term 'happy accidents,' is referring to." I muttered.

Esabelle's cheeked curled into a mischievous grin.

"Accident? What makes you think this was an accident?"

I couldn't help myself; I was madly infatuated with this woman. I rose up from the floor and spun her quickly around just as fast she pivoted to the right of me, unhooking us from each other again and ran all the way to the other side of the room.

"I've got an idea," I shouted as I came to a stop. Then I bent over, panting and grabbing my knees. Esabelle looked at me strangely, still standing in the middle of her bedroom. She had a nice bedroom too. A beautiful aqua-green with paintings of white daisies on her walls. For as tough as she acted, I never would have figured her to be the type to have a soft spot for Mother Nature.

"I want you to run as fast as you can from that end, and I'll run as fast as I can from this end. I would like to call this little exercise…target practice," I said.

I was surprised how easily I managed to get her to take part in this. We didn't talk about how any of this might actually get us killed simply because we didn't know what we're doing. Whatever happened after we hit each other at full speed could have been tragic. But that's the risk we must take when training to save the world.

"One," I called holding up a single finger.

"Two."

Esabelle crouched forward. The tip of her tongue stuck out of the left corner of her lips.

"THREE!"

For a few moments, you couldn't hear anything except for two people's socks striking the carpet with mad force. Then, with only a few feet in between us I reached out my arm. Esabelle matched my speed as she stuck hers out too. *Are we really doing this right now?* I thought. When we collided with each other, our bodies spun in a circle while connected at the wrist. We twirled and twirled as if we both got sucked into the center of a gigantic whirlpool. She smiled at me, laughing hysterically the entire time.

If this happened back in that hidden palace where the Silver Cannabis ambushed us, we would have probably gotten ourselves beheaded or some other extremely painful outcome. But none of that mattered right now, Esabelle and I were having fun. Her back hit the end of the bed with a hard flop. My eyes traced every feature of her face, whatever the significance of how all of this started, it didn't matter anymore. I wanted Esabelle and she wanted me.

I yanked my arm free from the bracelet link and then kissed her on her lips. Even if I wanted to stop kissing her, I wouldn't be able to, it was just impossible not to. I couldn't focus on anything else.

"Go to the gala with me," I told her. Esabelle simply hugged me and whispered "Yes…well maybe, we shall see," then she nuzzled against my shoulder.

Soliel Oupary

THE GLOWING MARKS are growing. All I can do is sit and stare at the marks as I unfurl a napkin from the table and place it in the center of my lap. Palace sat on the other side of the table, topping off my near empty wine glass. I had a puzzled look on my face. Everyone was dressed sharp and dapper. Palace had gotten one of the most coveted reservations in the city. By all accounts I should be happy that he's taken our…well whatever you would call us to the next level. I didn't know how to tell him about what was really happening underneath my sleeves.

We had spent so much time working through my fears of becoming some sort of monster because of the prophecy of Nubara. So, why of all days of days did this have to worsen now? Even though Ashley was the only one who I know of that could see all the sacred markings, that didn't mean that they might not evolve somehow. It's been happening for so long already, only time would tell if it would happen again.

"Don't even try to deny it…"

Palace didn't even bother to pretend that I wasn't feeling upset. Not that it wasn't hard to see. It was most likely written all over my face.

"It's nothing," I pushed back.

"It's never nothing with you."

"Do you think this dinner is too much too soon?" he asked sipping on his glass of wine.

"Never. What I'm feeling doesn't have anything to do with you."

By the look on his face, I immediately knew that was the wrong thing to say. He gave me that look most people give when they think that they've reached the end of their rope with you. Like there's absolutely nothing they could do now because I was simply too damaged to be worth the trouble.

"Ok," I finally fessed up.

"A-ha! I knew something was wrong."

Not something many things. I thought.

There was no way I was going to tell him the whole truth, I had to only tell him just a small part.

"My brother, Rex, he um….called me this morning."

"That's unusual?" Palace asked.

"We haven't said a single word to each other since we were children."

He looked at me a little differently now. I couldn't really describe it, except that I could tell he knew that I wasn't OK.

"I wish you would have reached out to me earlier, I would have made this a date for four. "

"It's fine."

"What did he want?"

"He wants to see me sometime soon. Too soon," I replied. Palace had a knack of facing all of his problems head on. Surely, I drove him crazy with all of my second guessing and general misunderstandings.

"You need to see him. This isn't even really a problem. It sounds like you're afraid of seeing him, especially after how long it's been since you've seen him but he is your closest family." Palace replied.

Palace has studied me well. I did intend on making amends at some point with Rex. It's just that bridging the gap gets difficult after you've gotten set in your ways about somebody. Rex and I had been separated for so long that I had gotten used to making him this distant relative. So distant, that it felt like I grew up alone.

"You could invite him here? That will make things a little easier. Less pressure. If anything goes wrong, I'll be here." Palace got up from his chair and moved behind me.

"No matter what happens, Soliel. I promise. You can always count on me."

Ashley Boylan

I'LL ADMIT, TAKING THE Queen Marietta's diary behind everyone's back wasn't one of my brightest ideas. Dr. Michaels…I mean Robert made it that much easier when he took up the position at the museum. I took the book with me into kitchen while drinking a glass of red wine. Robert had gotten totally obsessed with the mystery of the map, hoping to find the tiniest morsel of a clue on its pages. He would spend roughly most of his nights examining the pages under a powerful microscope to examine if there were any sort of invisible inks or dyes.

He would even go as far as carbon dated the pages. What he wanted was to see if those pages were actually truly of another world. Turns out, that all the tests Robert performed were inconclusive. However, when I looked down at the page, I saw blue lines lighting up the page, just like the ones on my arm. The light faded in and out, and that's when I had an epiphany. What if the two lockets we found are a part of a bigger puzzle?

What if they could only reveal two parts of a much bigger picture? I quickly pulled open a drawer shaking free the two lockets that had the strange symbols that no one in our group had seen before. I placed both lockets down right next to the journal and that's when I saw it. I wasn't sure whether it would really work but it was worth a shot. *Does this have some connection with my doppelganger? The Auracle?* I wondered.

Everyone else could pretend all they liked, but I wanted to know the truth. If there's a mystery, then I want to solve it. If there's an unanswered question, I need to find the answer. I don't know any other way to live. Maybe that's why I could see how Robert was driving himself a little crazy. He tends to have more of a personal attachment when it comes to his research.

I'm cold and impersonal, nothing like the Ashley most of my colleagues recognize. I whipped out my camera again, took a photo of the map and cross-referenced it with the New York City map. It didn't direct us underground as I previously thought, but instead the map from the back of Marietta's diary overlapped with the narrow pathways of central park. At the very end of West and 86th Street, I noticed that there were very light blue marks, just like the ones marking our arms. It glowed strongly on that street, and it must have wanted me to find it.

It was the only clue I needed. After seeing that, I grabbed my coat. Even though, I knew my mentor would advise me against it, I still decided to go check out the place alone. The buzz of my cell phone on my coffee table caught my attention. Feeling impatient, I picked up.

"How did you get my number?" I asked.

I could almost see Curtis smiling over the phone.

"Need a study partner for the exam? You free?" Curtis asked.

"Sort of busy, I've got other plans?"

"The plot thickens…plans? Like what?"

"The kind that isn't any of Curtis' business," I snapped.

"You're not going to do what I think you're going to do."

"You think?" I teased.

"It's that diary, isn't it? Were you seriously thinking about doing it on your own?

I wanted to end the conversation right there, the last thing I needed was Curtis' dead weight yammering in my ear the whole time.

"You better invite me," Curtis told me. "Or, I'll tell the Dr Michaels."

"You wouldn't…"

"Oh, I very much would," Curtis replied.

I wasn't sure whether he was joking or kidding but I couldn't take the risk. I wanted to do this on my own, even if I had to have the big mouth, Curtis Anderson tag along.

"By the way, who came with you to the dance?" Curtis asked slyly.

I didn't understand how Curtis could feel comfortable asking me this in the middle of the showroom.

"No one," I replied.

"Well, that's perfect because then we can meet up with each other."

None of this was at all what I was expecting when I picked up Curtis' call.

"O...k..." I replied.

I didn't know whether I was saying yes or whether I was just saying what Curtis wanted to hear, I was just so confused. Curtis and I couldn't stand each other at all. I was speechless at the randomness of all of this? I'm a smart girl, and I've dated here and there, but I draw the line at dating classmates. There was something that compelled me to break my own rules.

Callum Morrissey

I COULDN'T TAKE MY EYES off of her. Her red hair was pinned delicately in a bun on top of her head. She wore one of my favorite polo shirts as she danced to the music playing in my living room. She looked like a completely different version of Esabelle; completely opposite of the one I first met on the subway train. I couldn't even find the words to describe her right now. She threw me off balance in a certain way, like no woman has ever done before. It was the same feeling I had when we first saw the vision, while standing side by side in the field.

As she turned, a red glowing light emanated through the tips of her fingers.

Can anyone else see this? I thought.

The red light kept spreading and the whole time, I felt a prickling in my skin. When I looked down at my arm wearing the immovable bracelet, I discovered my fingertips also began to glow. There was no question now that Esabelle met for a reason that day on the subway train. That was the day my life changed and I'll never forget this night as long as I live.

Staring at Esabelle was like staring at the only light in the room. I admit, these thoughts were heavily clouded by my emotions, but when I think about the day we met, there's no way we only met by chance. I have even been thinking about all the small coincidences that happened that day. Why is it that Esabelle and I specifically ran into each other?

There was obviously something beyond simply happenstance that brought the two of us together.

Esabelle swished in my direction, pulling herself close to me. Our fingertips touched and the latent power intensified. Then I held her gently in my grasp and dipped her backwards. Esabelle scarcely looked away from my gaze.

Soliel Oupary

I ROSE UP FROM MY BED at the sound of banging on my door. After I brushed my hair out of eyes, I darted to my front door. When I looked through the peep hole, I couldn't believe who I saw. I swung the door open slowly and allowed her in. She was a small woman, bundled up in a heavy coat yet still trembling; she rushed in through my door as soon as it was wide enough for her to pass through.

"Carrie, what are you doing here? Where's Rex?" I asked.

I had only met Carrie once, the day after my brother got married, but that was ten years ago.

"If you don't help me, your brother will be dead," she insisted.

After I shut the door, I helped her out of her coat.

"I'm surprised he's alive. He called me one day out of the blue and expects things to be like old times."

"He's hard up, Soliel. Rex fell into playing high stakes poker and has several thousands in gambling debts. And now it's time to pay up."

"Why do you think I want anything to do with my brother?"

Carrie exhaled as she sat on my couch.

"Because you're family."

Great, I thought. *Emotional Blackmail.*

"Carrie, I...I'm running late for my class. Your welcome to stay here, I won't be long & then we can continue our conversation. Is that alright?"

She looked over at me & nodded her head in agreement.

I then grabbed my bag, coat & keys & left. Slamming the door behind me I stood there for a minute or so and suddenly felt that anger that kept me warm in the Arctic. That loneliness that frustration of having the worlds burden on my shoulders.

Then I brushed it off and left before I got late for class.

Soleil Oupary

ALL OF US LEFT OUR LECTURE, Robert waited for us out in the courtyard as Curtis, Ashley, and our other classmates left the auditorium.

"Robert" I shouted. He was standing there with a smile on his face. I hadn't seen him since everything that happened in the subway. He had spent so much time at the Natural History Museum, allowing his brother to take over most of his courses.

"How's the new position?" I asked.

"I'm going a lot less crazy. That's the biggest change. It's good, exactly what I needed."

Several minutes later, Ashley approached.

"Is the exhibit getting ready for public view?" she asked.

Robert smiled. "That's actually why I'm here."

Neither of us knew what he would say next. Tickets to the Winter Premier Gala were the most coveted tickets in all of New York City. There's no way even Dr Michaels could score such hard to obtain tickets.

"The thing is this job has many perks. One of them is some of the best tickets in town."

"No Way!" Ashley interrupted him before Robert had a chance to finish. Curtis then looked over her way to make sure Ashley kept her end of the bargain. Ashley intentionally kept her eyes down. I thought more about whether Palace would be interested in taking me to the gala. I had been so cold recently. He's been nothing but a saint for supporting me. Most people probably couldn't stand even being in the same room with me, given how I've been moping around. I was just finding it hard to cope. A brief chill of unease rippled through me. I figured it was only nerves.

Ashley Boylan

CURTIS FOLLOWED ME as I headed off to my next class. I sped up, hoping that I would leave him far behind but it didn't stop Curtis from slowing down his pace.

"How long are you going to keep running away from me?" he asked.

"What do you want? To rub it in?" I asked. "Is it not bad enough that you're blackmailing me for a date?"

"Well, since I am black mailing you for a date, I thought we should get to know each other a little better. So, tell me. Who is Ashley Boylan?"

"I'm an overworked grad student who just learned only a few weeks ago that she's a part of some grand legacy that pits the darkest corners of the cosmos against the fate of humanity."

Curtis shrugged. "Okay, enough about you. Now, I'll tell you about how awesome I am?"

"Are you really this obnoxious?" Ashley asked.

"I'm an undergrad who skipped out on medical school because I was more interested in finding the answers to the greatest secrets of humanity and the universe. It's why I applied to Rolling Hill's anthropology program."

Honestly, I was a little shocked thinking that maybe Curtis wasn't the annoying privileged smart-ass that I pegged him as.

Soliel Oupary

CARRIE WAS STILL SITTING heavily distraught in my living room when I got back and I was still having trouble with even the thought of having anything to do with my brother. After how he had treated me, he didn't deserve any help from me. Part of that was always my problem. It was hard for me to forgive people, even my own family.

Out of the corner of my eye, I noticed my blue scars flaring up around my elbow.

My eyes followed the rippling line up my body which was immediately intensified by a terrible pain.

"God!" I shouted.

The pain not only shot up my arms, but spread through the rest of my body as well. I collapsed hard on the floor, I had lost total control of my shivering body. I heard the muffled footsteps of Carrie running into my kitchen, my arms and legs trembled violently, it felt as if I was having a seizure.

"Soliel!" Carrie screamed not sure of what to do. Quickly, she reached for the phone to call 911 but for some reason the phone would not dial out. My lips parted and a blue energy burst free. Blue veins zigzagged all across my face. I was slowly losing myself; becoming someone else or something else. I started thinking differently, feeling differently, seeing things differently.

Carrie approached me from behind when my body stopped moving. She knelt down low and turned me over so she could see my face. Carrie gasped, not knowing if she looked at me or a monster. I rose up. My eyes were glowing blue and crackling with a power that I've never felt before. I turned and spoke.

"I am Lunati."

Chapter 15

I dialed three times now—still no answer. Here I stood all dolled up in pearls wearing a black sequined dress. In my free hand, my heels dangled on the ends of my fingers. I exhaled and dialed again

"C'mon...C'mon pick up!"

Carrie, my sister-in-law stood behind me with an eager look in her eyes. Her fingers were interlaced and she stood completely still, hoping for a voice to pick up on the other line.

"That's his number. I'm sure of it. Just look at the address—it's maybe a block away from the opera house in the city. You could easily walk there in no time. I don't know what's there, but it's all I have," Carrie whispered.

I shook my head. "Carrie, you know I'd try a couple more times if I could. But it's almost 9:00 and Palace is waiting for me downtown. He's been planning this for weeks and..."

Carrie backed away and sat stoically on the couch.

"I understand," she replied. "Just please. Take this with you."

Carrie folded the address and stuck it into my small clutch purse.

My heels fell on the floor with the thunderous clack just before I slipped in my toes.

"Now, it'll be awhile before I get back. So, don't worry about waiting up," I told her while shuffling my shawl around my shoulders. Carrie didn't say a word. She only pulled her legs up underneath her lap and then stretched out on the couch. Just as I slipped through the door, I took one more look behind me. By now, Carrie had her back turned and facing me.

I exhaled again, bowed my head and shut the apartment door.

Boy, that was a close one, I thought as I hastily left the scene. Carrie could have sworn I said to her that I was Lunati and that my eyes were glowing blue. I convinced her that my eyes were the result of a reflection of a car driving by and as for the words I muttered, it was just me saying I am losing it as in fed up with Rex's antics. That seemed to convince her after a while. I was worried that I could be losing myself to my alter ego, without knowing it. The thought started to frighten me but intrigue me as well. Lunati was a strong and fearless warrior of Nubara; I on the other hand, was the complete opposite.

Palace greeted me with a smile as he grabbed me into his arms, I didn't really know what to feel. Carrie waited alone, back in my apartment without any answers to the where about of her husband, my brother. The thought still weighed heavy on my mind too. Besides the drama happening here, another drama was taking place hundreds of miles away. My best friend, Shoba Ali, had to leave suddenly last night after everything had been going so well with her mother. She got a call during the night informing her that she suffered a cardiac arrest and went into a deep coma. The doctors are not sure when she will wake up from it.

We didn't even get to see each other to say goodbye. All I got was a late-night phone call from the airport only minutes before Shoba would fly away back to London. So, a lot of things were on my mind and I was just trying to figure out how to handle them all without going insane.

"Is everything okay," Palace asked.

I smiled. "Not if we don't hurry and get to our seats," I said dodging his question.

Palace grinned even wider. "It's a special production of L'Orfeo by Monteverdi. Got a pair of the best seats in the house. Balcony seats."

The two of us walked arm in arm up the stairway leading to the balcony. Just at the top of the stairs, an attendant stood by a velvet curtain. He nodded and bowed and pulled back one of its sides. Palace let me through first, and I shuffled into my seat. The musicians were already sitting in the small room underneath the stage.

"There's something else to tell you," Palace told me.

Just then, the lights dimmed and Palace's face slowly disappeared into the darkness. The actors immediately filled the stage as the sounds of violins and piano resonated through the theater. To be honest, going to an opera would never be my first choice. But Palace loved being cultured and despite my reservations about the strange bellowing voices and colored tights, it was actually quite entertaining.

A noise vibrated from Palace's pocket.

I leaned over his shoulder. "Hey, don't you know to turn that thing off?"

"It's important. My investors are calling about this business venture we've been discussing for the past couple of months—I got to take this. Do you mind if I..." Palace said, pointing back to take a step behind the curtain.

"Sure, I'll wait right here."

Palace was careful to maneuver through the couple sitting right next to us. As I sat there, I reached in my purse to look for a piece of gum. I needed something to keep my mind from worrying about my brother Rex. He made his choice to get in with the wrong crowd. Why should I have to go rescue him? Especially since he only contacted me for the wrong reasons.

As I dug in my purse, something cut my finger.

"Ouch!" I exclaimed underneath my breath and then sucked my finger in my mouth. When I open my purse wider, I saw the sheet of paper that Carrie had given me with the address. *You're not really going to do this? Are you, Soleil?* I asked myself. Where did the address lead anyway? There was only one way to know. Palace was still on his phone in the hallway, which meant I had to find another way to exit. Another attendant stood in the aisle. I shuffled out of my seat and approached him.

"Excuse me sir. Where's the nearest bathroom? " I asked.

"Yes, there are two. One is through the curtain and down the hall, the other is behind me but only employees of the opera house are allowed back there, it's a restricted area.

"I am so sorry it's just I really have to go," I insisted. To make myself seem even more dramatic, I held tightly on my arms and tap danced right in front of him. The attendant looked worried.

"Fine," he said, hoping that I wouldn't make a mess where I was standing. "Follow me."

I made sure to leave my shawl over my chair so Palace wouldn't get worried. He led me down a narrow pathway where the actors escape to change costumes between sets.

"The bathroom is straight ahead. You can't miss it. Be quick, all right. My job's on the line," he said and then turned back down the pathway.

I rushed forward, moving through the crowd of actors and then exiting through the back door.

Curtis Anderson

She can't see a thing. I snickered to myself. *Very Good* said Curtis all smugly.

Ashley shambled forward with her arms stuck out, feeling her way through the hallway.

"You better not be leading me over a cliff!" Ashley said still taking careful and deliberate steps.

"Well, now that you mention it..." I pretended to consider.

Ashley punched me in the shoulder. "Curtis I'm not joking." She laughed.

I wondered if she could feel the cool breeze blowing against her skin. I took careful steps behind her, still giving her enough room to find her own way. Ashley felt along her side to notice there no longer were any walls.

"Just stay still," I said.

She allowed her arms to relax at her sides. Carefully, I approached her from behind and untied the blindfold from her face. Ashley blinked a few times to adjust her vision, and then she gasped.

"Okay, this is totally unreal!" She said gazing at the dazzling lower Manhattan skyline with all of its life and twinkling lights. Although the sky was clear, you could hardly see the stars.

"You really amaze me..." I told her.

"I know, I'm a great girl, but I'm nowhere near as great as this view! I never expected this in my wildest dreams," Ashley said moving closer to the railing. The two of us shared a treasured moment on the rooftop of the apartment building where I live. I wanted to do something special to show how my much former enemy—now my girlfriend— meant the world to me.

Anyone who knew us, in our classes, would never believe the two of us got together. Ashley loves being competitive in understanding how everything worked mathematically. I, myself, had a competitive streak of my own and that's why we always butted heads. Not to say that we don't fight, because we still get into arguments every now and again, but no matter what happens we both have each other's back.

I invited her to sit down to the table that I prepared with two empty wineglasses and bucket of ice with a bottle of white wine in the center. "Go on, take a seat." I urged.

Ashley looked up at me out of the corner of her eye, a little apprehensive about what might happen next.

"No, it's not what you think this is. It's not a marriage proposal. So no pressure," I reassured her.

Ashley smiled awkwardly. Although both of us are in grad school, neither of us are ready for marriage.

"Okay then, so what's the fancy romantic dinner on the rooftop for then?"

"It's for state survivors—you and me. And for you taking me and giving me a chance."

Ashley seemed dumbfounded, it was clear that she couldn't believe this was happening. A part of me guessed that so many of our classmates and colleagues saw her as the tomboy brainiac instead of this intelligent woman who could be so much for someone else.

"What are we waiting for? Pop the thing open," Ashley said grabbing the bottle of wine out of the ice. That's when I noticed that after I set everything up earlier this evening, I forgot the bottle opener in my car.

"I'm sort of having a crisis," I told her.

"Why? What happened?"

"I forgot the bottle opener." I chuckled. "It's just like me to leave it in the car. It'll only take me a second to get it."

"Way to ruin a party just as it's begun..." She told me teasing.

Ashley Boylan

THIS WHOLE EXPERIENCE was something new to me. Not just because it's Curtis, but because it's so rare that I get dressed up and go anywhere—even if it's a roof. It's obvious Curtis tried to make this night something special between us. I set down the bottle of wine and looked over the balcony railing. In the distance I saw something moving around. It could be anything, a stray dog or a homeless man seeking shelter; in any number of possibilities here in New York. But something about this figure gave me an eerie feeling.

Whoever it was standing on the other building rooftop, was wearing a ragged trench coat and was staring directly at me. And in the blink of an eye, the figure strung an arrow to a bow and was aiming it in my direction. I froze, half in fear and half in shock and the only action I could do to defend myself was to cup my hand over my mouth. I wondered if this was how I was going to die. Alone on a rooftop with an empty wine glass, the figure disappeared in one swift motion but I did manage to catch a glimpse a tightly wrapped bun on the top of their head.

"Got it!" I heard from behind. Curtis rushed back up to my side, holding the wine opener in his hand.

"Now, where were we?" He whispered against my ear.

He popped open the cork and a soft hiss escaped from that bottle as air touched the aged liquid for the first time in years. I took the two glasses and handed him one. Curtis was careful to pour the wine slowly in each of our glasses.

"Cheers to another many more years of laughter and learning," Curtis said giving a toast. Our glasses clinked.

My eyes scanned the skyline again. "It's amazing, isn't it?"

"Not nearly as amazing as you," Curtis said and then pressed his lips against mine. In my head, this was all kind of cheesy, but his heart was in the right place. When he kissed me, all of my nagging questions about the girl with the bow and arrow melted away. That didn't matter now. I was trying to focusing on being in the moment, but I couldn't get the thought of that girl out of my head, and I want to know who she was.

After all, what kind of researcher would I be if I didn't investigate? Okay, I'll admit it. Maybe worrying about this now was not the right time, being that I was on a date and all. It's just that something about that girl seemed very familiar. There was something about the weapon she carried; I know I've seen it before. I've seen them when we are trapped in the tunnels. It's perfectly rational to think that I was hallucinating. I did have a bit more to drink than I intended. And, I did feel slightly queasy from it all. But I'd rather know for sure.

Maybe I should tell Curtis. That way I don't have to worry about lying to him later.

"While you were getting the wine opener from the car, I saw something."

Curtis raised a brow. "What do you mean you saw something?" I looked over to the rooftop and pointed to where I first spotted the girl.

"I could have sworn I saw a girl standing there wearing this long coat, but even stranger, she carried the same bow and arrow Soleil used in the tunnels when fighting the Centaur."

From the expression on Curtis's face it was obvious this wasn't something he was ready to talk about again, at least not just yet. Then again, neither was I, but the curiosity pushed away all my doubts.

"Sounds to me that what you're really saying is that you want to leave here and go on some kind of witch hunt?" Curtis asked.

I nodded slowly. "That's sort of the gist of it. Yeah, sure."

Without saying a word, Curtis grabbed our coats and handed me mine.

"Let me tell you something. You're crazy, but I'll go with you."

Even though I tried my hardest to hide the smile spreading across my face, I couldn't help but feel like Curtis had my back through thick and thin. The two of us traveled together down the stairwell and then to the elevator, which we took to the lobby. Curtis ran ahead, I looked at the building one more time. The windows were all broken and blacked out. It seemed that no one has lived here for decades. I felt hesitant, and then I ran forward trying to catch up from behind.

Lunati

I SAW EVERYTHING FROM a crack in the door. I haven't seen him in years, but I recognized his face sure enough. It was Rex. My brother.

Rex sat slouched over in the chair leading onto one side. His wrists and ankles were tied to the legs and arms. His eye was all bruised up, purple and black. Blood gushed from his lower lip and coating his teeth giving them a dark red tint. He could barely speak without mumbling his sentences.

"If you just listen to what I'm saying..." Rex then made a gurgling sounds and spat out a stream of blood. "I don't have the money yet. I just need a few weeks..."

I saw that there were four other men standing in the room but I couldn't make out their faces through the crack. I noticed that the one in the middle had rested his hands on his belt as he approached my brother. *He must be the leader.* I thought

"Now now Rex. The time for negotiation has ended. Your time is up. How would you feel if you were nice in enough to loan some poor desperate soul some money and they pissed it away playing blackjack in some low-rent district of the city? Hmm. It really doesn't matter, because you see I always get what is owed to — one way or the other."

One of his goons interrupted. "—with interest."

The man in the center chuckled. "You know, you got a good point there Tommy. You definitely got a good point."

The four men in the room broke out in laughter. Judging by the way Rex lowered his head, it must have made him feel five times smaller.

"Well, Alfred. You're not going to get shit from me!"

Alfred, the thug in the middle, didn't answer right away. He just stood there, letting Rex sweat. Then he lowered his hands to the buckle on his belt and he un-notched one end and then slowly yanked it from one side. I followed it as he cleared the belt through the loops on his pants. Alfred took a single step backwards, lifted his arm in a cocked position above his head and then slammed the belt down buckle end first straight across my brother's face. I watched in horror as my brother cheeked ripped open send a thick splatter of blood soaring through the air and landing inches from the door I was crouched behind. I felt a sudden rage well up inside me as my brother spit out his two front teeth along with another stream of blood that pooled out of his mouth. *I'm going to kill them!*

"Don't think for a second I will kill you," Alfred said through clenched teeth. "The next thing, and the only thing, I want to hear out of you is where is my money. And if you don't have my money, where can I get my money?"

Rex sat there, tied to a chair broken, whimpering with a gaping hole in his cheek, the flesh was still attached and hanging down, flapping every time Rex moved his head up to breath. He clearly had no answers for Alfred. Alfred was out of patience and meant to kill my brother with the next blow. I couldn't let that happen. He swung back his arm in the cocked position again; ready to slam the belt right across the other side of Rex's face. He brought his arm down in another violent descent towards my brother's tattered face but in mid-swing, a swooshing noise cut through the room. There was a slight hint of heat and a distinctive smell of burnt flesh filled the air. A shocked Alfred looked down to his hand a smoldering stump were it previously was mere seconds ago. There was no blood; it was as if something so hot had passed through seared the wound shut instantly.

"Boss? Are you okay? Oh my god look?" One of his goons asked while pointing to the wall.

Alfred was still piecing together the events that left him handless and when he turned his head to the wall, he saw what took his hand. His belt was pinned high on the wall by an electric arrow blazing multitude shade of blue swirling around each other with an occasional white light in the middle; it gave off an immense heat. They immediately drew their guns and aimed it frantically by swinging it left and right. Another bright blue energy arrow streaked through the sky and they all aimed directly at it. But before they could pull the trigger, the arrow split into several smaller electrified arrows and split off in all directions around the room. Gunfire pieced the air and then suddenly stopped. Leaving nothing but an eerie silence.

Rex struggled to lift his head to see what happened and why it was suddenly so quiet.

He then noticed each of the arrows had burned straight through each of the goons' hearts including Alfred. Ribs and muscle were completely disintegrated as ll four bodies lay on the cold cement floor fumbling around in jerking movements as if they were having seizures. That's when I stepped into the room, and it was almost like I was seeing a ghost.

Rex must've heard my footsteps because he looked up too.

"I don't have any money alright estimation point" my brother said probably halfway delirious and half blind as well since both his eyes were almost completely swollen shut.

"Don't worry; it's not money I want. I'm here to save you."

I quickly made my way to my brother and cut his restraints free using the tip of one of my arrows and since he lacked the strength to hold himself up, his body fell limp into my arms. I held him for a minute, stroking his blood soaked hair out of his battered face.

"Who are you?" He asked it was clear, they probably had them tied down here for days.

His lips were dry and split and he looked like he hadn't eaten in days. They must have tortured him for several days prior. Besides the gaping gash on his face, he also had scars raking up and down his arms as well as small burns from cigarette butts.

"I'm the person that's going to kill you if you keep making these stupid mistakes," I said. My face was still mostly concealed by the shadows, and even if I did step into the light and reveal myself, he was too out of it to what reality was and what wasn't.

Curtis Anderson

ASHLEY STILL HADN'T CAUGHT UP yet but I saw a single light flooding through the crack of a slightly open door about 10 feet ahead. I walked slowly, being careful that I didn't splash any puddles in my path or make any noise as I stepped closer to the room.

"Do you see anything?" I heard from behind me.

I held my hand out to Ashley, signaling her to stop.

"You need to keep your voice down. We don't know who's around or who might be looking..." I warned her.

Ashley nodded and did as I said immediately. She moved in close to my left shoulder and we both approached the door. The same girl in the trench coat that Ashley spotted earlier was sitting on the floor cradling a man who was practically covered from head to toe in blood.

"If we don't do something, she's going to kill him!" Ashley whispered harshly.

I couldn't tell what was going on, but as I looked past the mysterious figure, I saw that there were four dead bodies sprawled out in a circle on the floor with huge smoking holes where their chests used to be. If the girl in the trench coat did this, then there is no telling what else she was capable of. Before I could make a decision, Ashley burst into the room and I had no choice but to follow her. The girl in the trench coat looked up alarmed and in a blur grabbed something from her back pocket and of her trench coat and hurled it at the floor. A black object followed by a blinding bright flash exploded up from the floor at our feet. A smoke bomb!

I held my hand in my chest, hacking and coughing, trying to get some air. I saw no sign of Ashley anywhere.

"Ashley!" I called.

Ashley Boylan

THE THICK HAZE OF SMOKE made it impossible to see anything in the room. I knew Curtis must have been lost somewhere back there. But I had to find the crazy girl in the trench coat. Moving much faster, I tried to reach out and grab the woman's arm before she can escape the shadows. I dove blindly through the smoke and extended my arms as far out as they could go.

"Gotcha!" I cried as grabbed a hold of the strange woman's wrist, but it was a useless attempt. She simply tossed me to the side and I smacked hard against the cement wall at the far side of the room. As fought to catch my breath and get back to my feet, I looked up and saw her standing above me. The smoke had cleared and I could see her features now. Her eyes were an icy electric blue and in the center were her pupil should have been, was a swirling mass of energy changing from different shades of blue and intertwined with a warm white glow and every so often an arc of electricity would revolve around it. And I could hear it crackle. She had dark blue markings all over her skin that were somehow very familiar & her face seemed to illuminate brighter and darker the angrier she got. And she was pretty angry right now.

"Soleil!" I exclaimed, recognizing her face immediately.

With a strong shove, she pushed me back to the ground and scattered off in the opposite direction. The glowing bow she carried in her hands vanished in thin air until I noticed a blinking blue tattoo appear on her wrist. She ran through the darkness until I could no longer see her. The smoke was finally all cleared and I saw Curtis staggering around trying to find his way. I grabbed him by hooking my arm around his.

"You okay?" I asked.

"It depends what you mean by okay…" He replied.

Soliel Oupary

"HEY, SLEEPYHEAD!" Was the first sounds I heard as I slowly regained consciousness.

Then I jolted up from my seat and looked down at the stage and saw the actors giving their final curtain call and bowing to the audience.

"You mean it's over?" I asked

Palace smiled. "It's been over for the last ten minutes." *What* thought Soleil. *What happened to me? Was I passed out? Sleeping or something else entirely. How could I miss all of this?*

I have to admit I kind of felt like a jerk falling asleep during the last act of the play. As the other members of the audience began to leave, Palace helped me into my coat.

"Psst..." He whispered. "I just want to let you know, I drifted off on the second act."

As we started to leave, I wondered if that all was a dream. Maybe it didn't happen at all? One can only hope. One thing was certain, I was ready to get some rest and forget about the whole thing.

Ashley Boylan

CURTIS AND I HAD MADE IT OUT of the building along with the stranger who was now lying on the floor in a bloody mess. We called the police and soon after they arrived. I could hardly hear myself think due to the wailing sirens.

""That girl I saw... the one with smoke bomb..." I said.

Curtis shrugged. "What about her?"

"She was no stranger. She looks just like Soleil, except she had these strange blue eyes. And these weird tattoos and scars covering her body. Like the ones Soleil got after she touched that bow..."

"Unless Soleil has a twin, I can't see how that was her, unless you think her Nubarian side is taking her over? No offence Soleil is fragile and not so agile, you know what I am saying." Curtis said.

I just looked over at him. The thing was he was right. Even though the young girl looked, and behaved very much the same as Soleil would, they weren't the same person. Even though, logically, I knew I should approach Soleil about this. I mean I guess it would be a good idea to let her know that a blue skinned version of her with dark blue tattoos and strange blue eyes that generated electricity was running around the city burning holes in people with blue energy arrows. That's info that everyone should know. I mean I certainly would want to know. The problem with that notion was that I didn't want to accuse her of something she was innocent of. So, for now, I'll just keep this whole thing to myself until I know more.

Soliel Oupary

KNOCK. KNOCK.

I awoke to a loud banging at my door. At this time of night, I didn't usually give visitors and I wasn't too happy to be receiving any either. Palace rolled over to the side as I slipped out of the bed and made my way to the living room.

Knock. Knock.

The banging started again.

"You better have a damn good reason why you're knocking on my door this late at night!" I yelled.

Angrily, I unlocked the door and pushed back the deadbolt. My mouth started to move, but when I saw who it was I couldn't get a word out.

"Rex?"

He had finally come home. When he stepped out of the shadows, I could see terrible bruises all over his face which was covered completely in dried blood and there was a wicked hole in the side of is cheek that was beginning to puss.

"What the hell happened to you?" I shouted. "We need to get you to the hospital. That going to get infected!"

Rex ignored me and shuffled his way to my couch, barely able to speak or move.

"Got into a situation with some bad people... And they wanted to kill me tonight. Then out of nowhere, this girl— I don't even know what to call her. But she freed me and killed everyone in the room."

"Who was this girl?"

Rex sat back and relaxed on my couch. He then raked his fingers through his hair trying to think back to when he was tied up in the chair.

"It's going to sound crazy, I know. But she's different."

I've heard that more times that I care to admit. It seemed like everyone I've met in the last few months has been "different" in one way or another. That even included me.

"Different how? Tell me about this girl who rescued you?" I demanded, all of a sudden forgetting that I haven't seen my brother in years and now he finally shows up battered, bruised and barely alive.

Looking in his eyes, I could tell that Rex was trying hard to think back and remember what he had seen earlier.

"It is hard to say, but before I say anything, I want to let you know that I've been sort of heavily involved in the unreal…"

"Go on…" I replied. I didn't want to react too soon. Only because I knew that reality wasn't at all as it seemed. I learned that hard lesson when we were stranded in the tunnels.

"I think the girl that rescued me is a MIKO. It's a special form of human. A meta-human. And they're not like you and I," he said.

Yeah, you don't know the half of it. I thought to myself.

"Miko's are para-dimensional beings. I've sort of been studying occult — thinking I can find some cool spell that would give me a leg up at the craps tables. I've reading something about these girls. Or, these beings rather. They've got these powers that are sanctified in ways we don't understand. Some would say is holy and given to them by a higher power. I don't know anything about that. And that's really all I know. "

Callum Morrissey

A GIANT TEAR RIPPED THROUGH the dummy position near the wall.

"Arrghh!!!" Esabelle shouted as she attacked using her bracelet to rip through the dummy.

I still couldn't help but be amazed at how far we've gotten with our powers and controlling the bracelets.

"I think we need to try and go full force again," I suggested to Esabelle.

She looked away from me. And I knew why. Going full force meant in intensity that neither of us felt like we could handle alone.

"Remember were doing this as a team," I told her.

Esabelle nodded and agreed. Both of us walked back to the furthest wall. And then Esabelle took my hand into hers. Our metal bracelets protruded the sharp blades and then, together, we charged forward.

White feathers released and flew up in the air. Both Esabelle and I laughed.

Then she hooked her arm around my neck and looked up at me. The way she stared at me, I couldn't help but stare back. Our gazes locked in pure passion. I couldn't fight the urge to kiss her, any longer and I leaned forward and pressed my lips against hers and she responded by pressings hers against mine. I was ablaze with white hot intensity as I pulled down her jeans revealing her white cotton panties. She pulled at my pants and helped me out of my shirt pulling it over my head and then slowly removed hers. Teasing me and biting her lower lip. A lump was forming in my throat as I took her beauty in. I couldn't believe this was happening but I wasted no time thinking about that. I dove into the moment and took her in my arms and threw her on our bed. She then kissed me again and I turned out the light.

"Time for another battle. This time we will do this one together" I snickered as I stripped down to my boxers briefs. Esabelle giggled slightly and pointed at the pattern of stars on my boxers. I quickly removed that distraction by yanking them completely off and threw them at her and what she saw next left her speechless.........for once.

Soliel Oupary

I AWOKE IN PALACE ARMS. Both of our bodies were glazed in sweat, after having slept with each other for the first time since I moved in. It felt a little strange, knowing that my brother slept only a single floor underneath us. Still, I was relieved that he was home safe. I planned on calling Carrie first thing tomorrow morning and tell her the good news. Palace gave me a final kiss on the back of my neck before drifting off to sleep. I felt this stabbing pain on my side but then my thoughts went back to what Rex.

There seemed to be so many historical lores that I couldn't even keep them straight anymore. Then I lowered my hand down to where I felt the surgeon pain. I looked down and saw a deep purple bruise on my side. When I looked further up my torso I noticed there were even larger bruises mottling up and down my body.

Wait a minute? Was I the one who rescued Rex? No, it was not me but it was her. The other me... Lunati.

I couldn't believe it. And there's some sort of supernatural amnesia that causes me to forget. When I looked over to my drawer that was slightly pulled out, I noticed a blue light glowing faintly inside. I lifted out the necklace and lay it down on the floor so I could get a clearer idea of what was happening. A written message illuminated the floor in my handwriting but not in English.

Instead, it was written entirely in Nubarian. And of course, I couldn't really understand much of it. I was too tired to try to figure it out anyways. Palace twisted around and I panicked. I frantically gathered up the pendant and necklace in both of my hands. Then I dumped it back into the drawer. Naked, I slipped back under the covers and tried to drift to sleep.

When I woke up, I thought it was the morning but really it was late afternoon. I heard the post man drop something at my door. After securing my robe around my waist, I headed downstairs. Rex was still asleep on the couch, he refused to go the hospital but luckily, Palace has some medical experience and after a few shots of whiskey. Rex was numb enough for Palace to stitch his cheek back together. He even had some strong antibodies on hand to help fight infection, Rex lucked out big time. He would live but he would have a nasty scar, since he didn't get the proper treatment, but at least he won't have a hole on the side of his face forever.

I made sure I was quiet when I unlocked and opened the door. A single envelope lay at my feet, and I picked it up and immediately ripped it open. It read:

> You are cordially invited to the Grand Holiday Gala as distinguished guests.

Dr. Palace Palace Michaels & Soleil Oupary are to attend the gala as you are being honored for the once-in-a-lifetime discovery of Nubara.

Chapter 16

Soliel Oupary

Even though it was practically the most important night of our lives, the reporters still hounded us for a story. Palace, Callum, Esabelle, Ashley and I all arrived together in a rented town car. Through the tinted windows, I could see a wave of reporters camping out on the front steps of the New York Museum of Natural History. The anxiety I felt when I first was called to Palace's apartment was now flooding back to me.

"It's never enough for the soldiers..." Palace whispered under his breath.

"Robert said that everyone would be here tonight including the archaeology Society along with many big names in the science world." Ashley said.

"They might as well call this event after Pascal and Shaw, since this whole event would be a failure if it didn't have the brightest and best minds in science here at the Museum. Pascal and Shaw funded this whole shindig," Callum added. A strange thought surged through Palace's mind when Callum said those words. Pascal and Shaw funded this whole thing, yet they never stepped forward regarding the discovery or said anything about the subway incident. They always remained in the shadows, which made him wonder what they were up to.

You could tell they spent a handsome fortune, a pretty penny on everything. Giant spotlights waved in front of the stairway to the entrance of the Museum and all the guests arrived in the most expensive evening gowns and suits as they hurried out of the cold and into the main lobby. My friends and colleagues started gathering their things and prepared to leave the car.

Palace rested his hand on my shoulder. "It's not as scary as it looks…" He said trying to reassure me.

"Yeah, well. It's just something I'm going to have to get used to. Being harassed like this, now that we are the survivors, it's only going to get worse." I said. Everyone else was exiting the car first, holding steady as reporters swarm them from both sides. Palace grabbed my hand to make sure he wouldn't lose me.

I tried to be careful not to trip over the hem of my dress as I gathered the front and balled it up into my hands. We stepped quickly further and further up the steps until we reached the main entrance door. Callum was nice enough to hold the door open for Palace and I.

After about five excruciating minutes, we were all inside. We would have been in sooner if we weren't ambushed by the media.

Just as we thought it was all over, a barrage of microphones were pointed in our faces and before we even knew what was happening, we were being flanked by reporters who had been hiding out in the lobby and jumped up at the chance to interview us.

"Ms. Oupary! Can I please get a statement! Or, Ms. Oupary! Do you have an explanation of why only a handful of people escaped from a train crash that has killed hundreds?"

Palace rubbed both my shoulders, trying to keep me calm. "Don't listen to any of them. Don't talk to any of them." I knew he was right, because if I said anything, it would only lead to more questions. If you want to make it through this night, we have to make sure we stick to the same story. You have to be consciously reminded of a terrible time in your life, the light being punished for something or for some crime I didn't know I committed. When we finally made it into the grand hall, we were mesmerized by the scenery.

The music playing was classical and played at the perfect interval that you could hear every melodic note yet still hear the conversation of the person next to you. The people here were all wearing the fanciest attire I had ever seen. One outfit was probably worth ten times more than I make a year. All the super rich people were mingling and socializing amongst each other and since the reporters were not allowed in the main hall room, the atmosphere was a lot calmer and relaxing. Yet I still felt uneasy. I couldn't shake this overwhelming feeling. As if an unknown danger was lurking behind every corner, waiting for me to turn it, so it can strike.

The rest of our group scattered off in different directions. Palace grabbed me by the arm.

"You think we can talk a second?" He asked.

Even though he hadn't said anything yet, intuition was telling me that something was about to happen to feed my uneasiness.

"It's just I saw these text messages on your phone. And none of them are easily read in English. The last thing I wanted to do was come off like some jealous boyfriend. When I really want to know is this; are you still trying to study those artifacts we found in the tunnels?"

"Here, take the pendent and research it all you like."

Palace then showed me the pendant and it flashed quickly in my eyes, blinding me for a second.

"Damn, that's not what I meant to do. Are you okay?" He asked. My eyes fluttered open, but still everything in the room was a blur. Streaks of color swayed along the dance floor. Somehow the pendant didn't blind me, but made me see things in a different way.

My body started to feel intensely hot, and the glowing energy surged through all of my veins. I blinked my eyes much harder. And when I opened them again, they no longer wear brown but instead they were bright electric blue. That's when I knew, my old self had left my body and now I was my alter ego.

Lunati.

For whatever reason, Palace was barely paying attention and he didn't realize that the person he held in his arms wasn't me. At least not entirely. If anyone wanted to find me and I mean anyone from the other realm, they would have a hard time recognizing me when I looked like this.

"I can't say I'm not concerned that something might happen tonight," Palace said.

I gazed at him with my electric blue eyes. "No one would be idiotic enough to start a ruckus during one of the biggest events in the city."

Palace took my coat and handed it to the attendant.

"Let's hope you're right." He said.

Ashley Boylan

I NEVER THOUGHT I WOULD LIKE WEARING A DRESS, earrings or makeup. But I guess there's a first time for everything thought Ashley. Curtis and I shared some hors d'oeuvres and we already had our second glass of wine. But the night had just begun. I wasn't going to let a little supernatural mumbo-jumbo get in the way of enjoying our success.

"You see, this could be fun. Sure, we have to deal with reporters being on our backs, but at least we can dance," I told Curtis.

Curtis was a little more irritated than me. He had gotten sick of having his entire life splashed across the papers. And believe me; I understood just how frustrating that could be. But I'm not about to let any bottom feeding journalists ruin my evening. Not tonight! I twisted out of Curtis's arms and pressed my back against his chest.

Curtis widened his eyes.

"Someone's having a lot of fun," he said smiling.

"Life is short, Curtis. You got to learn how to have fun no matter what's going on around you," I told him as he wrapped his arms around my waist.

Then Curtis suddenly dipped me backwards making me giggle like a kid and accidentally stepped on my foot.

Curtis cringed. "Whoops, sorry about that…"

Callum Morrissey

"DON'T WORRY ABOUT IT, just come here…" I told Esabelle. She gave me one of those I'm-not-sure-if-you're-serious sort of looks.

"To be honest, it's very surprising that they're even dancing," she said while her red hair whipped about her face. Sometimes I wonder if I'm still somewhere sleeping and I haven't woken up yet. It just seems that someone like me doesn't deserve all this sudden happiness. I've spent so much of my time being a failure. Failure in my career, a failure in life and a failure in my relationships. Now that I finally met somebody who liked me just the way I am. I'm still unwilling to receive it. *What is wrong with me?* I thought.

I wanted to do something special for Esabelle. Even though she adored me as a lovable klutz, I still wanted to show her that I could be one of those cool romantic guys. And due to the events that happened over the winter, we never got a chance to celebrate as a couple. So I wanted to do something, even if it's a small something, I know she'll still love it.

"Is everything okay? You're sweating all over," Esabelle told me, wiping her finger tip against my forehead.

Okay, so I guess I was a little nervous. The thing I hate most about dating was buying gifts. I never knew if the gift I bought was the right choice. Even though people say it's the thought that counts, I didn't want to give her something that she would try to hide in the dark in her part of the closet.

"Callum, just go on give it to me. Don't think about it too hard," she reassured me. I knew she was being hones so I took a deep breath.

"I got it in here…" I said as I dug in the back pocket of my jacket. Then I pulled out a box with a red bow. Esabelle swiped the tendrils of her red hair behind her ears and looked at me with those piercing green eyes.

"Callum, you shouldn't have!" Esabelle exclaimed and then punched me hard in the shoulder, as she always did. She looked at me one more time before grabbing one end of the ribbon and pulling it free.

Then Esabelle furiously ripped open the box, throwing the red tissue paper aside. At the very bottom she found a small bottle cap with the name of her favorite indie band The Reapers.

"No you didn't! I used to listen to these guys when I was in high school. You know I was going through that 'angry no one understands me phase 'and I used to rock out to this while jumping on my bed after school," Esabelle said clutching the bottle cap in her palm.

I breathed a sigh of relief, thankful that she liked my gift.

Esabelle smiled widely and embraced me in her arms giving me what must have been a hundred kisses on each of my cheeks. She almost knocked my glasses off the end of my nose. In the midst of the volley of kisses, I had to readjust them to fit my face.

"Uh, I think I got a few smudges on your face," Esabelle said as she dug in her purse for her mirror." I jerked back when I saw my face in the mirror with at least twenty different lipstick smudges all over my face. Esabelle dutifully fished out her handkerchief and patted down my cheeks.

"Callum, I'm so happy I met you. Before you, I was meeting all the wrong type of guys. Just guys that would give me attention for my looks. But you— you love me for all that I am," she said before kissing me one more time on the lips.

"How could you have even remembered this? Given everything that was going on down in those tunnels, I can barely remember everything that's happened."

"Well, it's hard to forget anything about you," I told her and then held her face in my hand. It was a gentle and treasured moment we shared. I've never seen Esabelle like this. Even though she pretends to have a carefree exterior, she was really guarded on the inside. She guarded her secrets. She guarded her emotions. It was really hard to figure out. Anyway, it may be so special that I'm the one who made her feel as she could open up about who she was. For the first time in my life, I felt like my life had matured beyond being a helpless bachelor.

I felt like a man. Finally!

Soliel Oupary & Lunati

BETTY MCTAVISH ENTERED the Gala in style as she strutted in her transparent blue silk dress. I turned around and saw her making her way towards a few students from the team. It had been so long since we all came together in one place since classes were suspended after the events in the tunnel. It was nice to see all of my colleagues again.

We all cleaned up nicely. Even Robert looked very debonair. The only person that was missing now and someone that I thought I would most likely never see again, was my best friend—Shoba. She meant everything to me, and she could even be here on one of the biggest night of our lives. She deserves to be recognized too. If it weren't for Shoba, I never would have risked going much deeper in the cave and found the Emblem in the first place.

I would never be selfish enough, to tell Shoba to leave behind her mother just to come dancing with us. Even though we don't see each other very often, we haven't completely lost touch. I just called her last weekend and we still write each other letters. Usually, I tell her about everything that's going on. How things are going with Palace and how things are going with school. But I feel like I'm missing my most lighthearted half. Shoba was great about seeing the good in everything and allowing yourself to laugh no matter how sad she felt.

I needed that attitude more than ever now. Yet, I've been learning slowly on my own how to have fun.

Betty came over and greeted me.

"Can you guys believe this?" She asked looking all around the ballroom. Really, I couldn't. How could I ever have known that we would find the secret to Nubara?

We saw one of the directors of the Museum walk across the giant stage in the front of the room.

"Welcome everyone. Welcome. I hope you're enjoying your evening thus far. I just wanted to let you know that in about ten minutes we are going to have our distinguished guests speak about this groundbreaking discovery of Nubara. I simply want to give you guys' proper notice so you would know when to take your seats," the director said before leaving the stage.

"Woah, I guess we'll be up soon," Betty McTavish told me elbowing me in my rib.

The thought of having to give a speech made me feel queasy. The thought of getting on that stage and talking to a large crowd such as this completely terrified me. I froze with fear just thinking about seeing so many faces staring up at me.

Palace had bumped my shoulder. "She's just joking. No worries, the only person that is going to be giving a speech is my brother."

That was certainly a relief to hear. But even though my anxiety about having to speak in front of the crowd dissipated, I still had this twinge in my stomach. I clutched my stomach harder as more pain churned through my gut. It was more pain than anything I've ever experienced in my life. Without a doubt, I knew that this had something to do with Lunati.

I was sure of it.

It seemed that no matter what I did, I couldn't escape the connection that I have with Nubara. I thought that the less I thought about it, and then it would go away. The pain in my stomach proved me wrong. Lunati would have her way, whether I wanted it or not.

"I hear Dr Michaels is going to talk about how Nubara could change the face of humanity. Change everything that we thought impossible. It's like our research is no longer just some vague information in the textbook. Now, it's this real tangible thing that's going to advance us for the next thousand years," Betty finished.

I simply nodded my head, not really listening as the pain got too intense to ignore.

"Hey guys, I don't mean to be rude but I have to go powder my nose. I'll be right back," I said still holding my stomach and maneuvering through the crowd to the restrooms. *Powder my nose. Did I just say that? Do people still say that? Way to avoid suspicion Soliel,* I thought, ridiculing myself. I glanced quickly back, expecting the group to be following me or at least watching me but they were focused on the stage where Dr Robert Michaels was delivering his speech.

"Good evening, everyone," Dr Robert Michaels said as he started his speech.

Palace Michaels

ALL THE GUESTS HAD ALREADY made their way from the ballroom into the conference hall. Their evening gowns sparkled underneath a low lighting. Everyone who knew anything about physics and the molecular makeup of the universe sat in the audience of the presentation. I looked around for Soleil, but she still had not come back from the bathroom. I wondered if she was okay, but nevertheless, the show must go on. Plus it was New Years Eve, security everywhere. Nothing could go wrong. *At least I hoped.*

My brother strutted with the microphone in his hand and a giant screen was on display behind him. The crowd hung on his every movement, anticipating every word about how the discovery was made. There had never been a discovery this huge since the work of Stephen Hawking.

"What we had discovered over these past few months, is it that there is a dimensional connection between our world and a more ancient timeless world beyond—" Dr. Robert Michaels said. "Here there exist people with technology much more advanced than anything we have created today. The Novae Emblem we found would propel us light years ahead of modern science. Unfortunately, this discovery didn't come without its flaws. We had lost a few students along the way and the scars still haven't healed for those of us who have survived.

But those lives were not lost in vain. This is a huge step and will change the course for mankind in a huge way."

Then behind him an enormous picture taken from a highly powered telescope flashed on the screen. It showed the crowd where the assumed location of the Nibiris, the planet where Nubara was originated from. For the longest time, scientists thought that the planet would have a straight trajectory with Earth. And ultimately, the two plants would collide, causing the near extinction event of all humanity."

More pictures of the Nibiris planet flashed across the screen. Robert moved out of the way of the screens to give the audience could see the screen which was now showing the short distance between our planet and that of Nibiris. I knew deep down that if the science was not soon discovered, there would be no way to stop the horror that was coming. The next slide displayed photos of the artifacts discovered from both the excavation in the cave and the tunnels.

The crowd murmured at the artifacts in the photos. They couldn't believe that alien life forms had left behind traces for us to study. That meant for the first time in recorded history that humanity might actually make a connection with life forms from another planet. And we might find out more about not only where they come from, but who we are and where our species will go in the future.

"At the stroke of midnight the greatest discovery of all will be revealed to all. Trust me this one will blow your minds away". Robert pointed at the gigantic mirror covered by a satin red fabric covering its contents for the grand reveal. Princess Omegaura of Nubara. The mystical mirror that contained properties unknown to mankind and was the cause of the earthquakes New York City was having.

Not to mention it was a bitch getting it from the cavern to the surface. It took a few days to make sure it was unscathed that & if it vibrated at all the workers would have been buried alive.

Soliell/Lunati

FINALLY, THE CROWD HAD CLEARED. And I was able to move to the other side of the atrium. I felt I needed go somewhere fast to either sit down or regain my bearings, I had no doubt that I would pass out if I did not find a place of solitude. As I headed for the bathroom, I heard footsteps right behind me. Then I turned and saw no one there.

Maybe this is all my head. I thought.

I didn't have any real reason to suspect that somebody might be following me, but I couldn't shake the feeling that I wasn't alone. My steps quickened until I reached the door. I grabbed it quickly, slung it open and rushed inside. Once inside, I posted my back up against the door to listen if someone else might be waiting for me on the other side. Okay, maybe I was just being paranoid.

I opened the door again and saw nothing but people moving around in the atrium, probably heading to the conference hall. The last thing I wanted to do was miss out on Robert's speech. Suddenly I felt violently ill and could hardly stand up straight. My reflection in the mirror stared back at me and I leaned over the sink, turned on the water as hot as it could get and then splashed it on my face.

Okay, hold it together, Soleil. I told myself.

Needing to take a breather was okay, but almost having a total freak out didn't make any sense. I was able to move comfortably again and reached out my hand to grab a couple of paper towels but when I looked in the mirror, I saw a dark figure standing behind me. My heart stopped and my body stiffened as a paralyzing fear course through my veins.

The stranger wore a black cloak which hid all their features except a very toothy smile that spread across their face.

"I'm terribly sorry for this but I need you out of my way," the figure said sarcastically and then grabbed me from behind and dragged me into a room that was used to identify artifacts. He threw me to the floor and then locked the door behind him.

A horrible realization came to me. The only way to rescue myself was to allow that intense inner power in me free. It scared me more to lose control than it did to be captured. I still wrestled with that thought. Yet it was crystal clear, if I truly did have these meta-human powers, then I better damn well better use them. And fast!

My eyes blazed intensely and began to fill up with a blue crackling flame. I could feel my muscles stretching and tightening, the strange blue power transforming my arms and legs into lethal weapons. My dress tore as my muscles expanded and my hair slowly shortened, my bangs no longer covered my face. When I looked down at what remained of my dress, I saw a sleek black fabric stretched snugly over my entire body and the glowing bow seemed to manifest from thin air into my hand. Finally, I noticed the all too familiar glowing tattoo appear on the back of my hand. I was once again Lunati! I could feel the power surge through me and was keenly aware of every molecule surrounding me. With minimal effort, I slipped out of the strangers hold. Then with a flick of my leg I kicked the figure hard in the back of their knee and swiftly pivoted just under the ventilation shaft as they collapsed.

Ashley Boylan

ROBERT CONTINUED TO SPEAK yet I couldn't shake the uneasy feeling I got every time I looked Soleil's empty seat. It just didn't seem normal. It didn't seem right. She should have been back by now. I looked around to see if I could spot Soleil, it was possible that she couldn't make her way through the crowd after all; they were getting more intense and impatient.

"The chief falling?" Curtis joked as he watched my face look a bit distressed.

However, I was thinking of this more seriously. I mean it's no secret that those strange beings that are connected to Nubara, specifically the Centaurs might be after us. I thought we are being much too lenient about it. Much too careless about it and I had a sinking feeling in the pit of my gut about it.

"You know what?" Curtis started to say. "I know naturally you're an analyst, but we don't have to over think things."

"AHHHHH!" I screamed feeling an intense pain shoot throughout my body. "No, please no!"

The entire crowd turned, shocked and afraid to see what was happening. My first reaction was to grab Curtis's arm.

"Babe," Curtis said clenching his teeth. "Do you need me to get you anything? You're sort of hurting my arm..." I could barely see his face as he was speaking; a white light was forming an aura all around my body. The entire room started to shake underneath my feet. And everyone else in attendance at the conference looked around and then turned their attention up to the ceiling.

"Oh my God!" I heard. And somebody pointed up to the chandelier shaking violently.

The chandelier was swaying from left to right until its gold colored chain snapped and the whole thing, all seven tears, came crashing down right in the middle the audience. People were panic and running in all directions trampling each other to get out of the way as the chandelier came crashing down. Curtis grabbed my arm shoving me to the floor and out of harm's way. Shards of glass spewed everywhere as the chandelier of death impacted in the middle of the ballroom. Bits and pieces hit the spectators injuring the ones closest to the point of impact. The guests were running around screaming and a few were tending to the wounds of the injured. The night had quickly taken a turn for the worse and I had a feeling that this was only the beginning.

"Ashley, you need to tell me what's going on," Curtis insisted afraid that he didn't know how to help me. He only saw the expression straining my face as I struggled to breathe. I had no idea what was happening to me, and so many people, innocent people were getting hurt because of it. The panicked screams could be heard coming from all directions but I stayed on the floor, rolling on my back and grabbing my head. *What was happening to me?* That was the last thought I remembered.

Lunati

A HULKING MAN STRODE through the conference hall. He wore leather cuffs on his wrists and had dangling tassels. His bulging muscles nearly ripped through his leather pants. Around his neck he wore a studded collar. His long blond hair covered his ice blue eyes. As he marched forth, he was careful to avoid the people screaming and stumbling in his way. I watch from afar, on the right hand of the conference hall stage. My bright blue eyes burned scanning the room and noticing another man. He was much smaller than the giant beside him with a scrawny lean frame and a windbreaker jacket rumpled over his shoulders, yet he stood confidently as he held some type of laptop or tablet in his hands. He pushed up his glasses and focused on something on the screen.

"I'm trying to make a match of the crypto security they have. I've got two of the numbers but I need the last one..." I heard from afar.

"Hurry it up. I want to get out of here as fast as possible" The giant man grunted.

"Will you two knuckleheads figure it out? I got all dressed up only to get a tear in my stocking. What kind of flipping world is this?"

A woman shouted. She wore a dazzling silk dress with dark black knee-high stockings. One of them had a long tear along her calf.

Who are these people? I wondered.

Obviously, they didn't come from our world. Unless you were in the WWE, no one sane dressed like the giant brute with the cuff leather wrist straps, especially to a gathering like this. The two scrawny sidekicks didn't quite make sense either.

"What are we waiting for Pike?" The woman said irritably. "How long is this going to take? Do you think I like coming down here and having to deal with this?"

The big man tightened his massive muscles, obviously irritated with the irritated woman. Beside him, the small man tapped his finger on the screen flipping things left and right.

"Okay. Gretsy, Barrison i'm doing my best here. You want me to tag along and code break remember, I could have stayed home and watched reruns of Lost, instead of being caught up in this madness…" Pike said shaking his head.

Barrison & Gretsy stopped in their tracks. They both waited patiently on the side of the conference hall until Pike could finish hacking the crypto security code.

Using my powers that were bestowed upon me by Lunati, I searched the databases of my encyclopedic mind that had the memory storage capacity similar to any government super computer. Anything I wanted to know, I instantly knew, it was downright freaky, but very cool at the same time. I stood very still and allowed my mind to work its magic. A few seconds later, I had names for all three faces of the assailants. Gretsy Demoine, Barrison Stanly and Pike Pitts were a trio of international thieves wanted as far as Morocco, London, Japan and France.

They're mode of operation was to steal as much rare art as they could and then sell it off to the highest bidder on the black art market. And tonight, they have their sights set on stealing the Emblem and the diaries that Prof. Michaels displayed during the presentation.

I wasn't about to let that happen! We needed those artifacts in order to find the second map that will lead us to the real discovery that we've been searching for.

"I got it!" Pike exclaimed pumping his fist in the air.

The muscle of the group, Barrison Stanly pummeled his chest with both of his fists as a gorilla demonstrating his dominance would.

"Good, let's get out of here". He roared.

Gretsy didn't say anything at all. She only moved away from standing around and followed them to the back room where all the artifacts were kept. I couldn't let them get away with only connection we had— and possibly the last connection— to Nubara.

Instinctively I rushed forward after the three thieves as they ran to the vault. They quickly packed up the artifacts into a giant black case as I made my presence known, appearing out of the shadows and damn near made the one called Pike piss his pants.

"Who is this chick supposed to be?" Gretsy snorted.

Barrison shrugged as he looked me up and down, slightly amused and possibly a little turned on. "I have no idea who this girl thinks she is. But lucky for her, I don't fight girls, they're no challenge to me; so puny and weak."

"I'm only going to ask you this once. Hand over what's in the bag to me now!!" I warned.

Barrison chuckled. "What are you going to do exactly? Straddle my face between your tight leather pants....I don't mind. Go right ahead."

I felt the power of Lunati surge through me and felt my face tighten into snarl as I buried my foot into Barrison's chest. He didn't have to time to react to my lightning quick attack as the impact sent him flying back hard against the back of the vault wall. Gretsy and Pike looked at each other, before looking back at me. I could see the fear in their eyes and it fed my rage and made me more focused. I stood there fixing my radiant blue eyes on them. I could hear the crackle of energy surge from them as my rage grew.

"Your move." I said calmly, narrowing my eyes. "This little girl is about to kick all your asses."

Gretsy looked me over before lowering herself in her fighting stance as the smaller scrawny guy, named Pike, scurried behind the display table. *Oh this is going to be fun.* I thought as I got into my stance and prepared for round 2.

"Sometimes it takes a woman to do a man's job…" Gretsy said.

I just smiled.

She instantly charged at me and whipped her body around and attempted to connect the back of her foot with my temple but she was way too slow. My instincts were not of this world. I easily dodged her attack with time to spare and gave her a weak palm strike to the chest. I didn't want to kill her......yet. Stunned and angry at her failed attempt, she pulled out two silver stars and expertly tossed them my direction. I effortlessly dodged the first one and caught the other one between my thumb and index finger and threw hit right back at her. It slammed into her mid thigh and buried itself almost half way with a sickening thud. She screamed, half in frustration and half I pain as she crumpled to the floor clutching her leg which was now covered in blood. After seeing his boss go down, Barrison got back up and was ready for another round. Wasting no time, he charged with at me like a rhino, head down and arms out. I calmly stepped back and withdrew an energy arrow out of my quiver and placed it in my bow and then gently spoke to it. "For you and I are both linked, hear me arrow, make that creature suffer." I whispered.

Then I released the arrow. The arrow streaked towards the charging Barrison and right before it was about to burn its way through his massive hulk of a body, a bright blue blast lit up the room and then all I saw was darkness.

I woke up shivering on the floor, my entire body felt drained, as if all my energy had been sucked out of me. When I stood up I couldn't keep my balance and I collapsed back onto the floor. I was slowly starting to come to when someone grabbed my shoulder.

"Please, wake up. Wait, I think she's alive…" I heard a voice say.

"Palace?" I wondered.

"No," the voice replied. "This is security."

"You have to stop them. They're trying to still artifacts!" I told the security officer.

Barrison Stanly

A BATTERED AND BRUISED BARRISON managed to escape with the rest of the trio into an unused section of the museum. If it wasn't for Pike's quick thinking who wrapped up Gretsy's bloody leg with a torn piece of the shirt he was wearing whom Barrison had to rip apart, they would have led a blood trail straight to them. As they were about to discuss their escape plan, the steel security plates slowly lowered over the windows and doors blocking the windows and exits.

"They're going into full on lock down," Gretsy said, as he lowered Gretsy down. She seemed able to walk and put weight on her injured leg. The dress she was wearing covered the bandage as not to draw attention to her.

"No one will be allowed in or out." Barrison said, pressing his hand against his wounds.

"Sorry old pal." Gretsy said blowing Barrison a kiss. "Pike and I'm just gonna have to leave you behind."

She and Pike calmly walked out of the room casually into a wave of panicked spectators running down the hall.. Security was setting up perimeter checks on every floor and doorway, but Pike and Gretsy had to easily blend into the crowd. Barrison on the other hand was left alone, shocked and stunned. After all, he had carried that ungrateful bitch out of the vault after her encounter with the strange glowing blue woman. *Now what?* He asked

Palace Michaels

I CAN'T FIND HER! I stressed. Soleil never came back. And now I feel like a fool for having let her leave my side. My foot stepped on something. I looked down and noticed Wilson Pascal's phone underneath my shoe. When I read his last text he wrote before we parted ways it said:

> **Can't hold out hope for security. If we are going to do something, we'll have to do it ourselves…Get me those journals on Nubara now!**

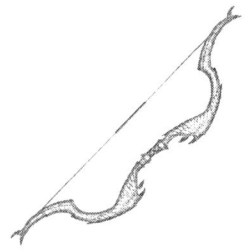

Epilogue

Palace Michaels

I was like a shark, stalking my prey from the depths of the sea as I snuck up on Mary, who didn't see me coming until I was with in arms reach of her. She tried to run, but it was too late. I grabbed her arm and pulled her out of the crowd.

"You better tell me what's going on if you know something…" I demanded.

Mary looked up at me shocked, as if she didn't understand a word I was saying.

"Uh, I have no clue what you're talking about. I'm just trying to find my husband. Don't think because you lost your little girlfriend that no one else matters," Mary replied in a sarcastic tone

"Don't try to deflect the question Mary." I demanded. "Are you part of this? Did you know this would happen?"

"Let go!" Mary shouted. "If you think I will tell you anything, then you've got another thing coming…" She threatened.

"I just want the truth. Where is Wilson?" I asked through gritted teeth.

Mary's eyes stealthily scanned over to the ball, where the artifacts were kept on display. I knew right then that someone must have tried to break into the vault.

"You don't have to. You've already told me everything I need to know," I told Mary and shoved her back, then made my way to where the artifacts were being held.

"Don't you dare go back there," she warned

"Why what you think you might find?"

"They told all the patrons to stay behind. If you go gallivanting off somewhere, where security can't see you, who knows what kind of trouble you can get into. And who also knows, if security will get there to rescue you in time," she said, issuing another warning.

"I'll take my chances," I told her.

Barrison Stanly

GET THE HELL UP!" Wilson shouted". "You only had one job and couldn't even do that right!"

Barrison was getting up slowly and was looking up at Wilson who stood a foot or two in front of him. Barrison was rubbing his head where Wilson had punched him.

"All I asked of you guys was to get the artifacts and get out. That's it! And you still weren't able to do that. By the way, where are Gretsy and Pike? They need to hear this rant too," Wilson said looking around.

"Those two bastards skipped out on me. They're traitors…" Barrison replied.

Barrison didn't actually believe that a group of thieves would somehow have loyalty to one another. However, he hoped that they'd wait at least until the job had been finished before backstabbing someone in their group. It came as no great shock, and he was still trying to figure out how he could escape without setting off the alarms or getting security's attention. It was a tricky situation.

Crushed glass from the display cases crunched underneath their feet as Wilson and Barrison hurried to the exit of the museum. They both knew that the security was heavy and that there would be a lot of questions, but at least they wouldn't get caught.

"Just follow my lead," Wilson said. "It's better to stay by my side; they know that I'm one of the directors and a law-abiding patron of the science's division. I'm the last person they would suspect right now."

Barrison only nodded. He was ready to get out. The only thing holding them back now was the total lock down in the museum. Barrison stayed walking by his side, until a group of security guards hurried towards them.

"That doesn't look too good…" Barrison mumbled.

"Let me handle this," Wilson replied.

The security guards held up their hands to Wilson and Barrison.

"Stop right there!" They demanded.

One of the officers spun Wilson around and pulled off handcuffs from their security belts and cuffed his hands behind his back.

"Wilson you're under arrest," one of the security guards said. "We know that you've been trying to break into the vault and steal the artifacts."

Before the other security guard could cuff him, Barrison shoved him with all his strength into a group of civilians heading for the exit and they all tumbled over like dominoes. Barrison quickly ran the opposite direction and disappeared back into the crowd, not really knowing what to do next. He knew every doorway would have security searching for him so it was very clear, he had to take drastic measures, but what?

Then it hit him, a sinister smile spread over the lower half of his face when he realized he would need to take a hostage in order to negotiate his way out. A few cops that had responded to the scene spotted him and immediately started running after him, but Barrison wasted no time and grabbed the nearest person to him. He quickly put her in a headlock and threatened to break her neck if the cops didn't back off. The cops backed off and he slowly backed up still holding the terrified red headed woman in his massive arms.

Wilson Pascal

"DO YOU KNOW ANYTHING of the thief or thieves that tried to steal the artifacts this evening?" The police asked.

Wilson was sitting in a secluded room. The room was empty except for a cheap metal chair and a rusted metal table. The walls were sparse except for the single clock hanging up near the right side. The last thing Wilson wanted to do was incriminate him. So he sat down and decided to co-operate to a certain degree.

"I'm sorry officer, I just have no idea what you're talking about," he said and shrugged

The officers were only questioning him on a hunch. They didn't really see him commit the crime but they figured Wilson was behind it. Wilson knew he should use this uncertainty to his advantage. As long as he kept the cops chasing members of his inner circle, then Barrison, Pike and Gretsy would not get caught. He would rather get a slap on the wrist then serve hard time. He had to continue biding his time and waiting for the storm to pass. Eventually, the cops would have to give it up because they have no real evidence beyond a hunch.

"Okay," one of the cops started. "Why are you trying to go after the artifacts?" One of the cops asked.

Wilson didn't directly reply.

"Why would you assume that?" He responded "as I said, all this is hear say and until I get my lawyer, you will hear no more from me."

The head cop, Officer Martinez, was speaking to his other officers outside of the room. The entire room was soundproof, which meant Mr. Wilson couldn't hear a word being said and vice versa. He sat back and relaxed, waiting for the cops to have their chat. He knew they didn't have enough to keep him.

They thought that by keeping in the dark, which they could make him sweat. It was a common tactic used to get an answer from a suspect but Wilson wasn't going to crack. He actually was enjoying letting the cops think that they had the upper hand. Outside of the interrogation room, he knew there was a completely different story happening. All three of his hired thieves were still free and could soon make their demands.

So he just had to buy time until the cops would come back in the room and try asking him the same questions again, but in a different way. As they always did. The doors opened and Officer Martinez and his men reentered the room. Wilson just smiled and nodded his head.

"Looks like we've got a situation," Officer Martinez said.

Wilson really didn't know what he meant. "You mean containing an innocent man illegally? Or even, letting him sit in a room alone for hours without his legal right to make one phone call?"

Officer Martinez shook his head. "No, security informed me the update of the evacuation situation. Turns out there is somebody holding guests' hostage."

Wilson smiled. "Okay. Okay. Okay. I'll give you two names. Gretsy and Pike. Those two were behind the entire thing"

Wilson was only trying to throw them a bone. He knew if he gave the cops a small morsel of information, he could then make them believe he was willing to cooperate. Even though he had to trade a couple of his cards he had on the table, he still had an ace in the hole. Barrison was still out there and he was the strongest henchmen that he had and could easily do whatever was necessary to take control. Besides, Gretsy and Pike were traitors. They allowed him to get caught without even trying to stop it. Wilson only now trusted Barrison to have his back.

"Who are these people? This Gretsy and this Pike?"

"I assure that those two who are the people you're looking for." Wilson said. "They came here to steal the artifacts regarding Nubara."

"You know this why?"

Wilson shrugged and considered playing dumb. Then decided to give the cops a little more.

"I vaguely know them. I can't be sure what those two were up to. I'm only telling you now because you asked for answers—so I'm giving them to you. There you go, you can keep me here and interrogate me… Or, you can go out there and find out who the real enemy is. Your choice but hurry time is running out."

Officer Martinez and the rest of the cops in the room stared at one another. They knew that Wilson was right. If there were more thieves out in the conference hall, they needed to be stopped. None of them liked the idea of taking a lead from a criminal. Especially one that had a good alibi, and was not directly linked to the actual crime. But if they wanted to save lives and prevent any of the precious artifacts from being stolen, then they had to take that risk.

"It's not him!" somebody shouted.

Wilson looked up and saw Mary, his wife, burst into the room.

"He had accomplices. Barrison. Gretsy. Gretsy. Pike. They are the ones that are really behind this. Please, let him go!" Mary pleaded.

The cops looked towards Wilson. "Is this true?" They asked.

Wilson nodded his head sadly, feeling defeated as he now knew he was implicated by his own wife. *Stupid woman, now I am in deep shit.*

"You heard the man. We need to put out an APB on the two following suspects of Gretsy, Pike and someone named Barrison. They're the ones trying to steal the Nubarian artifacts. Their still in the building somewhere, find them!" The other cops stormed out of the room, leaving Officer Martinez and Wilson alone.

Then Officer Martinez looked over at Wilson. "Stick around as you apparently had accomplices according to your wife."

Wilson hung his head at his sudden turn of bad luck. He was angry at his wife but he knew she was only trying to help. Yet all she had to do was stay put and not do anything. But there was nothing he could do about it now and besides, there was something far worse coming and somehow they were all apart of it.

Soliel Oupary

"SOLEIL!" SOLEIL!" I heard someone shout my name.

My body still felt like a hundred Bricks had slammed on top of me. I couldn't move or speak. I had a throbbing pain surging through my head. I just wanted all this madness to end. My eyes started to shift and they fluttered open. I looked up and saw Ashley leaning over me. She had a worried look that distorted the features on her face.

"its okay, Ashley. I'm not hurt or anything. I just got the wind knocked out of me. That's all," I said, trying to reassure her.

Yet Ashley's face still looked contorted and anxious.

"What's wrong? Is there something else?" I asked.

"It's total chaos out there. People are panicking. No one knows what's going on and haven't been able to contact Robert yet. Then we couldn't find you and…" Before she could say anything else, I took her hand. Clearly, Ashley had been panicking for several hours now. She was probably trying to find where everyone had scattered off to. I could also tell that she was worried about the artifacts being stolen, as they were our link to our individual pasts.

"What happened in here?" Ashley asked looking around at all the mess.

I did my best to recall, but most of the memory just came up in pieces. I knew that I transformed into my alternate self—Lunati. After that, everything became this crazy haze that I couldn't quite comprehend.

"I remember coming into this vault to stop somebody from trying to steal the artifacts. Once I found them, I lost control my body and then Lunati took over. I shot blue energy arrows at them as I tried to stop them." I stopped, *did I openly just admit to being Lunati?* I think I did. As if this was a normal occurrence, although these past few days it seemed to prove otherwise.

Ashley shook her head as it dawned on her that the girl who saved Rex was indeed Soliel overtaken by her alternate ego…Lunati. From the look she was giving me now, I knew she was pondering why someone would want to steal the artifacts found in the cavern of Nubara.

Why would anyone want to steal the artifacts? Yeah, sure they were an important discovery to science but that didn't quite mean they are priceless except for the loss of information they would provide.

"Do you know anything about them? The thieves that is? Such as the color of their hair? Their faces? Anything at all?" Ashley asked.

I could barely understand what happening right now. Everything was happening so fast. So, trying to understand or remember who tried to steal the artifacts was even more impossible to remember. All these questions were feeding my anxiety. Everyone was looking at me as if I was the leader. But I don't know how to lead. I'm just a student who is trying to study a legacy that turned out not only to be beneficial to humanity, but also beneficial to understanding who I am. I just wanted to be left alone and sort things out in my head.

I knew deep down that would be impossible, as now I was a vessel for the spirit to come through me and change everything about who I am and what I am to do. It's a terrible and scary feeling. To feel like a monster. A monster that nobody understands. Now, I have these powers and I don't know how to control them. But people look up to me to be some kind of... hero. But I'm not a hero, am I? I'm just a girl doesn't have her parents any longer. I'm just a girl who doesn't even know who her brother is anymore. How can anyone look up to me for anything?

Ashley was still looking at me for answers. "All I can tell you Ashley is that they got away, which means that they must still be in the Museum somewhere. Obviously I didn't see where they went to. I just know that they escaped from the vault, but the good news is that they didn't steal any of the items."

Hearing the news was of no relief to Ashley. Yes, the age old artifacts weren't stolen, but people's lives would be at risk as long as the thieves were hiding amongst the regular patrons.

Ashley said. "I overheard that Wilson was also in on it. Him and his wife. They had hired some of these thieves to steal the artifacts. It just goes to show you that you can't really know who your friends are."

Ashley was definitely telling the truth. Who we can trust anyone now that our whole world has been turned upside down. Honestly, I think we've been too gullible. Thinking anyone and everyone we met since then has our best interest at hand. The truth is we had to be careful, and keep our deepest darkest secrets guarded from everyone. That would be easy for me. I'm private person anyway. But for Ashley, she thrived on being around people, even if they could hardly understand her because of her genius over analytical mind.

I was finally able to move a bit and Ashley helped me up from the floor. I was still a bit wobbly, so I held onto Ashley's shoulder as I attempted to find my bearings. I felt so bad for Dr Michaels, this was supposed to be his most important night and he spent months preparing, only to have it ruined in a matter of minutes. Besides Robert, I also hope that Palace was okay. I haven't seen him since I left to find the bathroom.

"Listen Ashley, we need to hurry and get back outside because now that Wilson knows what those thieves he hired had planned for the items from Nubara, our friends are still out there unaware of the danger that they're all in."

I finally was feeling confident that I could walk again and let go off Ashley's shoulder, dusted glass off of my dress and made my way to the vault's exit, but Ashley stood there, unmoving.

"Ashley, are you coming or what?" I asked. Yet she still stood there looking down at the floor. "Ashley, are you Ok?"

I quickly walked back towards her and grabbed her hand and as soon as I did she jerked her head up and looked into my eyes and then I noticed that her eyes had turned completely opaque and she spoke. "The Chandelier will fall revealing the beginning of Earth's destruction"

Callum Morrissey

"ESABELLE! ESABELLE!" I shouted as I lost track of her in the crowd.

She didn't answer and I turned back to see if she was behind me. To my horror, I saw a huge hulking man with a wild devious grin stretching across his face clutching Esabelle's head with his massive arms in an inescapable headlock with one arm and with his other arm, he was aiming a gun at a large group police officers who were all holding their hands out showing this monster of a man that they intended to make no sudden moves. My heart felt like it skipped a beat as looked into Esabelle's terrified green eyes and I felt a rush of anger wash over me. I wanted to tear this beast head off! I didn't care how big he was. My love for Esabelle made me feel invincible.

"Now don't do anything drastic..." One of police officers said keeping his voice mild and gentle.

Barrison laughed. "Drastic, huh? You mean like this?" He then aimed the gun right at Esabelle's head. Esabelle surprisingly didn't cry out or scream. She just close her eyes and breathed very slowly, controlling the rhythm of her breathing. I could tell that she didn't want to give him any satisfaction whatsoever. Esabelle was strong like that, even when she was scared to death. A true warrior. It's part of why I loved her. She continued to remain very still in Barrison's hands and I continued to want to kill this man.

"You're not going to get away with this," Esabelle muttered frustrated.

"Says the woman who has a gun held to her head..." Barrison replied. "Look, little girl. You're in no position to give me orders."

That's never stopped Esabelle before. If there's anything you can count on, she was being herself and she got into your mind. That was what worried me the most, he could get easily frustrated and end her life which I did not want to see happen.

"Now listen up pigs. If it isn't already obvious, I'm going to take one hostage at a time and end their lives one by one so I would appreciate it if you could radio your police buddies and escort me and this lovely little girl out of this museum," Barrison demanded. "Otherwise people will start losing their lives, starting with this red head"

The police officers started looking at one another; they knew they had no choice but to do exactly as he said.

"There has to be another way, can we talk about this? What do you want with her anyway?" I asked, trying to do something to distract Barrison from killing my girlfriend. He snapped his head in my direction and narrowed his eyes at me and smirked.

"Hmm. You must be this one's jealous boyfriend. Well boy! I've already said everything that's needed to be said. Now I just need you to keep your scrawny little mouth shut as I show your girlfriend the night of her life." he turned his attention back to the officers.

"Now officers, I'm going to need you to follow through my requested action. I'm not interested in making deals or negotiating. You either allow me to exit this wretched place, or I start killing."

I swallowed hard at the sound of the mallet clicking in Barrison's gun.

I knew I had to act fast.

Think Callum. Think.

I could always jump between him and Esabelle, but that could have a very deadly outcome. I knew if I stood here thinking that Esabelle would be dead either way and since the big man with a gun had his back mostly to me, he wouldn't see me coming, so without further thought I was ready to attack. I would have to grab the gun first. And as I took my first step...... Someone shouted

"Wait!"

Ashley grabbed me by the back of my shirt.

"Don't do anything stupid, Callum." She insisted.

I looked at her with desperation in my eyes. There is no way she could understand the pain I was feeling. The idea of losing Esabelle was something I didn't want to fathom. If Esabelle died, so did I.

"Trust me, I know what you are thinking but that's a bad idea. Instead of just waiting it out, you put both of your lives in danger. Just stay here with us and wait for the police to think of a plan, okay?"

That answer wasn't good enough for me. I looked over to Esabelle and saw her trembling. I didn't know how long until she would collapse. Barrison lowered the gun from her head to her neck. He wiggled his fingers over the trigger.

It was like he was taunting everyone. Telling me us that we had no control.

I didn't know what to do next but I knew I had to something and fast. The best idea had was still to jump right for her. So I went with it.

I lunged out, fast and swift, and grabbed her arm, a blade tore through my nice shirt slicing deep into Barrison's forearm just as he was pulling the trigger.

"NO!" I screamed at the top of my lungs and landed hard on the floor rolling head over heels a few times before I stopped in the upright position. I felt disoriented for a second but then the twinge of pain in my left leg brought me back to my senses. I slowly scanned my left leg and immediately discovered a geyser of blood gushing down my calf.

"Oh my god! Oh my God! I've been shot!"

Ashley cuffed her hands over her mouth, too afraid to say anything at all.

"I'm shot!" I yelled, unable to believe it myself.

Palace rushed over, tearing down his shirt mid-run. He slid on the floor and glass ripped up the knees of his suit. He then took the ripped part of his sleeve, lifted up my pant leg, and tied it around my calf.

"You need to stay very still. If you lose too much blood, you'll pass out. I'm no doctor but I know losing this much blood is not good."

Of course, what I did was stupid. But stupid was the only plan I had.

"As crazy as this whole scene is," Barrison said, he was still holding Esabelle but his left arm was now bleeding profusely. It didn't seem to phase him as he dripped blood all over the floor and still pointed the gun at the cops.

"I didn't pull the trigger. Can't you see? There is no smoke coming from the barrel of my gun."

"He's right. There's another shooter in the crowd," Palace said.

Frantically, I turned my head around trying to focus on everyone's face. A large amount of people standing, idling & horrified as they watched us sitting on the floor. That's when I saw something glinting in the center of the crowd. It was a woman with red stockings, and mascara running down her cheeks. There was something about the way she stood there, staring directly at me.

"There she is!" I shouted, pointing my finger in her direction.

I knew I was right when I saw Barrison look over at her and smile shockingly.

"Gretsy, I thought you turned tail like some coward. Nice to know that there is still loyalty among thieves."

Gretsy shrugged. "Well, I figured we still needed to keep you around. Now, let that dumb broad go so we can ditch this place," Gretsy said holstering her small pistol against her thigh.

Barrison nodded and then threw Esabelle hard to the floor and as she tumbled, she grabbed Callum's leg which triggered her blade on her arm to shoot out and slice Barrison's thigh as he dashed towards the doors.

Robert darted after Barrison who was moving slower than normal; he was finally showing signs of pain from both cuts administered by Callum and Esabelle. *What is he doing? Why is he trying to be a hero?* I wondered as Prof. Robert Michaels threw himself under Barrison's feet tripping him and sending him tumbling head over heels but after the second roll, he managed to regain and his balance and turned his focus on the Dr who was still getting up.

Barrison grabbed Robert by the collar and dragged him up by his side. Then he sprinted towards the exit with Dr. Michaels dangling in his grasp.

Barrison held the gun right at Robert's head. We knew we had to be careful, as Barrison was running out of ideas and now that he was injured he was desperate.

Palace helped me get up to my feet. "Callum, what you did back there was really stupid. I mean totally idiotic. But you saved Esabelle's life."

I smiled. Wrestling back the mess of my hair.

"I know, but I couldn't let anything happen to her. But I agree that wasn't the most rational thing to do. But at the time it seemed the only thing I could do. So now what do we do about your brother?"

"I'm hoping I can come up with my own crazy plan," Palace replied.

As Barrison got closer to the exit, I was afraid that we were running out of options to save Robert. We really needed a miracle right now.

"Callum, are you all right?" Esabelle asked me.

"There's a little pain in my calf, but I'll survive."

Esabelle glanced and pressed her hand at her own calf.

Gently, I rested my hand on her wrist. "Do you mind if I take a look?"

That's when I lowered my head to the hem of Esabelle's dress. And I saw that she also had a bullet wound in her calf.

"How can that be?" I asked. "Does our connection also mean that if I get hurt, then you'll get hurt too?"

All of this was a new dimension for both of us. Obviously, there was some link between us. But I had no idea, that our lives are also linked in some delicate supernatural balance. And I couldn't think of anything else worse for us right now. It just made our love much more vulnerable and now that we knew, we would have to be extra careful.

"You just have to remember, Callum. When we opened the Pandora's Box of Nubara, we have to take the bad with the good. Sure

that means we have bracelets that protrude sharp blades and sure that means that we are intrinsically linked. It also means that I met you and that never would have ever happened if I were not on that subway train that day."

I finished her sentence. "With Soleil."

We looked over to the exit and Barrison was almost there. A white light streaked out of nowhere catching everyone's attention. Barrison, still holding Dr. Michaels, looked up confused. The white light made contact with the majestic chandelier that lay directly above. There was a sizzling sound of electricity coming from the chandelier and the lights began to flicker.

"No way. This can't be happening. Not right now." Barrison said, muttering under his breath as a dark shadow covered his entire body. He threw Robert into safety as the chandelier made contact with his body.

CRASH!

Glass went flying in all directions and I covered Esabelle eyes to make sure that she got nothing in them. After a few minutes, I lowered my hand and saw that Barrison was bleeding from new wounds up and down his whole body and was now crawling on the floor towards the exit. Bleeding badly, his only goal was to get out of the museum anyway he could.

"Do you think some chandelier is going to stop me," he said spitting up blood. Barrison tried to stand up. He searched the room for Pike and Gretsy, but neither of them could be found.

"Bastards!" He shouted, furious that he had been double-crossed again. As he tried to take steps forward, he collapsed to the ground again. His Achilles tendon had been sliced by the glass. There was no way for him to escape now, not with the speed that he was crawling and the cops were approaching quickly.

CLANG! CLANG!

A low pitched metallic noise caught our attention. The clock hanging on the wall struck twelve. It was midnight! The New Year had finally arrived and despite all the chaos, time never stood still.

"Is it really the new year?" Ashley asked with Soleil at her side, who had transformed back to her original self.

"Yes," Soleil said in a grim tone. There was a giant glass window on the wall behind her that ran from the ceiling all the way to floor.

Barrison who was still crawling on his hand and knees had managed to grab a hold of the red satin sheet covering the mirror that harbored Omegaura within it. As he fell forward, he somehow gracefully removed the sheet straight off of the mirror. And as he did, I knew that something was drastically wrong.

Robert looked at his brother with a very concerned look, while Esabelle clutched my shoulder in awe. Ashley stood wide eyed and confused next to Soleil. It was Curtis who broke the silence.

"Where is she...where is Omegaura?"

The mirror was grand as it stood in place but the reflection of the Princess of Nubara was missing. Where could she have gone? Soleil's last thoughts were of what Ashley said in her trance like state, "when the chandelier would fall a revelation of Earth's destruction would be made known to everyone present."

Omegaura.

The end of humanity.

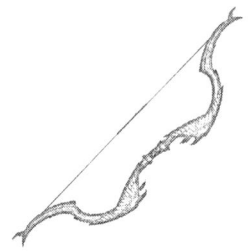

About The Author

Alex is an easy-going & youthful writer devoted to creating the best experiences for his readers by letting his imagination paint a picture step by step which then gets translated into words.

Alex has been writing since the age of 18 & is interested in all genres, especially Horror, Thrillers & Sci-Fi. He hopes that everyone will enjoy his "Nubara" series, "The Second Husband", "Something Sinister Is In This House & other novels releasing by next year.

https://www.facebook.com/AlexHSingh
https://twitter.com/NubaraRises

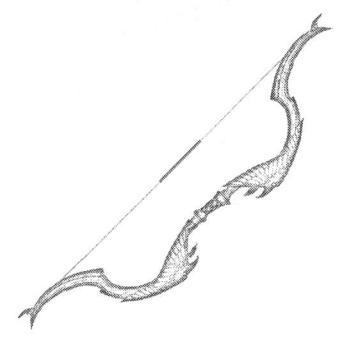

Coming Soon

Origins Of The Risen…Nubara 2
Surfacing In A Landmass Near You!

The Second Husband

Made in the USA
Lexington, KY
05 September 2015